THE
RESTLESS
TRAIL HOME

A WESTERN FRONTIER ADVENTURE

ROBERT PEECHER

Print ISBN – 9798324769475

CONTENTS

1

Tommy Duvall's eyes lit on the woman standing in the door-way of the saloon, framed by the door, silhouetted by the fading light outside. She held his Winchester Yellow Boy in both hands, a curl of smoke rose from the muzzle.

To his left, crammed up against the counter inside the saloon, at least a score of Mexican men who'd just witnessed three killings. To his right, pressed against the wall, a dozen more. To a man, they all seemed to be holding their breaths, waiting to see what would come next.

They'd already seen Duvall walk up to a table and shoot a man out of his chair. They'd seen him trade shots with another man, and chase him out into the yard behind the saloon and kill that man even after he tossed down his gun. Then they'd seen the woman shoot in the back a third man. Duvall figured it was more bloodshed than the residents of this border town were accustomed to. But then again, maybe not. Border towns, at least those in Texas, had a reputation.

He must have been a fearful sight.

He didn't know how bad he was shot, but Duvall could feel blood on the side of his neck where he'd been grazed by a bullet. He might've been shot in one or two other places. He didn't feel any pain, but he also hadn't examined himself, and some of those shots had been a mite close.

Duvall stepped over the body bleeding in the middle of the floor. He kept the Smith & Wesson Model 3 in his hand, held high where everyone in the place could see it clearly. He wanted it to serve as a warning for all of them to stay back.

What Duvall knew that the rest of them didn't know is he was just about empty. Maybe he had one shot left.

There on the ground, near the body, were three pairs of saddle-bags. Duvall kneeled down and picked up one pair, his eyes roving over the men watching him. He flung the first pair of saddlebags over his shoulder, then he took a deliberate look around the room to make certain no one was coming at him. He flung the second pair of saddlebags over his shoulder on top of the first. They were weighty. Heavier than a pair of saddlebags would typically be. And it was a solid weight, too. It felt different.

The third pair of saddlebags he started to lift from the floor, intending to just carry them out, but one of the bags wasn't buckled, and something slid out of the flap as Duvall shifted the bag to pick it up. Duvall kicked it back in with his toe, but too late. One of the men standing not far away breathed the words.

"De oro."

Duvall shot a look at the man, a severe look that he intended as a warning.

He picked up the saddlebag and started for the door, stepping over the other dead body to get to it. At the doorway, Duvall spun around. The Mexicans either side were starting to advance from the walls into the center of the saloon, but they stopped now as he turned back to face them all. They could easily over-power him. But as far as any of them knew, Duvall still had at least one live round left in the cylinder, and none of them wanted to be the one to catch that shot. He didn't know if a single one of them spoke any English.

"Don't nobody follow me," Duvall said. "I see any of you on my backtrail, I'll kill you like I done to these others, here. You see I ain't a man to be trifled with."

But he didn't move. His neck was wet and sticky. The saddlebags hung heavy on his shoulder. The stares of anger and horror from the men watching seemed to pin him to the spot. He worried that as soon as he turned his back to the room, started out the door, that maybe someone would decide to take a shot at him. Maybe a deputy, or whatever sort of law they had here, or maybe someone who'd noticed the glint of gold from the brick that slid partway out of the saddlebag.

"Tomás," a woman's voice called from behind him, and Duvall twisted to look. Turning his neck stung like the devil, but he knew the wound wasn't threatening his life. Just a grazing wound. He'd been lucky, but it wasn't the first time he was lucky.

Marisol Rosales sat the saddle of her piebald pony, and she held the reins of Duvall's flea-bit gray.

"Vamos," Marisol said, encouraging him to come on.

Beyond her, Duvall saw that Pablo Peña sat in his saddle, and he'd collected the horses that belonged to the three dead men.

Duvall turned back for one last look around the saloon.

"Don't none of you try to come after us," Duvall said again.

He turned his back on the saloon, bracing himself to feel a bullet smash into him from behind. But no gun barked. No bullet smashed.

He shoved the Smith & Wesson into his belt and stepped painfully into the stirrup. He had a wound in his side more serious than the one on his neck. A bullet hole from a ricochet and probably a cracked rib. That one hurt far worse than the stinging in his neck. But it was more than a week old now, and what hadn't yet healed, he'd more or less grown accustomed to.

As he swung himself over the horse, he noticed a fresh hole in the flap of his coat. As he got into the saddle, he held the end of his coat up and looked at the hole. Stuck a finger through it. In the chaotic exchange of gunfire, Duvall had felt a slight tug as Rodrigues fired a shot at him. He concluded now that the tug he felt must have been one of Rodrigues's bullets cutting through the tail of his coat. Damn thing shot through his coat, and missed him by less than inches.

The trio of riders went at the gallop.

Duvall heard shouting behind them. He wondered again what sort of law there was in Puerto Palomas and how far that law might go to capture or kill a man who'd committed murder at a Palomas saloon.

Pecas Gris, the flea-bitten gray with the black mane that Duvall had stolen in Texas years ago and ridden to New Mexico Territory and now all the way down into Mexico, began to out-pace the other two horses. Duvall touched his knee to the horse's shoulder and turned east, like he was riding for Juárez, some seventy miles away.

There were federales guarding the border, Duvall knew. He'd seen them there earlier. Not many of them – he'd counted three outside a little guard house on the only road out of Palomas leading to the north. Three federales on the border, even five or six, didn't worry him much – except they were all armed with rifles. Duvall didn't want to risk that a lucky shot might hit one of the three riders. So he turned east, driving for the desert.

Of course, they would not go as far as Juárez.

The man they'd stolen the gold from – Juárez was his stronghold. They maybe didn't know in Palomas yet that a million dollars in gold had been stolen from Señor Manuel Arellano Hermosillio, but they surely knew in Juárez.

And maybe nobody in Palomas would recognize Señor Arellano's daughter, but they would know her in Juárez.

But at least one man in Palomas did know Marisol Rosales, and he did recognize her.

When she appeared at the door of the saloon, having just shot Emster in the back, a man leaning against the bar immediately recognized her.

Juan Pedro Guerrero stepped out of the saloon and watched the three riders turn to the east.

"Soto!" he called to one of his hired men in the bar. "Go and saddle my horse. Bring a couple of the men, and tell them to arm themselves. Pack for a few days in the desert, just in case. And send a rider to Juárez to Señor Arellano. Tell him his daughter Marisol from Santa Catalina has just shot a gringo in Palomas and that I am following her into the desert. Have him send word what he wants me to do with her when I have caught her and the gringo she rides with."

NÉSTOR LOZANO DRANK FROM his canteen and then replaced the cork. He hung the canteen from the saddle horn and looked out across the desert. As far as he could see, the tracks left by his own horse and the riders with him were the visible signs that any human or horse had ever come this way. He rocked slightly in the saddle to get the horse moving. The sandy earth crunched under the weight of the horse. Hard and crusty on top, but the weight of the horse was plenty to break that hard top layer and get to the soft sand below. And then the hoofs sank nearly two inches into the sand.

"If they came through here, they would have left tracks," Lozano said, as much to himself as to anyone else.

His men possessed no opinion one way or the other. Or if they did possess an opinion, they certainly did not express it. Lozano was not the sort of captain who required or welcomed opinions in others. His opinion was the only one that matter, and these men had ridden long enough with Lozano to know that about him.

Still, Lozano was puzzled. The gringo surely came north, fleeing for the border.

But no one had seen them. Not the vaqueros working cattle in the pastures. Not the people in the villages between Santa Catalina and Juárez. Not the farmers on the road driving produce to one village or another.

"It is important to me that I be the one to find the gringo," Lozano said. "I do not want anyone else to find him."

The sky was as blue as it could be. Not even a wisp of cloud. And the sun stood bold and hot in the middle of the sky, beating down on them and acting like it would not move, would not set, would only hang there in one space and cook them for eternity.

When Lozano was a boy, twelve or thirteen years old, he stole bread from the bakery on the street where he lived. His aunt, who had raised him and his cousins, had recently died. Just days before. And he stole the bread to feed himself and his little cousins.

Manuel Arellano Hermosillio saw him steal the bread. Even then, almost twenty years ago, Señor Arellano was one of the most powerful men in the state of Chihuahua. Certainly the most powerful man in Juárez. Señor Arellano grabbed Lozano in the street as he tried to get away with his stolen bread, and the man beat the young boy. Slapped him, boxed his ears, knocked him to the ground and kicked him.

"I'll tolerate no thieves in my town," Señor Arellano had said. "This baker works hard to feed his family. You pay or you do not eat his bread."

And then, after kicking him and beating him, Señor Arellano gave Lozano a job. And when he learned that Lozano had two cousins, young orphans, he found a home for them.

He mucked stalls at Señor Arellano's ranch for two years. Then he worked with the vaqueros. First he cared for their horses and their gear. Then he rode with them and learned from them. But even at a young age, it became evident that Lozano's talents tended toward other work. He became adept and tracking and killing cattle rustlers, and for some years that was his primary job. He worked in this desert south of Juarez. He tracked rustlers to their hideouts in the mountains. He taught them not to steal from Señor Arellano, and he made certain they learned a permanent lesson.

Then he moved into Juárez. Though the nature of the work didn't change, the men he dealt with on behalf of Señor Arellano were a different sort of men. They were political men, business men. Rivals. And Lozano did not track them to mountain hideouts. He raided their haciendas or found them in saloons or stores. He traveled through the state. Bullying. Threatening. Killing. He never asked why. He never asked what these men did to deserve their deaths. He simply dealt with the men Señor Arellano told him to deal with in the way Señor Arellano told him to do it.

Just a few weeks ago, Néstor Lozano received his reward.

Señor Arellano sent Lozano to Santa Catalina. A lovely little village on the bank of the Rio Santa Maria in good farming country. Hilly country. Pleasant views in every direction, cool breezes, shade trees. A choice assignment.

Run things, Señor Arellano told him. Oversee my cattle. Look after my hardware store. I will send men to you, and I want you to train them like a military so that when the time comes, they will be ready.

And the other thing Señor Arellano said to him: Go and see my niece, Marisol Rosales. Pay attention to her. When I come to see her, I will suggest that she should marry you.

Néstor Lozano knew what all of this meant. Train an army? Had the rumor not been going around for many months that Señor Arellano was involved in a plot to spark a revolución. Señor Arellano intended to be El Presidente over all of Mexico, and he had many political connections and friends in the military who were loyal to him.

Lozano also knew that Marisol Rosales was not Arellano's niece. She was his illegitimate daughter – one of many children in villages across the state. And Lozano knew, too, that Arellano employed his sons as his surrogates, and where there was no son, he used his daughters to forge bonds of familial loyalty among his men and his friends. He would give to Lozano Marisol's hand in marriage in return for lifelong loyalty.

And it might have all turned out that way, as Señor Arellano intended and as Lozano imagined, but then the gringo showed up in Santa Catalina, and Marisol – foolish, flighty girl – fell in love.

"Señor Lozano?" Guillermo Gomez said. He spoke tentatively, afraid of offending.

"Qué es?" Lozano snapped.

"Perhaps they went west beyond the mountains," Gomez said. "We found their hideout in the mountains. Maybe they went to the valley beyond the mountains and turned north there. It would take them to Palomas. They might plan to cross the border at Palomas."

Lozano sniffed.

It was possible. Señor Arellano had sent from Juárez to Monterrey two wagons loaded with guns and almost a million dollars in gold bricks and coins. Bribes for the army posted at Monterrey to join him in his revolución. He'd sent the wagons under a light guard, hoping not to draw the attention of the federales or soldiers loyal to the current regime. Those two wagons were meant to be the spark of revolt.

But several miles north of Santa Catalina, the wagons were ambushed – the guard murdered. The bodies showed evidence that they had been assassinated.

Lozano only discovered the contents of the wagons when Señor Arellano himself arrived in Santa Catalina two days later.

Every man in Santa Catalina began the hunt for the men responsible, but Lozano knew that Marisol's gringo was among those responsible.

And then Marisol disappeared from her home. She'd gone off with that gringo thief.

His intentions now were to kill the gringo and recover the gold. What rewards would Señor Arellano have in store for him if he achieved such a feat? Surely far greater than a flighty daughter. But he would take Marisol, too. She was the most beautiful woman he'd ever seen. Surely, the most beautiful in all of Chihuahua and possibly the most beautiful in all of Mexico. Her love of the gringo mattered little to Lozano. If he could not win her heart, he could at least beat her into submission. But perhaps that would not even be a choice. Lozano had seen Señor Arellano's rage, and he suspected that Marisol's father would prefer to see her hanged than redeemed.

"We will ride to Juárez," Lozano said, wishing he'd gone himself to the mountains to try to track the thieves. "We will send a rider to Palomas to see what we can learn."

2

THE BABY CAME, WITH still no word from her father.

Hazel had lost count of the number of weeks, now. Ten weeks, or maybe twelve?

Her husband had left in February, saying he was going to town to find work. He needed to raise a stake, he'd said. Enough money to replace at least some of the cattle they'd lost over the winter. With snow still on the ground, he saddled the only good riding horse they had and rode to Las Vegas.

"Two weeks at the most."

That's what he said. He'd be gone two weeks at the most. Back in time for the baby to be born. Back with money, if not with new cattle. They'd lost some steers to the bitterly cold winter. Rustlers had ridden off with some. More than anything, though, it was incompetence that led to their downfall.

"Your daddy never did know nothing about cattle," Hazel whispered to the baby, gently rocking her to and fro and watching out the open front door. "But he could pick a piece of land."

The cabin sat up on a hill below the big pines. It looked out to the east, so that every morning out the front door there was a painted sky, lush with the promise of a new day. It made the first cries of morning a bit more bearable because Hazel knew she would not miss the sunrise. Though the first cries of morning often came not long on the heels of the last cries of night, and life now seemed to be a vague haze of never asleep and never fully awake.

Below that morning sunrise, rolling hills all covered in tall grass, perpetually waving in the constant breeze – except when it was all covered over in snow and killing the cattle. And the narrow Sapello River cut through the open country. Her husband had promised that river was the key to their success. Year-round water for the cattle.

At times, Hazel would stand holding the baby and look out at the brown grass framed by the door, the rolling hills, the morning sky lit like a fresh peach, and she would imagine that she was looking at a painting hanging in some grand hall and she would wonder what brush stroke the artist used to make the grass appear to blow back and forth like that.

Now, a wagon cut out across the field, coming toward the house. She bounced the baby in her arms.

"We're about to have visitors," Hazel said. "Jorge and Maria, I think."

How terrible it all would be if not for Jorge and Maria. They lived in a little village not far from Hazel's cabin. Mostly Spanish speakers in that village, families of Mexicans who'd been here since this land was all part of the former Spanish territory. Indifferent to political boundaries, this land was their land for as long as they could hang onto it.

When Hazel's husband left to look for work, Maria helped. She was there when the baby was born. They brought her food. Jorge chopped wood to make sure that she had fuel for the stove. He brought water up from the well. He helped to plant the garden. Maria came up sometimes just to take the baby, to give Hazel time to sleep or to work in the garden. They were an older couple, their own children grown or teenagers.

Jorge went to Las Vegas to search for Hazel's husband, but he came back with no answers.

No one there knew her husband, anyway. They'd been here only a year. Just long enough to build the cabin, buy the cattle, get Hazel pregnant, and watch the cattle die. They'd come from the east where things were different.

"I hope we have not come too early," Jorge said.

Maria took the baby from Hazel's arms.

"Not too early," Hazel smiled. "I'm always happy for company."

"Si," Jorge said. "I have a box of food for you. Smoked meats, vegetables, beans. Also some flour and corn meal."

"So much?" Hazel said. "What do I owe you?"

"No. Nothing. We are happy to share what we have."

Hazel dropped her eyes. Receiving charity was hard for a proud woman.

Jorge saw her reaction and quickly changed the subject.

"We come early today because we are riding into town in a little while. You said the next time I go to town you wanted to send a letter with me?"

Hazel sighed heavily and slowly nodded her head.

"Yes. Thank you. I'll give you money for the post."

"Please. No," Jorge said, holding up a hand to stop her. "I am happy to do it."

Hazel found the envelope. The letter was written. It had been written for more than a week now. The envelope addressed and sealed.

"It's to my parents in Chicago," she said. "I am reluctant to send it, but I think now I must face the truth that my husband is not coming home."

Jorge stiffened and sent a glance at Maria. Maria shushed the baby in her arms.

"I'm asking them if they will send money sufficient to get me back to Chicago," she said. "I cannot stay here. As kind as you have been, at some point I've got to find a way to do for myself."

"Many things can happen to a man," Jorge said. "A fall from the horse. Thieves. Sometimes the Apache still come this way. If they caught him ..."

Jorge left the thought unfinished.

He had his own beliefs that he had shared with his wife. A man whose cattle are all died with no money and no prospects? Maybe the man ran off. Some men find it easier to run than to face their own failures. Maybe he turned the gun on himself, his body still at the foot of some ravine somewhere. It happened a lot, especially among the lonely cow punchers. But a married man who cannot take care of his family? Maybe him, too. No man takes well to failure, and the man who finds himself deep in a hole and carries the shame of failing the ones who rely on him? Well, many things can happen to a man, Jorge thought.

"Thank you," Hazel said. "I have resigned myself to the thought that I will never again see my husband, and I am now trying to resign myself to the thought that I will never know why."

3

"I THINK I'D LIKE to find a place near a big river. The Mississippi or the Missouri – a big river. With hardwood trees on the banks. Maybe someplace up in the mountains where it ain't so hot in the summer."

Marisol laughed.

"Have you had enough of the desert, Tomás?" she asked.

"Had my fill, no doubt about it," Duvall answered her.

"What about you, Pablo?" Duvall said to his last remaining friend. "When we get back across the border, where'd you like to go?"

"I just want to go home, hombre," Pablo said. "I miss mi madre and mi bed."

They rode east out of Palomas, following a pretty well established trail straight for Juárez. But about an hour east of the town, Duvall turned the horses into the desert. It was full dark by then, and not enough of a moon to really see by. The sand was soft here, and not much vegetation. Come morning, if anyone from Palomas cared to follow them, they'd be easy enough to find. They were leaving tracks that would be no problem to follow.

Pablo had brought along the horses that belonged to Emster, Liller, and Rodrigues, and six horses turned up a lot of sand. In truth, anyone who followed them would likely be able to see them in the morning with a pair of field glasses and wouldn't even need the tracks in the sand. Six horses also made a pretty large moving object out in the middle of the flat desert. They walked the horses some distance to the south, deeper into Mexico. Maybe they should have turned for the border, but Duvall had it in his mind to try to go the way no one would expect them to go, to try to disrupt any pursuit. When they'd walked for a couple of hours and were well south of the road, Duvall suggested they stop and make camp.

They had no fuel for a fire, so camp consisted of six hobbled horses, jerky, and blankets – no coffee, no hot beans.

Now, with the stars like hundreds of thousands of pricks of light in the sky overhead, they huddled in their blankets and put their backs to the cold wind and tried to sleep.

But the promise of the future did not sweeten their dreams this night. Instead, the three of them all laid with their private sorrows and fears.

Marisol knew that in the morning they would turn north and make for the border. She would cross into a strange country and an unknown future with a man she hardly knew. She thought of her friends back in Santa Catalina, especially of her close friend Dulce. She thought of the cantina that had been her mother's, the place where she'd earned her living since her mother's death. She thought of the little home she'd left with its courtyard garden that she had tended so meticulously. She'd built such a pleasant life for herself, and she'd given it up on a whim. This American held her future, now. Good or bad. Though she had known him only a short while, she trusted him. She believed that he loved her the way she loved him, with a passionate, bright burning flame. But what life would they be able to build together in America?

She heard Duvall moving under his blankets and opened her eyes and watched in the direction where she knew he was sleeping. There was just light enough to see the dark shapes of the horses moving. And then a spark and hiss and a glow at Duvall's face as he struck a match and lit a cigarette. He shook out the flame from the match.

When he exhaled, Marisol thought she could see a light cloud of smoke blowing away in the starlight.

Duvall's thoughts were not on the future but on the past. He thought of his dead friends – Bull, Richie Hull, and Chuck; Bassett, too, and even Coyote Johnson, but especially Billy Muggs. Billy, who'd been like a younger brother and best friend to him. They'd left Texas together so many years ago and settled in New Mexico Territory in Las Vegas. That's where they fell in with Bull and Pablo and Richie and Chuck. A good group of pals. Troublemakers, but not outlaws. Tough boys who wanted to be tough men, but they'd never make it now, except Pablo. Pablo and Duvall were tough men, now. They'd seen their friends gunned down. They'd murdered for gold and Duvall had murdered for revenge.

Coyote Johnson led them all into this – his big stories of being a tough outlaw. Probably all lies. The younger boys, Bull and Billy and the others, they'd thought Yote Johnson was something else. They admired him because he had an easy way and talked a lot.

Duvall never did care for Yote Johnson, and when Yote started recruiting the boys for this Mexico adventure, Duvall had planned to stay out of it. But all his pals were going, and Billy, and Duvall felt like he should go, too. He didn't want to miss out if all the boys came home with a million dollars in gold. And he didn't want Billy Muggs going down to Mexico and stirring up trouble without him. He'd come to protect Billy – at least, that was part of it – and now Billy was dead.

Pablo's thoughts ran along the same lines, but as the night wore on and the cold wind and fear of the black desert continued to keep him awake, his mind began to drift to other things.

"Hey, Duvall," Pablo said, seeing the glow of the cigarette as Duvall took another drag.

"Yeah?"

"How much gold was in them saddlebags you grabbed?"

"I don't know Pablo. I never looked. I reckon two gold bars in each of the bags, maybe some coins. Each bar is worth six hundred dollars, or thereabouts. So maybe twenty-four hundred in each pair of saddlebags. What's that three times over? Seventy-two hundred?"

"That's a heap of money," Pablo said.

"It is."

"We gonna split that?" Pablo asked.

"I figure so."

"Split it in half?" Pablo said, thinking of Marisol and wondering if Duvall intended to give her a cut. Sure, she'd shot Emster in the back, but it wasn't like she was part of stealing the gold.

"Split it into threes," Duvall said. "I'm going to take a third to Bassett's wife. I can't return her husband to her, but I can give her some of this gold."

"Huh," Pablo said. "Si. I reckon that's only right. I hadn't thought of Bassett's wife."

"It's the right thing to do," Duvall said.

"I've got two of them gold bars myself," Pablo said. "Should I kick one of them in for her, too?"

"You don't have to," Duvall said. "I've got two bars that Bull left for me, but I ain't planning on giving her any portion of that."

"Si. That's fair, I guess," Pablo said. "It was mucho oro, Duvall. You never did see it all, did you?"

"When you boys unloaded the wagons, I was passed out," Duvall said. "That was just after they took that bullet out of me."

"Mucho."

"Well, truth is, Pablo, ain't none of us ever should have seen it. We should have stayed home."

Duvall said it, and he believed it, but at the same time he wouldn't be here with Marisol if he'd not come south across the border with the boys. He didn't know how to feel about that, but it didn't matter. He was here now. And he was with Marisol. And the boys was all dead.

"I was just thinking," Pablo said. "We came down here for all that Mexican gold."

"Uh-huh," Duvall grunted. "And we should be glad we're getting back across the border with any of it."

"Si," Pablo said, a hint of uncertainty in his voice. "I'm just thinking. It's a shame not to get what we came here for."

"It's buried, Pablo. We had it, and then we lost it."

"Si," Pablo agreed. "I'm just thinking, is all."

Duvall cursed as the fire from his cigarette got too near the tips of his fingers and burned him. He shoved the cigarette into the sandy earth.

"We could search for years and still never find that gold," Duvall said. "We ain't got a clue where they buried it."

"I'm just thinking," Pablo said again.

"Well, stop it," Duvall said. "If we get out of Mexico without stretching a rope, we can call this whole enterprise a success. We've got some gold, and we should be satisfied to get out of Mexico alive and richer than we were when we come down here."

JUAN PEDRO GUERRERO ADJUSTED his sombrero to block out the morning sun.

"They left the road here," he said, looking at the fresh tracks in the sand. He studied them for a moment without swinging himself down from the saddle. "Si. Six horses."

Guerrero had two men with him – Soto, who was his best man, and a prizefighter called Alvarez. The prizefighter hadn't been with him very long, but Guerrero knew that Alvarez had run into trouble for throwing fights. A man who lacked scruples could sometimes be useful to have around. Alvarez had done most of his fighting in Juárez, but he came originally from a little village south of Palomas that fell under Guerrero's area of control.

"Why would they turn south?" Soto asked. "Why not go for the border? If they turned north, they would have been less than five miles to the border."

"Si," Guerrero said. "Maybe they do not want to cross the border."

"They killed three men in Palomas. They should want to cross the border."

Guerrero laughed.

"Si. Maybe they are not very smart. Maybe they do not know north from south. Or maybe they do not think they will be in trouble. Marisol Rosales may think her father will protect her."

"Will he?" Soto asked.

Guerrero gave a shrug.

"Who can say? It depends on why she shot that man, I suppose. And who is the gringo she is with? And what does her father think of her being with him?"

"Who was the Mexican?" Soto asked.

"The third man? I do not know him. I have never seen him before."

They'd ridden as far as they could in the dusk and made camp along the side of the road after nightfall. Guerrero preferred that his quarry get farther away than disappear into the night.

He'd sent a rider to Juárez, but it could be days before he heard anything back from Señor Arellano. In the meantime, he would track Marisol and the two men, and when he caught him he would decide how to deal with them based on their behavior. If they co-operated, he'd take them back to his hacienda and make them his guests. If they declined his invitation, he would detain them – force them to be his guests.

Guerrero and the others rode some ways from the road, following the clear tracks left in the desert floor.

Soon enough, they found the spot where the trio had camped down in a small depression. Tracks showed where the horses had been tied overnight, but there was no sign of a campfire.

"They spent a cold night," Guerrero remarked with some satisfaction, though Soto noted to himself that their own group had also spent a cold night.

"The morning tracks also lead to the south," Guerrero said. He was off his horse now, looking off to the southern horizon. "Perhaps they are going to Santa Catalina. That is where the Rosales woman is from, I believe."

"Why not simply take the road south when they left Palomas?" Soto asked.

Guerrero shrugged. "There is no water to the south, no forage."

But the tracks did not lie. The three men, Gurrero, Soto, and Alvarez mounted and followed the tracks to the south.

"Rio Casas Grande," Soto said.

"Ah. Si," Gurrero said. It was not much of a river. Most times of the year it ran dry, though there might be water in it now. And there were a few little villages south of Palomas that sat near the river. "Well, wherever they are going, we will be able to follow them."

Guerrero got back in his saddle, and without waiting for the others began to ride to the southwest, in the direction the tracks took him.

"What is the name of that village where the Santos girl lives?" Guerrero asked.

Soto grinned.

"Guadalupe Victoria," he said, knowing that Guerrero knew the name of the village. Guerrero's grandfather had fought with the man the village was named for in the war of independence from Spain. He knew the name well enough.

"Well, if we are lucky, maybe we will lose the tracks of the gringo and Marisol Rosales, and we will find ourselves very near Guadalupe Victoria. And with nothing else to do – because we have lost the tracks – I will go and visit the Santos girl."

Soto laughed.

"Si. And maybe I will ask her if she has a friend." He gave a glance to Alvarez. "And we will ask her if she has a goat for Señor Alvarez."

Guerrero laughed. Alvarez scowled at Soto, but he was accustomed to being the butt of the man's jokes. Señor Guerrero always wore a smile. He always was looking for a joke to laugh about. Soto achieved his position as Guerrero's right hand by being ready with the jokes, and they came at the expense of anyone who was nearby. Alvarez didn't care. He had a comfortable life in Puerto Palomas. He was well paid and did not have to work very hard. If he sometimes became the butt of a joke, what did that matter to him?

Guerrero led the other two men south, following the tracks. The riders made for a small mountain visible on the horizon, only four or five miles south of where they'd camped. There, they left the soft sand, riding over rocky terrain. It became difficult to follow the trail. Guerrero had to hunt for sparks on rocks that showed where a shod horse stepped down and chipped a rock.

"One of the men we are following has done his share of tracking," Guerrero declared. "He knows the tricks for hiding his tracks. They have ridden in circles here among the hard ground to try to confound anyone following them. He is either a tracker or an experienced thief."

From the mountain, the trail led west. Still desert, but with more grass and desert greasewood. The trail remained complicated. Guerrero had to stop at dusk for fear of losing the trail altogether.

In the morning, they tracked Marisol and the two men to the road leading back to Palomas, and there it became impossible to follow the trail. Too much traffic on the road in recent days to identify any one set of prints from another.

"Did they go north, back to Palomas? Did they just ride in a big circle? Or did they turn south, to get farther away from the scene of the murders they committed?" Guerrero asked himself.

In the end, he decided to turn south. There were a couple of little villages there, places where travelers on the run could rest and eat, and Marisol and the two men likely would have been able to reach the first of those villages before dark the previous day – rest their horses overnight at the livery and spend the night themselves in a warm and safe place. Perhaps she even knew someone there.

4

THE OLD MAN STUDIED Duvall and Pablo, sitting their horses behind Marisol and holding onto the spare horses. Marisol spoke to him. She spoke to everyone they encountered. She'd told Pablo his Spanish was too poor and that he was easily recognizable as American-born. So she talked to the old man while Duvall and Pablo stayed back and waited. But they were near enough to hear the conversation, and Pablo leaned toward Duvall, and in a hushed tone he translated.

"She's asking if he's seen strangers in the village in the last few days," Pablo said.

Duvall grunted.

"It's a long shot," Duvall said.

Pablo hushed him so he could hear, but the old man was still studying him and Duvall, looking past Marisol. He wore a wide-brimmed sombrero and dusty clothes. A fine layer of desert dust covered everything around here. Duvall and Pablo and Marisol all wore dusty clothes, too. They'd been two days in the desert before finally coming out into a little village south of Palomas. But not this village. This was the second village they'd come to.

"No," the old man shook his head, and said something more.

"You ain't got to translate that," Duvall said. "I get the gist."

Pablo frowned.

"Now he's talking about some Americans who came through here a year ago," Pablo said. "That ain't who we want to know about."

"I got a feeling that old man would know if strangers came through his village," Duvall said.

After their first night in the desert, they'd broken camp just after sunup. Before setting out, they went through the saddlebags to see what they had. More gold than they'd suspected. Two of the pairs of saddlebags had six gold bars each, thirty-six hundred dollars in gold just in those. The other had four gold bars. There were also coins totaling a thousand dollars. More than ten thousand dollars in gold. When they got back to Las Vegas, they would give a portion of it to Bassett's wife, assuming they could find her, but even then, it would leave a substantial amount of money for both Pablo and Duvall.

Enough that we can feel good about riding for the border and leaving behind whatever else is buried in Mexico, Duvall had said.

But then they'd found a piece of paper in one of Emster's saddlebags. It was a hand-drawn map, probably drawn by Rodrigues because the places marked on the map were written in Spanish. El placito. El cementerio. La misa.

The map showed an unnamed village drawn as a square with a church and the plaza marked, a cemetery positioned to the northeast of the town. It could have been any of a hundred villages, except that there was a mountain range to the southwest of the village that was marked as Boca Grande and a river drawn as a squiggly line north of the village marked as Rio Casas Grande. There were two villages that the map might have depicted. The first one they came to out of the desert was promising because it sat right on the road north that Rodrigues and the other two had traveled after stealing the gold and then fleeing for the border. But in that village, the cemetery was south of town and the plaza and the church were separated by a block. They'd come out of the desert and taken their horses to the livery to rest them and get them fed. Then they'd walked through the town and discovered that the town did not match the map.

They paid the hostler to spend the night in a one-room cabin behind the livery, and in the morning they asked him about other nearby villages. He knew of only one other village around there that sat between the Boca Grande mountains and the Rio Casas Grande.

Guadalupe Victoria sat a few miles off the main north-south road running from Palomas south to the heart of Mexico. But only a few miles off the main road, that would have made for an easy detour for Rodrigues, Emster, and Liller.

They could have easily gone to the village, buried the gold, and then resumed their trek north to Palomas.

In addition to the map, the piece of paper bore a series of numbers. Fifteen. Three. Five. Six. Two.

The numbers meant nothing obvious and there was nothing else with them. Duvall guessed that they were paces – fifteen paces, three paces, five paces, six paces, two paces. But where to start counting? Which way to turn once the paces had been walked off? But maybe they weren't paces at all. Probably the only three people who could explain what the numbers meant were all now dead in Palomas, but Duvall didn't care.

When they discovered the map, Pablo looked it over and said, This is where they buried the gold. We should go and find it.

Duvall objected, arguing instead that they should get across the border.

"We came here for the gold," Pablo said. "All our amigos are dead, hombre, and if we go back without the gold, then what use was it for them to die?"

Duvall still argued against it.

"We don't know what's coming up behind us, Pablo," Duvall said. "We don't know if we've got Señor Arellano's men tracking us from Santa Catalina or if we've got the law in Palomas coming after us.

Unless we want to join our amigos buried all over Mexico, we need to get across that border."

"You yourself said you wanted to do what they wouldn't expect us to do," Pablo said. "That's how we get them off our trail. Let's turn west, at least see if we can find the village on the map. If we don't find it in a couple of days, we'll ride for the border and get out of here. Look, Duvall, we probably ain't never gonna be back this way. This is our one chance, in our whole lives, to get that gold we came for."

Pablo Peña made a compelling argument, though Duvall still debated it.

"It might not be a bad idea to have a look around," Duvall told Marisol. "If we can find the gold right away. We'd never want for anything the rest of our lives if we found that money."

Marisol gave her head a small nod, but she closed her eyes and frowned.

"I thought, Tomás, that we would never want for anything the rest of our lives as long as we were together," she said. "That's why I came with you."

Duvall nodded at her and smiled.

"That's right. But if we find that gold, we can be together and be rich, too. Surely, that's preferable. A day or two is all we'll spend."

They made southwest through the desert and came to the road leading back to Palomas. It was there, at the road, when Duvall finally made his decision.

"We can turn south," he said. "We can try those villages near the Boca Grande mountains and see if we can find the gold. If we don't figure out where it's buried, then we'll ride on."

"We can't go back through Palomas," Marisol said.

"We won't," Duvall told her. "We'll skirt around the village and cross the border in the desert. Then we'll make for Fort Selden."

So they rode south at the road to Palomas. They went to the village nearest the Palomas road, but quickly discovered that village did not match the map. They spent the night and rested the horses. And now they had come to Guadalupe Victoria and the old man sitting on a cracker box. The village was right. The cemetery to the northeast, the church there beside the placita.

But the old man didn't know about any strangers coming to town.

"He says we can check down at the livery," Marisol said, turning her piebald pony back toward Duvall and Pablo. "But he thinks if there were strangers in town that he would have seen them."

They stepped their horses along the street leading into Guadalupe Victoria. A gust of wind picked up and blew hard, bringing with it sand from the road. Duvall had to reach up to catch his hat to keep it from blowing away. The late-afternoon breeze felt hot, and Duvall had a sudden sense of foreboding.

"We shouldn't be here," he said. "We should've gone on across the border when we were so close. We need to get out of Mexico."

"It won't hurt to look around the village," Pablo said. "We're here, Duvall. We should at least look around."

Duvall shook his head.

"You think that old man misses anything that happens in this village?" Duvall said. "I'd wager he spends every waking hour sitting on that old cracker box and watching every coming and going in this village. If Rodrigues and them others came here, he'd know it. Besides, they wouldn't bury that gold in the village where someone might see. They'd bury it off in the hills."

"Maybe that old man doesn't spend all his waking hours on that cracker box," Pablo said, and he nodded in the direction of the man.

The old man watched the trio ride along the street, and then he rose abruptly and cut down another street.

"Where's he going?" Pablo asked. "I'll bet all the gold in my saddlebags that he's going to tell someone about us – and about us asking about Rodrigues and Emster and Liller. Wait here for me."

Without pausing for argument, Pablo dropped down from his saddle and started to follow the men.

"Tomás," Marisol said. "You are right. We should not be here. We need to leave this village. Señor Arellano has sent men to follow us. Word will soon spread of the dead men we left in Palomas. It will only be a matter of time before Señor Arellano's men are here in Guadalupe Victoria looking for us. We should be gone before they arrive."

Duvall nodded his head.

"I agree with you. We'll let Pablo follow the old man, and then we'll tell him we're going."

"The gold does not matter," Marisol said. "I did not flee my village – my life! – because I wanted money. I came with you because I wanted to be with you."

Duvall watched Pablo disappear around the back of a building, following behind the old man.

DUVALL AND MARISOL HITCHED the horses in a shady lot beside a small cantina very much like the one Marisol had owned in Santa Catalina. The cantina was within sight of the spot on the road where Pablo had left them, and Duvall figured that would be a good spot to wait for him to come back. Duvall didn't want to leave the horses unattended because of the gold stashed in the saddlebags. So Marisol went inside to get food and returned a short while later with a tray of birria and flat bread and two beers.

"I tried a bite inside," Marisol said with a grin. "Not as good as mine, but it will do."

They sat on the ground in the shade a little ways from the horses and put the tray of food between them.

"Maybe when we get back to Las Vegas, we should take some of that money and buy you a new place up there," Duvall said. "It would be a shame to deprive the world of your cooking."

Marisol smiled at him.

"I would like that. I loved owning the cantina in Santa Catalina."

"Of course, all this gold we've got, you wouldn't have to ever work again if you didn't want to."

Marisol gave a small shrug of her shoulders and tucked a strand of loose hair back behind her ear.

"It's a joy to me to work. To see people happy with the food I make. To see friends all day. I'll have to make new friends in Las Vegas, and there's no better way to make friends with people than to feed them."

"As good as your cooking is, it won't be hard to make friends," Duvall said. "I reckon just about everybody will want to be your friend."

"What work will you do?" Marisol asked.

"All I really know how to do is ranch work," Duvall said. "I reckon I'll go back to that."

"There is enough gold, you won't have to work if you don't want to," Marisol said.

Duvall nodded his head thoughtfully.

"I suppose not, but I'm kinda like you. I wouldn't know what to do with myself if I wasn't working. But I don't care to work around people. Cows is terrible to work with, but they're a sight better than most people I've met, and the best people I know are hosses. So, I'd rather work cattle on the back of a hoss, anyway."

They ate and drank and waited for Pablo to return, but he was more than an hour getting back to them, and Duvall was starting to get restless. Marisol sat in the shade watching as he paced back and forth, looking up one street and down another. At last, Duvall saw Pablo walking along the main street in their direction.

"He went to the funeraria," Pablo said. "He was in there a long time. Then when he came out, I followed him down to the livery. He talked to the hostler for a while, and then he went to a cantina. When he went in there, I came back here."

Duvall gave a shrug.

"Okay. So he went to the undertaker and he got a bite to eat. Let's ride on out of here before it's dark."

"Don't you see?" Pablo said. "He went to the funeraria?"

"So?"

"Rodrigues told you they buried the gold with Billy and Bassett."

"Liller said that," Duvall said.

Pablo grinning and shrugged.

"It don't matter who said it, hombre. The point is, they said they buried Billy and Bassett with the gold. And that old man went to the undertaker, Duvall. Don't you see?"

Duvall glanced at Marisol.

"Pablo, are you saying you think they buried the gold here in the cemetery?"

"Si. That's what I think. I walked down to the cemetery to see for myself. There's five fresh graves."

Duvall frowned.

"Five graves seems like a lot for a village this size," he conceded. "Are they marked?"

"With wooden crosses."

"Are there names on them?"

Pablo shrugged.

"All Spanish names. What I think is Rodrigues and Liller and Emster rode into this town with Billy and Bassett already dead. I think they had the undertaker bury them. I don't know how the old man knows about it, or how he might be involved, but I think he went to warn the undertaker that we were here asking questions."

Duvall nodded thoughtfully, but his jaw was clenched.

"What?" Pablo asked, seeing the look of doubt on Duvall's face.

"Some old man going to talk to the undertaker don't mean there's a million dollars of gold in the cemetery," Duvall said.

"Si, it don't. But I followed that old man to the livery, too. And do you know what I saw there?"

Duvall shook his head.

"In the corral, more than a dozen good looking horses. I mean really good horses, Duvall. And I think maybe I recognized them."

"Recognized them?"

"When we ambushed the wagons with the gold, we took Señor Arellano's horses that the escort was riding. That's how Rodrigues and them packed out the gold, on those horses. Remember?"

"I remember."

"Those are the horses at the livery. I'm sure of it. I think Rodrigues and them other two brought the bodies here, brought the gold here. I think they buried Billy and Bassett with the gold in the cemetery. I think they sold the horses to the hostler – or, hell, maybe they just left them at the livery. But I'm telling you, Duvall. That old man knew more than he was saying. He may not know about the gold, but I think he knows Rodrigues and them were here in Guadalupe Victoria."

Duvall shrugged his shoulders and chuckled.

"What do you want to do, Pablo? You want to go dig up the cemetery?"

Pablo shrugged.

"Maybe."

"Maybe you're right, Pablo. Maybe they buried that gold right here in the cemetery. But we don't know that. And we don't know which of those five fresh graves they might have put the gold in. We do know that we've got people in Mexico looking for us, and we can guess that they'll be around here soon. Word is going to get out about those killings we did in Palomas. And that's going to bring Arellano's men looking for us. We need to get out of Mexico before they find us."

"We may be too late for that, Tomás," Marisol said.

Duvall glanced at her and saw that she was looking out to the road that led in from the east, the road they'd taken here. In the distance, not yet in the village, he could see three riders coming toward them, and his stomach dropped. Just at a glance, Duvall could see these men weren't local farmers riding to the village for supplies. They came on tall, strong-looking horses. They wore big sombreros. These were vaqueros or, more likely, gun hands who knew their business. They didn't belong in Guadalupe Victoria any more than Duvall and Pablo did – maybe even less.

"Mount up," Duvall said. "We need to ride out of here now."

"What's going on?" Pablo asked.

Duvall was already over at Pecas Gris giving a tug to the flea-bitten gray's cinch strap.

"I got a feeling them boys is here for us. Walk the horses out of the lot up to the road," Duvall said. "No reason to draw attention to ourselves."

Even as he said it, though, the three riders brought their horses to a gallop, making to cut off their escape.

NÉSTOR LOZANO DOZED ON the sofa in Señor Arellano's hacienda in Juárez when the rider came in from Palomas.

The hacienda consisted of a large compound of houses, horse barns, bunk houses, smokehouses, and other buildings. Most all of them were built of adobe. The main house, where Lozano now rested, had wide windows that opened like French doors and let in a cool breeze, even on hot days. An orchard behind the house shaded and cooled the air that blew through the house. The sofas were made of mahogany and cushioned in soft fabrics of brilliant colors. Tapestries and paintings hung from the walls. Rich, earthy colors mingled with vibrant fabrics and paints so that every corner of the house was pleasing to the eye.

Lozano had never seen a place more luxurious than Señor Arellano's hacienda in Juárez.

In some ways, his move to Santa Catalina had felt like a banishment. This hacienda was where Lozano worked and lived prior to his move. Of course, he lived in one of the bunkhouses and then in a private room in one of the servants' houses. It was nicer there, though neither compared to the main house. In Santa Catalina, as Arellano's official overseeing his businesses in and around the village, Lozano had the luxury of living in Señor Arellano's hacienda outside of Santa Catalina, but it did not compare to his home in Juárez. Just working in Juárez and being around this house on a daily basis was far better than anything Santa Catalina could offer.

As far as Lozano knew, Señor Arellano was still in Santa Catalina. He did not like to travel, and having just ridden there, he did not want to turn around and come immediately back to Juárez when he learned that his gold had been stolen. So he sent Lozano after the thieves, saying that he would remain for a while in Santa Catalina.

When Lozano finally arrived in Juárez with still no clue about the whereabouts of the gringos who stole Señor Arellano's gold, he decided to rest for a day. He sent riders out to watch the border crossings. Palomas was the only village on the border to the west within any proximity, but east along the Rio Grande there were several places where they might cross – San Isidro, San Agustin, even as far as Guadalupe was not out of the question.

He sent other riders to some of the villages to the south and west to ask about gringos who might have traveled through there in recent days.

Lozano felt certain the gringos had not yet escaped Mexico, but he also knew that time was running out. Any day they might cross the border. For a million dollars worth of gold, Señor Arellano would send men into los Estados Unidos. Even if they had to commit murders and fight the authorities, the border would not stop Señor Arellano from regaining his gold. But across the border, they would be far more difficult to track.

Lozano sent four riders across the border to Mesilla.

He sent the Basurto brothers, Luis and Armando. Lozano had no authority to send them. They were not gun hands or ranch hands, men who Lozano could order about. But they were the best to send into the United States. They had sense enough to not get themselves into trouble, and they had experience in the United States. Both brothers were lawyers – the sorts of men Lozano had little use for. So he sent two others with them, Javier and Ricardo. Javier and Ricardo were gun hands.

It seemed most likely now that the gringos had gone west of the mountains near Santa Catalina, riding north through the valley on a road that would take them to Palomas. No one crossing the border at Palomas would risk going west in New Mexico Territory because there were too many Apache roaming the hills that way. If the gringos crossed the border anywhere west of Juárez, they would turn east and eventually pass through Mesilla.

Lozano cast a net of spies, certain that the men who stole the gold would be seen.

When the rider arrived, Lozano did not immediately go to see what was happening. He did not even open his eyes from his nap. If it mattered to him, someone would eventually come and get him.

But through the open windows, he heard voices in the yard outside. Hurried voices. Urgent voices. Someone shouted for Señor Valdez, one of Señor Arellano's top men in Juárez. That roused Lozano's curiosity, and he now rose and went to the window.

The main floor of the house stood high over the basement where the kitchen was located, so when he stepped out onto the little balcony, he was looking down into the yard. There he saw a half dozen men, including some of Señor Arellano's ranch hands. They were gathered around two men who had just dismounted from horses.

"What is going on?" Lozano shouted down to them.

The men all looked up at Lozano, and one of the riders answered. "We come from Palomas with news for Señor Arellano."

"Señor Arellano is not here," Lozano said. "He is away at Santa Catalina. What news do you bring?"

The two riders looked at each other, uncertain if they should give their message to someone they did not know. But one of Señor Arellano's hands who stood near them said something, and that must have been enough to convince them.

"Two days ago, three men were killed in Palomas."

Lozano narrowed his eyes.

"Who was killed?"

"Strangers. Two of them were gringos."

Lozano's eyes opened wide at that.

"Gringos?"

"With a Mexican," the man said.

"Ay, caramba," Lozano breathed. "Who killed them?"

"Another gringo, traveling with a Mexican and a woman. A woman known to Señor Arellano."

"What woman?" Lozano demanded.

"Marisol Rosales!"

Lozano pointed a stern finger at the two men.

"Do not move!" he shouted, and he turned swiftly, almost running to the back door of the hacienda, across the wide patio, and down the steps into the yard.

"You have seen Marisol Rosales?"

"We did not see her, but our boss, Juan Pedro Guerrero witnessed the killings." The man speaking gave Lozano a dark look. "Señorita Rosales shot and killed one of the gringos."

Lozano felt himself flush with anger.

"Where are they now?" he demanded. He wanted to strike the man for the way he spoon-fed the information. "What else do you know? Tell me your story?"

"Señor Guerrero rode after them. He intends to bring them into his custody and wait to hear from Señor Arellano."

Lozano turned on one of the ranch hands.

"Saddle my horse and the horses of my men. Fetch my men. Tell Guillermo Gomez to get here to me this instant!"

The man nodded and ran to do as he was told, and a couple of the others went to the barns to saddle the horses. Lozano directed his attention back to Guerrero's messenger.

"You will take us to Guerrero," Lozano said. "Get fresh horses and be ready to ride out in an hour."

"Señor, it will be dark soon. Perhaps we should start for Palomas in the morning."

"We will ride through the night," Lozano said.

5

THE THREE RIDERS CAME at the gallop, cutting off the escape with guns drawn. They rode right up in front of Duvall, Pablo, and Marisol, leading their horses out of the vacant lot.

The lead rider smiled as if amused by some private joke.

"You don't remember me, eh, señorita?"

"I do not," Marisol said.

He nodded his head, grinning at her.

"I remember you. A very pretty girl. How old would you have been? Fourteen or fifteen, maybe? Your father took much pride in you."

Juan Pedro Guerrero slipped down from his saddle. His man Alvarez did the same, but Soto stayed in his saddle, a rifle across his lap. Guerrero motioned to Alvarez, and the man stepped forward, walking up to Duvall and taking the converted Colt from his holster. Then he stepped over to Pablo Peña and similarly disarmed him. Alvarez didn't touch the rifles in their scabbards on the saddles, nor did he bother with the holstered Model 3s on the saddles. Just the guns immediately available.

"You don't mind if we get those out of the way?" Guerrero said in English to Duvall. "I saw how dangerous you are with your pistolas back in Palomas."

"You were there?" Duvall said, realizing that if that was the case these men had followed them for two days through the desert.

"Si. I was there," Guerrero said. "I was in the saloon when you started – what do you say? Burning powder?"

"That was personal between me and them," Duvall said. "If you don't mean me no harm, I won't put no harm on you, neither."

Guerrero laughed, seemingly delighted with the response.

"I mean you no harm, amigo," Guerrero said. "But you come to my village and kill three men, bringing with you the niece of mi amigo who happens to be a very powerful man in Chihuahua. You understand why I've followed you?"

"I reckon," Duvall said.

"My name is Juan Pedro Guerrero. Who do I have the pleasure of speaking to?"

Duvall clenched his jaw.

"I'm Duvall. This here is Pablo Peña. And Señorita Rosales."

Guerrero smiled.

"Indeed. Señorita Rosales. Marisol. What are you doing here so far from Santa Catalina?"

"We are traveling to las Estados Unidos," Marisol said. "And if you know that Señor Manuel Arellano Hermosillio is my – uncle? – then you'll know that he won't be happy that you've interfered with us. Mis compañeros are in a hurry, Señor Guerrero. I must ask that you not delay us any longer."

Guerrero answered with a smile and a chuckle.

"If you are in such a hurry to get to los Estados Unidos, why not cross the border when you were in Palomas and so near? What are we doing here in Guadalupe Victoria, much further now from the border than you were two days ago?"

"Are you the law here?" Duvall said, interrupting. "What right do you have to arrest us?"

"I am not arresting you," Guerrero said sharply, the smile dropping from his face. "I am inviting you to be my guests. But the answer to your question? Señor Arellano is the law here. And I am in his employ, to oversee the village of Palomas. I am not arresting you and putting you in a jail. I am inviting you to be my guests. Out of respect for Señor Arellano and his fondness for Señorita Rosales, I am offering you the courtesy to come with me to my hacienda. We will wait until we have word from Señor Arellano, and when he says what he wants me to do, then we will see if you will stay with me a while longer or if you will continue on to los Estados Unidos. I am being nothing but a gracious host, extending to you – what is the word? – hospitality."

"What if we ain't interested in your hospitality?" Duvall said. "Fact is, we want to ride on and go without being bothered."

Guerrero's smile returned. He stretched his hands wide.

"Mi amigo, if Señor Arellano wishes that you go on without being bothered, then that is fine. But for the moment, if you reject my hospitality, then I would be deeply offended, and Señor Alvarez, here, he would not want to see me deeply offended. Eh? Si, Alvarez?"

Alvarez, who didn't appear to understand a word of the English conversation, nodded his head vigorously.

"Si, Señor Guerrero," Alvarez said.

"If it comes to it, we will force you to come with us," Guerrero said. "But I don't think it is necessary to force you. Come. Be my guests. If it is a personal matter between you and those men you killed in Palomas –" Guerrero gave a small shrug. "Well then, that is fine. We do not care about two dead gringos in Palomas. Not if Señor Arellano does not care. Si? And if Señor Arellano does care about the dead gringos, then that will be a matter that he can take up with you. In the meantime, hospitality."

Duvall cast a glance to Marisol, but she had only a hopeless and frightened look on her face.

"Alvarez," Guerrero said, nodding at the horses.

Now Alvarez went around removing the weapons from the horses. They were too much for one man to easily manage, though, so as he took up each weapon, he removed the live rounds, emptying them into his pockets. As he did so, Guerrero unloaded the two revolvers Alvarez had already taken – Duvall's Colt and the Model 3 Pablo had carried. Soto remained in his saddle, his hands on the rifle in his lap, though he did not wield it in any threatening way.

When the guns were unloaded, the rifles, too, Alvarez and Guerrero returned the empty weapons to Duvall and Pablo.

"It is too late to ride to Palomas today, and we do not want to have to spend another night in the desert. Eh, Soto?" Guerrero said with a glance back at the man still in his saddle.

"Si," Soto said.

"I suspect you would prefer a bed, would you not, Señorita Rosales?"

Marisol frowned.

"I would prefer to be left to continue our journey," she said.

Guerrero laughed.

"Please. Let's forget about los Estados Unidos, for now. I am sure once we have heard from Señor Arellano, you will be able to continue on your way without any further delay. But if Señor Arellano does not want you to travel to los Estados Unidos, certainly you would want to know that and not defy him. Correct? So, we will go and find a casa where we can spend the night in comfort. You and your amigos will remain polite guests, and I will remain a courteous host. Come. You will see, this is all for the best."

"You're safe here, señorita," Guerrero said, speaking Spanish now. He walked across the large bedroom and pushed away the sheer curtain hanging over the window so that he could look out to the courtyard. He stood with his back to Marisol for several moments, then he turned back facing the room and strode across to a writing desk and sat in the chair there.

He crossed his legs, a smile on his face.

"Your protection is most appreciated, but equally unnecessary," Marisol said.

Guerrero nodded.

"I do not know what sort of trouble you're in, señorita."

"I am in no trouble Señor Guerrero. I assure you, I am quite safe."

Guerrero nodded his head.

"Si. I am happy to hear you say so, but let me say this – I have separated you from those two men so that you can speak freely. If they are forcing you to accompany them against your will, I can protect you from those men."

"I do not need protection from those men," Marisol said. "I just want that mi amigos and I be allowed to continue our journey."

Guerrero narrowed his eyes.

"Si. If your uncle Señor Arellano agrees, I am happy to let you continue on your way. But we will wait for him," Guerrero said. "You understand my position, surely? If your uncle does not want you to cross the border with these men, and I allow it, then it will be me who is in trouble with your uncle. You know the man. I do not want to find myself explaining why I blundered to Señor Arellano."

Guerrero paused and watched her closely for any sort of reaction, but Marisol tried to remain impassive.

"But this is a small thing," Guerrero said, continuing to smile broadly at her. "I am sure there will be no problem. Once I am certain that your uncle approves of you going across the border with these men, you can be on your way. Of course, if there is something else going on that you have not told me – if these men have you against your will; if these men have broken some law or are in some sort of trouble."

Guerrero shrugged his shoulders and leaned back in his chair. He left his statement unfinished. Waiting. Giving Marisol a chance now to change her story.

He had taken them to what Marisol believed must be the finest house in Guadalupe Victoria. A sprawling adobe home in the shape of large horseshoe. A family called Salinas owned the house and it sat on a large estate. Guerrero knew Señor Salinas, and after speaking to the man for a few moments, he ushered them all into the house. Señora Salinas took Marisol for a bath. Guerrero took Duvall and Pablo Peña to a room and left them both inside. He took their guns, saying he did not want anyone to have an accident in the Salinas home. But Guerrero showed no interest in taking the saddle-bags they'd slung over their shoulders. Marisol knew that Guerrero would be able to take those saddlebags anytime he wanted. For the time being, on the small chance that Señor Arellano had no interest in these men, Guerrero was willing to let them keep the saddlebags.

But he locked them in their room and put his men Soto and Alvarez to guard the door.

After Marisol had her bath and put on a dress that Señora Salinas left out for her, Guerrero took her here to this room.

He did not say that she was being held as a prisoner, but she also had no illusions that she could leave if she wanted to.

"Now is the time to tell me," Guerrero said. "If there is something going on here that you haven't said – something I need to know about or something your uncle would not approve of – now is the time to tell me. And I'll say this to you, too. Let's say you are in Santa Catalina, and you meet this gringo. He is handsome? He is charming? Let's say that you fall in love with him. But he is in some sort of trouble, and so you agree to go with him to los Estados Unidos. Si? Maybe it is something like that. But now, knowing that he has been caught and that your uncle will soon be aware that you are here with him and that you all are under my protection – and you are scared that you have made a wrong decision. Maybe he is not so charming if you think you are going to be caught up in whatever trouble this gringo is in. If it is that, all you have to do is say so to me. Even if you are afraid your uncle will be mad at you, your uncle and I are very close friends. I can speak to him on your behalf. Just tell me."

Marisol's chest tightened as Guerrero spoke, and she felt like she could hardly breathe. For the first time, Marisol wondered if Guerrero knew something. Had he heard about the gold? But she dismissed that fear. If Guerrero knew about the missing gold, he would be much more urgent. They would be on their way to find Señor Arellano, not sitting here in a house in Guadalupe Victoria.

"It is nothing like that," Marisol said.

Guerrero nodded his head.

"Well, I did not think so," he said. "But just understand, if you change your mind and feel there is something that you need to say to me, Marisol, I will be happy to help you."

A knock on the door, and Marisol felt like she could breathe again.

"Come in," Guerrero said, looking at the door.

Señor Salinas opened the door and nodded his head to Marisol. He spoke then to Guerrero.

"Dinner is on the table in the dining room," he said. "We have set places for you and your three guests."

"Fine. Thank you," Guerrero said. "Soto and Alvarez will eat later."

He turned to Marisol.

"Let us go and eat," Guerrero said. "I am sure, after spending two days riding through the desert, that you and your friends must be very hungry."

Alvarez and Soto led Duvall and Pablo into the dining room where Guerrero and Marisol were already seated at the table. The moment he saw them come into the dining room, Guerrero burst into laughter.

"Amigos!" he said. "You carry your saddlebags even to dinner? Do not be so suspicious! Do you fear that we will go through them and steal your valuables?"

As Guerrero spoke, Alvarez directed Duvall and Pablo to two seats across the table from Guerrero and Marisol.

"I reckon it's hard not to be suspicious when a man takes you prisoner," Duvall said.

Guerrero waved a careless hand at him.

"Oh, please, señor. Prisoner? No. You are my guests."

"Guests can leave when they want," Duvall said.

Guerrero chuckled. Still delighted by everything Duvall said.

"Well, yes. There is that. You are not free to leave. You are my guests, whether you want to be or not. But you are looking at it in a very negative way, Señor Duvall. Let's look at it in a more positive light. Weary travelers plucked from the road for a comfortable night of repose and nourishment. Si? Tomorrow we will ride back to Palomas, and you can remain as my guests at my hacienda. In two days, or three, I am sure we will have heard from Señora Arellano. And at that point, assuming everything is in order, you will be on your way. No harm. Si?"

Guerrero did most of the talking through supper. He did not ask about the three killings, or what prompted them. He did not ask where the trio were going or why they were in a hurry. He did not ask what business Duvall and Pablo had in Mexico. He truly seemed disinterested. He'd done his part by arresting them, and was satisfied to let Arellano work out the rest.

Instead, he talked about himself. He talked about the bullfighting he'd done when he was younger. He talked about tracking rustlers through the desert. He talked about his cattle and his ranch hands and how much trouble it was to find water in the summertime.

Marisol cast across the table worried looks at Duvall. Though she was certain he understood, she wanted to stress the severity of their situation without saying words. She wanted to convey to him some silent encouragement that no matter what, she was still in this with him.

Marisol understood that Guerrero had divided them to try to pressure her. She was sure that Duvall realized that, too. But she wanted him to know that she could be taken away from him physically but no one could divide her love for him. She would stay true, no matter how much she feared her father's imminent arrival.

As the plates emptied – or emptied as much as they were going to – Guerrero pushed his plate away from him and leaned back in his chair.

"Señorita," he said. "You have hardly touched your food. You should eat."

"I've eaten all I care for," Marisol said shortly.

"The trouble with being a chef is that no one's food can match your own," Guerrero said with a smile.

"The food is fine," Marisol said. "It's the circumstances I dislike."

Guerrero laughed his hearty laugh and clapped his hands.

"I have tried to be a good host," he said, feigning disappointment.

"I would like to have a walk in the yard with Señor Duvall," Marisol said.

Guerrero pursed his lips and thought about it for a moment. Then he smiled.

"I think that is unnecessary," he said. "I think you should return to your room and rest. My intention is to rise early, before dawn, and set out for Palomas so that we can do the most of our riding during the cool of the morning. Soto, please escort Señorita Rosales back to her room."

Marisol cut a sharp look at Guerrero, but he merely smiled in response. Then her eyes softened and she gave a small smile to Duvall.

He did not smile back. His face was drawn, and he appeared worried. Marisol stood up, and Soto followed her as she walked out of the dining room and back toward the room where she was being held.

When they had gone, Guerrero then told Alvarez to take Pablo back to his room. And then he turned to Duvall. "Come, Señor Duvall, you and I will walk in the yard together."

Pablo didn't move.

"Oh, Señor Peña, let's not be foolish," Guerrero said. "I will return Señor Duvall to you."

"It's all right," Duvall said with a nod to Pablo.

Pablo had two saddlebags he slung over his shoulder.

"Please, take them all," Guerrero said. "I'd hate to have Señor Duvall burdened."

Duvall helped Pablo get the other three saddlebags over his shoulders. Alvarez reached out his hand to take one of them, but Duvall ignored him and slipped the saddlebag onto Pablo's shoulder. The moment one of these others lifted one of those bags, they'd realize the weight surely meant gold bars, and Duvall wanted to delay that as long as possible. Chances were probably good that if Guerrero found out how much gold was within his reach, he'd kill Duvall and Pablo on the spot to keep the gold for himself.

Now alone, the two men sat facing each other at the dining room table.

"Would you care for a cigar?" Guerrero asked, opening a brass cigar holder and extending it to Duvall.

"I'll smoke with you," Duvall said.

"Let us step outside. I detest smoking inside and having the air thick with smoke."

Guerrero stood and held out his hand to usher Duvall toward a back door. At the door, Guerrero struck a match and held it for Duvall to get his cigar burning. Then he struck a second match to light his own cigar.

They stepped outside into the evening air. It had cooled off a little and was pleasant enough. The grounds of the house did not match the immaculate decoration inside. With so little water, there was not much that could be done outside. But the yard did feature tall, narrow Italian cypress trees and decorative cactus. A stone walk ran to a horse barn and carriage house on the side of the main house. From where he stood, Duvall could see Pecas Gris in one of the stalls of the horse barn, and he felt a pang of regret. He felt a deep tenderness toward the horse. Outside of his pal Billy Muggs, now buried with the gold they'd come to Mexico to take, Pecas Gris was Duvall's constant companion for the longest stretch of his life. It seemed likely that short of a miracle, his life might be getting down to just a few short days left, and he wondered what would become of the horse when he was dead.

"I do not know what you are doing in Mexico, amigo," Guerrero said, puffing on his cigar. "I suspect you have been up to no good. And I think that when we hear from Señor Arellano, I am going to learn some things about you. What do you think of that?"

Duvall shrugged.

"I don't know what to tell you," he said, unwilling to make a confession. "I'm just trying to get across the border, back into America."

"Si," Guerrero said, smiling and nodding his head. He gripped his cigar between two fingers and drew on it, exhaling the smoke that immediately disappeared in the wind. "Maybe you know. Maybe there is nothing to know. But I think you should tell me if there is something to know. And before you deny anything to me, I think you should hear what I have to say. Señor Arellano is a very generous man, very kind to the people who live in this desert and the mountains around here. He is well-loved because of his generosity. But he is also a – what is the word in English? – like a judge?"

"Just?" Duvall offered.

"Si. Yes. He is a just man. And that means that he is a man who loves justice. No?"

"Sure."

"If you have committed some wrong in this country for which you should be punished, a just man will see that you are punished. He is generous, but just. You comprehend what I am saying?"

"I understand you," Duvall said.

"You seem like a man of adventure to me. You seem like an honorable man. If justice is coming to you, I think you are the sort of man who will accept his fate. Tell me if I am wrong?"

Duvall said nothing, but his thoughts went to the men he'd murdered so that he could steal Arellano's gold.

"An honorable man accepts justice when it is given to him. But an honorable man would also seek to protect others. Si? Señorita Rosales, for instance. If your adventures have led you into trouble, and if you are going to be punished for that trouble, why must she face punishment alongside you?"

"She ain't done nothing," Duvall said.

"Has she not?" Guerrero said. "I myself saw her shoot a man in the back."

"To save me," Duvall snapped.

"Ah. Si. To save you. And now I ask that you return that favor to her. Confess to me what you have done. Let me protect her from Señor Arellano. Separate yourself from Señorita Rosales to save her. Confess to me what you have done. I will protect her from Señor Arellano. You know he is her father. Si? All this about him being her uncle is a lie that Señor Arellano says to spare his reputation. And as her father, he will be inclined to forgive whatever she has done."

Duvall took a draw from the cigar.

"Turn us loose to ride across the border and I'll protect her myself."

Guerrero laughed.

"No, mi amigo. That will not happen. You do not known Señor Arellano. His fury would sweep me away like a desert wind. If it turns out that you have committed some crime in his country and he is seeking your head and he learns that I had you and allowed you to go? No, mi amigo. It would go very, very bad for me. You love the girl?"

"I do."

"Then do this thing for her. Protect her."

"I could pay you," Duvall tried.

"There is not enough money in the world."

Duvall drew on the cigar. Blew a cloud of smoke into the wind.

"Try me. Name a price," Duvall said. "Fifty thousand dollars?"

Guerrero laughed.

"Señor Arellano has made me a very rich man. There is no amount of money that would convince me to betray him. But I am getting a sense of why you are running for the border. Have you stolen from him? If you are offering me fifty thousand dollars, you must have taken a lot."

The smile dropped from Guerrero's face, and he gave his shoulders a small shrug.

"It is nothing to me. Whatever happens next is between you and Señor Arellano. We have some time. If you change your mind and want to try to spare Marisol from her father's wrath, tell me. I will do what I can. But you are rapidly running out of time."

"They're going to hang us," Pablo Peña said.

"If we're lucky," Duvall sighed.

After his walk with Guerrero, Duvall returned to the room where he and Pablo were being held. Duvall told Pablo the things that Guerrero had said to him and how the man had tried to convince Duvall to confess.

"We should try to hide this gold in the saddlebags," Pablo said. "Maybe here in this house?"

"I don't know," Duvall said. "There might come a time when we can try to bribe our way out of this."

Pablo shook his head.

"I already tried a bribe."

"Did you?" Duvall frowned.

"The man Alvarez. When he brought me back to the room after supper. I said to him that we know where there is half a million dollars in gold. Get us out of here, and we will tell you where it is. I even opened the flap on one of the saddlebags to show him that we had gold."

"He didn't go for it?"

"No. Sadly, he did not. And now I worry what will happen when they find this gold on us. If they open up these saddlebags and find the gold, we're dead. But if we get rid of it, maybe we can tell them we weren't involved in the robbery?"

Duvall shrugged.

"Maybe. At this point, I don't think anyone will believe us if we say we weren't involved. If you want to get shed of the gold, we can do it," he said. "But I reckon it don't make much difference, par'ner. The moment Arellano shows up, I think they'll kill us. But they're going to want to know where the rest of the gold is, and I expect they'll torture us to find out."

Pablo nodded his head, a grave look on his face.

"We should've listened to you," Pablo said. "You tried to tell us back in Las Vegas that we shouldn't partner up with Yote Johnson and Rodrigues. You told us this was a bad hand before the cards was even dealt. Look, hombre – I'm sorry for how this all turned out."

"Don't feel too bad about it, Pablo," Duvall said. "Hell, I didn't even listen to myself. I'm here with you. Ain't I?"

"Yeah, but I know you, Duvall. You're only here on account of us. You came here to watch out for us."

"Poor job I made of that. Billy and Bull are both dead. Chuck and Richie. I didn't look out for anyone."

"You tried," Pablo said. "That counts for something."

Duvall nodded his head, thinking about his dead friends. It was true what Pablo said. From the start he'd been opposed to riding into Old Mexico to try to ambush a wagon load of gold. He'd warned the boys away from it. He didn't trust Yote Johnson or his Mexican friend. He knew when Emster and Liller joined their outfit at Fort Selden that a bad deal had turned worse.

A setup from the start. Emster, Liller, and Rodrigues had devised this plan to ambush the gold wagon. Rodrigues recruited Yote Johnson who, in turn, recruited Duvall's friends – Bull, Billy, Chuck, Richie, and Pablo. They'd recruited Bassett, too, who Duvall had never met before this. After the fact, it was all pretty plain. Yote and the other boys were supposed to take the fall. Emster, Liller, and Rodrigues were supposed to ride off with the gold.

The plan didn't quite work out. Duvall objected when Emster proposed splitting up. So Billy and Bassett rode with Emster, Liller, and Rodrigues – along with most of the gold.

Bull and Yote and Pablo, along with Duvall, were supposed to lead Arellano's men on a wild goose chase. Each of them carried a couple of bars of gold. At the time, it had seemed like a genuine offering to show that everyone would get their share of the million dollars they'd stolen. But now, Duvall realized that Emster and Liller had insisted that everyone get some gold so that when the others were killed the crime would be hanged on them. Emster and Liller thought they could bury the gold, escape across the border, and then come back later and dig it up with Arellano never even knowing that there'd been others involved in the theft of his gold.

But that turned sour in a hurry. Duvall was shot during the ambush of the gold wagon. While he recuperated at Marisol's home in Santa Catalina, Yote, Bull, and Pablo led a short chase through the desert that ended with Yote and Bull getting killed and Pablo narrowly escaping.

Meanwhile, Rodrigues and those others killed Billy and Bassett and buried the gold. But they'd never dig it up, now. Duvall saw to that at the border village of Puerto Palomas.

Every bit of it had gone wrong, and it had gone wrong for everyone involved.

For a moment, right after Marisol Rosales shot Emster in the back at that Palomas saloon, it seemed that Duvall and Pablo would survive to tell the tale. Maybe they didn't have all the gold, but they'd at least get across the border with their lives.

"Damned greed," Duvall breathed.

"Si," Pablo agreed.

"When we was running from Palomas, after I killed Liller and Rodrigues and Emster?"

"Si?"

"I turned us south back into the desert. What do you think we were? Four miles from the border? Five miles from the border?"

"Si. About that," Pablo said.

"I told myself I was turning us into the desert to confound anyone who wanted to follow us. It wouldn't make sense to them."

"Not so bad a plan."

"It was a terrible plan, Pablo. If I'd turned us north for the border, we'd have been across the border before sunup. We'd be half the way to Fort Selden now, and on our way home. I turned us south into the desert because somewhere in the back of my mind I knew that if we left Mexico we'd never see that gold again."

Pablo shrugged.

"Is a lot of gold, hombre," Pablo said. "Even now, trying to think of how we might escape all this, I'm thinking about getting that gold."

"We'd better stop thinking like that, par'ner. We'd better start thinking about crossing that border and nothing else. It's going to take a miracle for us to escape. Too bad Alvarez didn't accept your bribe."

6

NÉSTOR LOZANO HELD HIS red coat in one hand and his riding crop in the other, and he beat the coat thoroughly with the small whip. Each whack kicked up a fresh cloud of dust, but still the bright red color of the coat would not come through.

He'd been days and days in the desert now. His clothes were thick with trail dust and sweat, probably ruined by it. But it was not the trail dust that caused him to hit the coat so hard. It was the rage boiling inside him, and he gave the crop another swing and it thudded against the coat.

"Where the hell did Señor Guerrero go?" Lozano demanded.

Luiz Sanchez shrugged his shoulders.

"They rode into the desert in pursuit of the killers," Sanchez said. "That is all that I know. I don't know anything about any gold shipment. I don't know anything about Señor Arellano's daughter."

"Niece," Lozano corrected him, though both men knew that Marisol Rosales was, in fact, Arellano's daughter.

Néstor Lozano seemed like a lunatic.

Sanchez knew the man's reputation and knew that he was one of the young guns valued by Señor Arellano. Luiz Sanchez had worked for Juan Pedro Guerrero for many years, and had worked for Guerrero's father before that. He was an old man now, nearly fifty, and he hadn't lived so long without learning the value of staying away from these men like Lozano. The Guerreros, father and son, were level-headed men. They kept their tempers. They enjoyed their lives. They accumulated wealth, and the people who worked for them got wealthy, too. They did not make enemies in the desert town of Palomas.

But Lozano seemed like a lunatic. Shouting and pounding his fists, demanding this and demanding that.

"Señor Guerrero rode in pursuit of the gringo and Señor Arellano's niece," Sanchez said. "That is all that I know. Where they are? I cannot say. When they will return? I do not know. You are welcome, Señor Lozano, to stay at the hacienda until Señor Guerrero returns. And then he can answer your questions."

Lozano had just ridden into Palomas and come directly to Guerrero's hacienda. And that's where he started making his demands and beating the hell out of his own coat. Some of Guerrero's ranch hands had taken Lozano's horse and the horses of the men who rode with him.

"How did he have the gringo in his sight and fail to take him as a prisoner?" Lozano said. "Tell me that!"

"I don't know," Sanchez shrugged. "I was not there. All I know is that three men were killed and the gringo and another man rode off with Señorita Rosales. Señor Guerrero rode in pursuit. Si? This is what I know, and nothing else. If you want, I'll make a room for you and find a place in the bunkhouse for your men."

Lozano shoved the coat at Sanchez.

"Get it laundered," he said. "Prepare a room. Find room for my men in the bunkhouse. Get us food to eat."

He stormed off across the yard, bound in no particular direction. His anger such that he could not get control of himself. Guillermo Gomez spoke to Sanchez in a quiet, almost apologetic tone.

"We have been many days on the trail of the gringo," Gomez said. "It is so much gold that he has stolen from Señor Arellano, and Néstor is very upset. He feels this will come back on him. It happened just outside of Santa Catalina."

"Si," Sanchez said without much sympathy. "But none of this is my fault. It is not Señor Guerrero's fault. The man needs to calm down. Relax. Señor Guerrero will bring the gringo back."

Gomez nodded his head.

"I hope so. We have sent word to Santa Catalina where Señor Arellano is. I do not know if he will come here, but if he does, that gringo had better be in our custody or dead."

Lozano was storming back across the yard in their direction now.

"How many men did Guerrero take with him?" Lozano said. "Everywhere I look here, I see idle men with nothing to do."

Sanchez frowned and shook his head.

"I'll see to your room," he said. But then he stopped and turned around. "Oh, señor, one more thing I forgot to mention."

"Si?"

"One of the men killed by the gringo?"

"Si?"

"He used to work for Señor Arellano."

"Qué dijo?" Lozano said. "What did you say?"

"Si," Sanchez said. "I recognized him when I saw the body. His uncle once worked for Señor Arellano. And his cousin, I think. His name is Rodrigues."

Lozano stared for several long moments, blinking at the man. Obviously trying to wrap his mind around the implications.

"Where is the body?" Lozano asked.

Sanchez chuckled.

"El cementerio."

"Buried, already?"

"Si. Of course," Sanchez said. "But I know it was him. I have met him before when I traveled to Juárez."

Sanchez turned now and walked toward the house to make arrangements for Lozano and his men. Lozano turned to Gomez.

"Do you understand what this means? One of Señor Arellano's own men was involved in the theft of his gold."

Gomez shrugged.

"Maybe. We do not know this yet. This man was killed by the gringo we are chasing. Perhaps he was trying to arrest the gringo and hold him before he escaped across the border."

"No," Lozano said, shaking his head. "No – it was this man Rodrigues and two other gringos. They had a fight among themselves over the gold. Surely that is it. Someone was trying to cut someone else out of their share? Or someone wanted it all for himself? Rodrigues – do you know the name?"

Guillermo shrugged his shoulders.

"I don't think so," he said. "But I seldom ever traveled to Juárez."

"Rodrigues," Lozano said the name again, thinking about it. "I think I do remember him. Maybe he was a ranch hand or something? A stable boy who thought he could make himself rich."

Gomez waited to see if Lozano had any other rants coming. The man still paced angrily around, talking about the "stable boy" and the gringo. When he was confident that Lozano's tirades were no longer directed toward him, Gomez said, "I will go see if I can do anything to hurry Sanchez along. The men need to eat."

"Si. Go," Lozano said.

Gomez hurried toward the main house, following in the way Sanchez had gone. Inside the house, he found Sanchez talking to a servant woman, instructing her to prepare dinner and giving her Lozano's coat.

"Tell me, what are the chances Señor Guerrero will come back here with the gringo?" Gomez said.

Sanchez shrugged.

57

"Señor Guerrero is a very competent man, if that's what you're asking. But who can say if he will catch the gringo? I will not follow him far if he crossed the border."

Gomez sighed heavily and looked back over his shoulder to be certain no one was listening to them.

"Señor Lozano – I have only worked for him for a few weeks. I do not know him well. But he has a ferocious temper, and this gringo has him enraged. I am sure the man fears for his position with Señor Arellano, that perhaps someone will blame him for what has happened because it happened near Santa Catalina. But he is loco about this gringo."

Sanchez nodded. He knew better than to get involved in someone else's problems.

"He will not hesitate to go across the border if he has to. Whatever it takes, he will hunt this man until he kills him. I'm just worried what will happen to those of us who have to hunt with him."

"Si," Sanchez said. "You must look out for yourself, too."

Guillermo Gomez nodded his head. He was exhausted and hungry, and he knew the other men were as well.

7

MARISOL CLICKED HER TONGUE and said "Fabiola" to get the piebald pony's attention. Then she dragged the right rein to lead the pony back over toward Duvall and the gray gelding.

"Are you okay?" Marisol said softly.

"I'm fine," Duvall said.

The morning was still dark as the group of riders left out of Guadalupe Victoria.

Duvall led the string of spare horses – those they'd taken from Emster, Liller, and Rodrigues. Guerrero made no effort to disturb his "guests," other than to disarm them. But even then, their empty rifles and revolvers rode on the saddles of the spare horses. Guerrero, Soto, and Alvarez had continued to allow Pablo and Duvall to tote their saddlebags and hadn't made any effort to get a look inside. Guerrero never even asked if they had boxes of shells in their saddlebags – they did. Plenty of ammunition. But it did them no good. Even with their guns somewhat in their own possession, they couldn't get to a gun, load it, and use it before Guerrero or one of the other two could shoot them down.

Duvall thought Guerrero's behavior as their captor walked a fine line between risk and confidence. But allowing them to keep the saddlebags, and ostensibly keep their guns, seemed to Duvall a bold demonstration of his superior position. Begrudgingly, Duvall admired the man.

"You must try to get away," Marisol said so softly that Duvall could barely hear her, even in the still of the morning.

Overnight, Duvall had moved all of the gold bars to his and Pablo's saddlebags. If they saw a chance to get away, they would have the gold with them and not on the spare horses. They'd both also stashed some bullets for their rifles and revolvers in their pockets. Just enough that if the opportunity presented, they could load them. The thought of escape was already on Duvall's mind. However, he saw little opportunity for it.

"Ain't likely we'll get a chance," Duvall grumbled back to her.

Alvarez led the way, riding out ahead of them on a chestnut gelding. Pablo followed Alvarez, then Duvall and Marisol. Behind Duvall walked the three spare horses, essentially keeping single-file. Soto rode there beside the tied horses, and Guerrero rode at the back. Alvarez and Soto both rode with rifles across their laps.

The road from Guadalupe Victoria to Palomas cut north through empty, flat desert. No place to hide, desert. No where to run, desert. See a man for miles, desert. How could they get away if there was no place to get away, too?

"Watch for your chance," Marisol said. "And when you see it, go. Do not look back for me. My father will forgive me, but he will kill you for the theft of his gold."

Duvall frowned.

"I ain't gonna leave you," he said. "Even if I see a chance. If I can't bring you with me, I'm not going."

"The important thing, the only thing now, is to live," Marisol said. "If you live, I will find you and I will come to you. But if you are dead, I will only be able to mourn at a gravestone. So, get away if you can. I will come with you if it's possible."

"Uh-huh," Duvall said noncommittally. He didn't intend to make a promise he might not keep.

They'd come up this way on their way to Puerto Palomas, before killing Rodrigues and the other two. Duvall cast his memory back, trying to recall if there was anything in this desert, even the tiniest glimmer of a chance, where they might be able to escape.

He could scatter the spare horses to cause a distraction. Maybe knock Guerrero or one of the others out of his saddle. Maybe in the process grab a weapon.

But then it would a race, and it would be a race he could never win.

In this desert, even if they got a mile or so in front of them, Guerrero and his men would always have Duvall, Marisol, and Pablo in sight. It wasn't a matter of overtaking, it was just a matter of keeping up.

All Duvall could remember was an area somewhere north of the Rio Casas Grande where the country west of the road was broken by hills and, maybe four or five miles in the distance, some high peaks. Not mountains, certainly, but tall hills that would have deep ravines where a man and a horse with a bit of a head start might be able to hide. And if that man had an empty rifle, but a few shells in his pocket, he might be able to make a stand – especially against just three men.

He'd have to get Pablo and Marisol away, as well.

Duvall suspected that Guerrero was exactly the sort of man who would put a gun to Marisol's head and threaten her life to draw out his quarry. But if the three of them could steal a chance and ride into those hills, they might be able to get out of this.

The sky overhead showed the first light of morning. Not a yellow light topping the eastern horizon, but a gray light at the center of the sky that slowly descended all around them, so that blackness became grayness and shapes became distinguishable. The nearby mass of some roadside brush, some greasewood growing up out of the desert. The far off, hazy blackness that slowly separated itself from the grayness of the sky until the riders could make out the shape of a prominent hill – one of those hills Duvall had remembered.

They were getting close. The sun would probably just be poking over the horizon when they reached those hills.

The horses were all pretty fresh, still. They'd only been at a walk in the darkness, and the temperature was still plenty cool.

Then Duvall noticed off to the side of the road a black shape. He couldn't put a name on it – just a shape – but what drew his attention was that it seemed to move.

"Make yourself small," he whispered to Marisol.

"What do you mean?" she asked.

"Something is wrong up ahead."

The thought hadn't formed clearly in his mind. Maybe it was just cows wandered out into the desert. Or maybe a coyote hungry enough to hang nearby as humans approached.

He saw no movement, now, and maybe it was nothing.

Duvall had put the lead rope for the spare horses on his saddle horn and given it a couple of turns, but he dropped his hand down now and unspooled it. He was going to tuck the rope under his leg so it wouldn't go anywhere, but he still had it gripped in his hand when one of the spare horses let out a terrible shriek and reared.

Duvall was so caught off guard by the sudden jerk of the rope that he fell out of the saddle.

The spare horse, it was Emster's horse, jumped and kicked out with its back legs, and Duvall had to roll clear to keep from getting stomped.

Guerrero rode away from the horse, getting himself safely clear.

Pecas Gris ran forward, and Marisol's pony Fabiola also jogged away. But the three spare horses were in chaos, and as Emster's horse rose up over him, Duvall saw why. The horse had an arrow shot through its neck.

THE YELL PIERCED LIKE the high-pitched shriek of the coyote, rising and falling.

It came solitary at first, but then it was taken up by other throats, growing in intensity until it drowned out the screams of the wounded horse and, for a moment, Duvall thought it must be the only sound on earth.

He couldn't guess if it was ten or a hundred. But he needn't wonder what could make such a terrible noise.

"Apache!" Alvarez shouted from the head of the column. The crack of a rifle immediately followed his shout.

On the ground, with that wounded animal jumping all around him and the shouts of the fearsome Indian warriors filling the air, Duvall remembered a nighttime raid that seemed now like a lifetime ago. He remembered seeing his pal Richie Hull standing in the driver's box of a wagon shooting a rifle at the attacking Apache. He remembered the brutal fighting – killing with a knife.

They would all die here on this road to Palomas, he thought. No need to fear Señor Arellano. The only fear now was that they might not be killed outright and would survive long enough to be tortured.

Duvall shook himself, feeling dazed.

"Tomás!" Marisol cried, and the terror in her voice helped to bring him to action. Her pony danced in a circle, rearing its head. Duvall leapt from the ground and dashed to her pony, grabbing at the bridle and pulling the pony's head down to try to bring it under control.

The charge of the Apache would have been enough to stir up the horses, but the screams of the wounded animal had spooked all the others.

And now the air was filled with flashes and thunder as Alvarez and Soto fired their rifles blindly into the dark of morning. Rifles out in the desert barked out an answer, but Duvall couldn't tell how many. Gunpowder burned in Duvall's nose. He took Marisol by the wrist.

"Come on down from there!" he said.

The wounded horse, snorting and breathing hard, dropped to the ground.

Soto's rifle rang out.

Duvall held Marisol close to him and led her toward the injured horse.

Guerrero shouted orders in Spanish.

Pablo Peña was there, dismounted, and standing beside Duvall.

"Grab those hosses," Duvall said to him. "We need our guns."

Alvarez fired a shot. Soto fired a shot.

Invisible Apache in the desert issued their war cry in defiance of the two rifles.

Duvall found his Yellow Boy rifle tucked into the saddle of one of the spare horses.

The wounded horse kicked out and let loose a terrible shriek as it tried and failed to regain its feet.

Duvall began feeding shells from his pocket into the rifle. His fingers moved expertly in the dark, no thought nor sight required for a task he knew well.

He pushed Marisol away, toward Pablo and told her to get down below the raised ground of the road. He knew Pablo was loading his own rifle, and in a moment the two of them would join Guerrero and his two men in the fight.

Duvall turned quickly and put the muzzle of the Yellow Boy against the head of the wounded horse and squeezed the trigger. The horse went suddenly rigid and then slack. Its wounded shrieks fell silent.

A dark figure darted toward them out of the desert, and Duvall swung the rifle up to his shoulder and looked to put his front sight on that figure. Without even registering the words she was saying, Duvall heard Marisol shout a warning.

"Behind you!" she yelled.

And then he felt the jarring thud against the back of his head as a club-wielding Apache knocked his hat off and sent him face first onto the sandy road.

He might have been unconscious for a moment, or maybe not. But he felt Marisol's arms around him, pulling him up from the ground. Duvall's head was spinning. He saw Alvarez, still mounted. He was firing his rifle harmlessly into the sky.

Guerrero was on his feet, but he was being overrun. Two or three or ten or twenty Apaches had come out of the desert and grabbed him. Some were beating him, one or two of them were dragging his rifle away from him. Duvall couldn't find the one who'd cracked him in the head, nor did he know where his own rifle had got to.

Pablo was sprawled on the ground. He'd been knocked stupid as well.

Soto was out of his saddle, no longer shooting. But in the gray light, Duvall could make out Soto's horse galloping away down the road the way they'd come, no rider on its back. Then one of the Apache – maybe the one who'd knocked him in the back of the head – gave Duvall a solid kick in the side, right where he'd been shot back when they ambushed Arellano's gold shipment.

Duvall tumbled over onto his side.

Marisol let out a yelp, and Duvall thought she'd been struck, too.

And then the same man grabbed him by the arms, wrestling with him. In the pale light, one of the Apache warriors appeared over him. Duvall thought he was going to be scalped as the man raised something up over his head, but then the Apache pulled a burlap sack over his face. They punched him a couple of times, in the body and the face, and then Duvall felt himself getting dragged away.

It was rough treatment. Beaten and dragged around. That sack was hell to try to breathe through, especially when he was already out of breath and gulping for air.

And then a man with a heavy accent spoke in English.

"I'm going to take this sack off your head. If you want to stay alive, you'll keep your mouth shut about what you see. Say if you understand." The words came from a thick Mexican accent and didn't sound anything like any Apache Duvall had ever heard.

"I understand," Duvall said.

Whoever yanked the sack from his head grasped a good handful of hair, too. But the sack came off, and Duvall took a breath and blinked.

Alvarez was standing over him, his rifle in his hand.

For a moment, Duvall didn't understand. Had Alvarez overpowered the Apache? He had a clear image of Alvarez during the fight, shooting his rifle into the air. Duvall's thought had been that Alvarez must've been shot through with arrow or rifle and in his death throes had fired a harmless shot at the sky. But Alvarez was fine. Untouched in the melee.

And then Duvall saw the Apache warriors standing behind Alvarez. Three of them. The ones who'd dragged him over here away from the road. And when he looked past them, at the road, Duvall saw Marisol and Guerrero with sacks over their heads. Soto had no sack over his head. Soto was lifeless and sprawled on the road. But he didn't see Pablo anywhere.

"You be quiet, gringo. Listen to me. Si?"

"Yeah. Sure."

"The gold? Where is the gold? Half a million dollars in gold. Where is it?"

Duvall blinked at the man.

His first instinct was to say nothing. His head was swimming from the knock he'd taken and the sudden rush of the attack out of the morning darkness. But now he was collecting his wits together, and he blinked at the Apache warriors standing behind Alvarez. And then Duvall saw it. They weren't Apache at all. They were dressed like them, but these boys was all Mexicans, disguised to look like Apache.

Alvarez had taken the bribe, after all.

"Our lives for the gold," Duvall said.

Alvarez threw a punch and clocked Duvall in the side of the face. It rattled his brain. He saw stars, and it took a few moments for Duvall's ears to quit ringing. The worst of it was, Duvall knew Alvarez hadn't even put much behind that punch.

"Our lives for the gold," Duvall repeated.

Alvarez chuckled silently and shook his head. He looked back over his shoulder.

"Si. You and the Mexican and the señorita. You give us the gold, and you will live."

"It's buried in Guadalupe Victoria," Duvall said. "But I won't say where until I know for sure that we're going to ride out of here alive."

Alvarez narrowed his eyes. His face twisted into a frown. Then he wrestled the sack back over Duvall's head, and Duvall could hear him walking away. When he'd walked some distance, Duvall realized where he was going.

"Don't tell him nothing, Pablo!" Duvall shouted.

He heard the footsteps coming at a run and braced himself. It was a shin that connected with the side of his head and knocked him to the ground.

Duvall didn't try to move, not knowing if those Mexicans dressed up like Apache warriors were still near him. He'd only heard Alvarez walk away. His head was still spinning and he couldn't reason out what Alvarez might do next, what would make sense. Guerrero was still alive, but his head was covered in a sack. Maybe Guerrero did not yet know the treachery, that his own man had staged this ambush.

Alvarez must have slipped out of Señor Salinas's house in the night and made arrangements quickly in the middle of the night, then returned in time to ride out before dawn. How many of these men dressed as Apache were there? Duvall didn't count them, but he figured there had to be no less than eight or nine of them.

Duvall couldn't clearly mark or even guess at the passage of time, but through the fabric of the burlap he could see that it was getting lighter out. The gray of pre-dawn was being replaced by the yellow light of sunup. And then Duvall heard footsteps again. Someone, grabbed him and dragged him up from the ground and back into a seated position on the desert sand, and then the sack came off his head.

"Where in Guadalupe Victoria?" Alvarez asked. "Where is the gold buried?"

Duvall tried to look past him, to put eyes on Marisol. But Alvarez shuffled a half step to keep himself in Duvall's line of sight.

"I won't say anything until I know we're getting out of here alive," Duvall said. "Take this damn sack off my head and let me stand up."

Anger flashed across the Mexican's face. Alvarez's fist balled, but he didn't swing it.

"I'll kill the girl if you don't tell me."

"You do anything to her, and you guarantee that I'll never tell you nothing. Same for Pablo. You kill either of them, and you might as well kill me, too, because I'll never talk. You let us leave here with our lives, and I'll tell you where that gold is buried."

"I let you leave here, then you'll lie to me about where it is buried."

Duvall saw his point. Alvarez hadn't thought this part of it out. Or he'd figured that Duvall or Pablo would tell him where the gold was without an argument.

He grabbed Duvall by the front of his coat and effortlessly lifted him up off the ground, standing him on his feet. The man was strong as an ox. Alvarez brushed some of the trail dust off of Duvall's coat.

"We will go back to Guadalupe Victoria," Alvarez said after a moment. "You will take me to the gold. When I have it, I will let you and the other two go."

"Let them go now," Duvall said. "I'll go back with you."

Alvarez blinked several times.

"Si. I will let them go now. You will ride with me. When I have the gold, I will let you go."

Duvall nodded. He didn't smile or shake the man's hand. He figured Alvarez would probably kill him as soon as he had the gold. But at least Pablo and Marisol could get away.

Alvarez gave Duvall a push back toward the road, back toward the horses.

As they neared the road, Duvall saw that Guerrero was hogtied on the road, his knees bent and his ankles tied to his hands behind his back. He was flat on his stomach, a burlap sack over his face.

"What about your boss?" Duvall said. "What are you going to do about him?"

Alvarez spat into the dirt. He slid a knife from its scabbard on his belt and fell with a knee in Guerrero's back. The hogtied man grunted when the knee hit him. Alvarez grabbed the burlap sack and wrenched Guerrero's head off the ground, bending it as far back as it would go, and Guerrero grunted again. Then Alvarez slid the knife across the front of Guerrero's throat, cutting it deep so that blood flowed out in a thick stream. The grunts were replaced by a choking and gurgling.

Alvarez stood and turned and pointed the bloody knife at Duvall.

"Do not try to cheat me."

EIGHT OF THEM, INCLUDING Alvarez. Seven dressed as Apache warriors.

Duvall looked around at their faces as a couple of them brought Pablo back over, still with a sack over his head. These pretend Apaches looked like they could all be Alvarez's cousins. Most of them were stocky, like Alvarez. They all had thick noses, like Alvarez. Was Guadalupe Victoria his family home? It would make sense how he was able to so rapidly put together an outfit to pull off this ambush.

A couple of them were rounding up horses, bringing them out of the desert. One was holding Pecas Gris and Fabiola and Pablo's horse.

The two spare horses, the ones that had belonged originally to Liller and Rodrigues, they were still tied to the dead horse on the ground and had not gone anywhere.

"Take the sacks off their heads," Duvall said with a nod at Marisol and then Pablo. "You want me to cooperate with you, then you better start treating us decent."

"You don't tell me what to do," Alvarez said. "You be glad I don't cut you where you stand."

"Uh-huh," Duvall said, feeling pretty good about his situation. "You can threaten to cut me if you want, but I know better. You just killed Guerrero, which mean's you're partnered up with me for good now. The only card you got left in the deck is getting that gold."

Alvarez clenched his jaw, and his eyes shot daggers. But he didn't argue the point. They both knew it was true.

Whatever else happened, someone was going to be asking questions of Alvarez sooner or later.

"You didn't plan on killing him from the start," Duvall said. "Did you?"

Alvarez said nothing, though Duvall let the question stand for several long moments waiting for an answer.

"Naw, you didn't plan to kill him. If you'd planned to kill him, you wouldn't have worried about covering his head with that sack. You cut his throat because you ain't happy with the way this has turned out. And now you're trying to reckon what to do about him being dead and having to par'ner up with me."

Still, Alvarez said nothing. But he didn't have to say anything. He had himself an ill conceived plan to accept a bribe for half a million dollars. Or a million dollars. Or whatever Pablo promised him. He'd only thought it out a little ways. Probably, Alvarez never expected Soto to get killed. Probably he had some plan to drag all of them into the desert with sacks over their heads. Out in the desert he would separate them. He'd convince Duvall or Pablo to tell him where to find the gold. Maybe he'd kill them or set them free. Then, maybe, Alvarez would put a sack over his own head and somehow he and Soto and Guerrero would get loose and escape.

Guerrero wouldn't know that Alvarez had been involved. He'd think he was lucky to escape the Apache.

Something like that, Duvall figured. Maybe he was off on a detail or two, but surely Alvarez's plan went something like that.

"That's all right, Alvarez. This can all still turn out okay for you. You set Pablo and Marisol free, let them ride off, and I'll work with you. You'll get your gold so long as I get a promise that you'll let me ride off, too."

"Si," Alvarez said.

Duvall tested his luck.

He bent down and helped Marisol off the ground. He pulled the sack off her head, but he held her face so that she looked at him and did not look at Guerrero's body on the ground. It was gruesome to see.

"We're going to be all right," Duvall said to her. "You and Pablo are going to ride out of here in just a couple of minutes."

Alvarez watched them and listened close to what Duvall said.

"You're going to ride north, skirt around that village of Palomas. Understand? Cross the border and make for Fort Selden. You understand?"

Marisol was pale and her mouth hung slack. She still hadn't been able to get her mind around what she'd experienced this morning.

"I understand," she said.

Duvall nodded at her, looking deep into her dark eyes, searching for recognition of what was going on. It had been a terrible shock for her. Who in the desert – New Mexico or Old Mexico, either one – didn't fear an Apache attack above all other things? Duvall understood her reaction. His own heart was still beating like drums inside his chest, and he'd known for a while now that it wasn't Apache. Marisol maybe still hadn't even realized it.

"Everything's going to be okay," Duvall told her again.

The two men leading Pablo over pushed him up to Duvall.

"Go ahead and take that sack off your head, par'ner," Duvall told him. "We're working this out with Alvarez now."

Pablo pulled the sack off and blinked at the morning light. His face was red. Alvarez must've knocked him around some.

Duvall glanced at Alvarez.

"We have an agreement?" Duvall said.

"Si."

"All right, Pablo. You and Marisol are going to ride out of here. Get on north across the border, but skip past that town of Palomas. You hear? Make for Fort Selden. I'll catch up to you there."

Pablo shook his head.

"What are you doing?"

"I'm riding back to Guadalupe Victoria to show Alvarez and his Apache friends here where to find that gold."

Pablo blinked again.

"You told me not to say nothing," Pablo said.

"I worked a deal," Duvall said. "Right now, our lives are worth more to us than that gold is."

Pablo sighed heavily.

"Dangit, Duvall," Pablo said, anger boiling up. He gave Duvall a shove and started to walk away.

"Pablo?" Duvall said. "We're going to get out of this alive. Forget about that danged gold."

Pablo turned now and looked at Duvall. He didn't say anything, just started with a real intense expression. Duvall frowned at him, but then he glanced at the ground and realized Pablo's angry pacing had carried him about eight or ten feet away to where he was standing over a Yellow Boy rifle just sitting there in the dirt. And that's when Duvall realized Pablo had cooked up his own plan.

"Don't do it, par'ner," Duvall breathed, but he was too late.

Pablo dropped his hands to the ground and grasped the rifle.

Duvall grabbed Marisol by the shoulders and spun her so that both of them fell to the ground.

He heard the rifle shot and saw Alvarez's eyes get wide with surprise as a bullet punched him in the gut.

8

DUVALL SPIT FORTH A string of expletives. He'd been willing to fight it out if it came down to that, but he'd hoped they could just ride out of here. Now Pablo had turned the thing to a contest of death.

Pablo Peña fought like a man who'd learned to enjoy it.

He dropped the lever on the Yellow Boy and swung it in the direction of two of Alvarez's Apache cousins, or whatever they were.

The rifle thundered. The action to dislodge the spent shell and chamber the next round took less than a second, and the rifle thundered again.

Duvall, hands and knees, scrambled across the hard caliche floor of the desert road. He reached Alvarez. The man was not dead, but his agony was writ across his drawn face. Gut shot down around the hip. Duvall had heard some of the old gun hands at Ben Callahan's ranch talk about what that sort of shot could do, and Alvarez's face suggested Pablo's shot had done it. A shot to the hip bone could ricochet from one hip bone to the other, bouncing back and forth across a couple of times and cutting all through the intestines. Duvall had heard of a man who took two weeks to die with a wound like that, but no amount of laudanum could relieve him of his pain or lull him to sleep.

The look on Alvarez's face suggested he was experiencing a wound nearly so serious.

Duvall grabbed for the man's holstered revolver, but Alvarez came to life. He snatched hold of Duvall's wrist.

With his free hand, Duvall punched at Alvarez's wounded stomach. The man bent double against the pain and released Duvall's wrist.

Pablo's rifle burst another shot, and then another.

Duvall jerked the revolver free and pushed himself to his feet.

He immediately found a target. One of the Mexicans dressed as an Apache charged past Duvall, going for Pablo. Duvall shot the man in the back and then thumbed the hammer back on the revolver to shoot him a second time.

Pablo had the rifle at his shoulder, looking down the barrel, and he didn't have to search to find a target. Three men were coming at him with knives. Pablo and Duvall both fired into the mass of them, and one of the men went down immediately with a head wound. Duvall thumbed back the hammer on the revolver and fired again. Pablo worked the action on the rifle and let off another shot. A second of the three stumbled and then dropped to his knees.

The third one was on top of Pablo now. Pablo parried the man's knife with the rifle, stumbling back. Duvall swung the revolver, crashing the barrel into the man's skull. The man dropped to the ground at Pablo's feet, and Pablo used the butt of the rifle to smash his head.

Duvall saw two men – the two who'd gone into the desert to collect horses – mounting their horses. The nearest horse to him was Guerrero's, a big black gelding that looked like it could run for days. Duvall climbed into the saddle and gave pursuit to the two just beginning to ride away.

Pablo's rifle barked behind him and one of the horses went hooves over head into the desert floor just as Duvall rode past.

Guerrero's horse reached and bounded down the road, rapidly overtaking the second man. Duvall was almost close enough to reach out and touch the man's horse when he finally leveled the revolver and fired. The first shot missed, but he thumbed back the hammer and fired a second time, and the man pitched forward in the saddle.

Duvall caught the horse and reached out for the loose reins. He pulled the horse to a stop, and the man tumbled over, badly wounded but not dead. Duvall dropped from the saddle, maybe a hundred yards from where they'd started their race. He used his last bullet to execute the man, and then he climbed back in Guerrero's saddle and rode back.

They were all dead or dying.

Guerrero and Soto. Alvarez. The seven men who'd dressed themselves as Indians and staged the morning ambush.

"He took the bribe, hombre," Pablo said to Duvall as the latter returned on Guerrero's horse.

"I'd say so. You didn't have to start killing, Pablo. I'd cut a deal with the man."

Pablo shook his head.

"He was never going to deal with us, Duvall. As soon as he got the gold, he was going to kill us."

Duvall shrugged. No point in arguing. And besides, maybe Alvarez was going to let Pablo and Marisol go, but he probably did plan to kill Duvall.

"We've got to leave out of here," Duvall said. "We've got to get the hell out of Mexico right now."

"Si," Pablo said. "Unless we go back to Guadalupe Victoria and try to find that gold."

Duvall shook his head as he dropped down out of the saddle.

"I don't want to be here when we run out of luck, par'ner."

Marisol still sat on the ground, her face in her hands. Duvall stepped over to her, put a hand in the back of her hair.

"Marisol?"

She looked up at him. He didn't know what to expect – tears or fear or something. Her eyes were wet, for sure, but a small smile crept across her face.

"You're okay?" she asked.

"I'm okay."

"Your head is bleeding."

Duvall nodded his head.

"It's pounding pretty good, too. But I'm okay. And we ain't got time to worry about a headache right now. We've got to keep moving."

Pablo had learned his lesson from the ambush of Arellano's gold wagon. Just as Emster and Liller had done on the road outside of Santa Catalina, Pablo now went around and killed those wounded but not yet dead. He shot Alvarez last.

Duvall took Marisol away to collect Pecas Gris and Fabiola while Pablo killed the survivors.

She jumped with each gunshot.

"It's terrible," she said after Pablo had shot the third or fourth man.

"It's necessary," Duvall said. "We can't have survivors. Survivors means someone can point in a direction and say, 'They went that way.' It ain't pleasant, but right now the most important thing to me is that we get across the border."

"They'll still come after us," Marisol said. "Someone will come along who knows that we were Guerrero's prisoners. They'll blame us for this."

"Probably," Duvall said. "But this here is a mess. Whoever comes along is going to find a bunch of Mexicans dressed as Apache. And my guess is, it won't take much to find someone who recognizes them and ties them to Alvarez."

"Alvarez?" Marisol asked.

She hadn't seen everything. She still had that burlap sack over her head when Alvarez cut Guerrero's throat. She hadn't worked out everything that had taken place.

"Last night, at the Salina hacienda, Pablo offered to bribe Alvarez. My guess is that Alvarez had some friends or maybe some relatives there in Guadalupe Victoria, and I think he left during the night and recruited some help. He had them fellers dress up as Apache, maybe hoping they wouldn't have to kill Guerrero. I don't know. But I guess he figured if there were survivors, he wanted them to say it was Apache."

"So Alvarez staged that whole thing?" Marisol asked, stunned at the revelation.

"He did."

"Those aren't Apache warriors?"

Duvall chuckled.

"If those were really Apache warriors, we'd probably all be dead now. No, them boys is all local Mexicans."

Marisol shook her head.

"There's nothing men won't do for gold," she said.

Duvall hung his head.

"It's nothing more or less than I did for gold."

Señor Salinas examined the dead man's face an recognized him immediately.

"One of the Alvarez brothers," he said.

The dead man wore a headband around his head, and tucked inside the headband were rags dyed black. Salinas gripped a corner of one of the rags and jerked it off the man's head. It was a crude costume, like a child would make.

Señor Salinas could make nothing out of the scene on the road.

"This is all too bizarre," he said to his son, who stood beside him. "These men are from our village. These men are cousins of Señor Alvarez who traveled with Señor Guerrero. Why would they disguise themselves and attack their own cousin and Señor Guerrero? It makes no sense."

Señor Salinas's son, Nando, shrugged his shoulders. The boy was nearly thirty years old now, and already he had taken over many of his father's duties in Guadalupe Victoria. He oversaw the family's small cattle production and its business interests. The older Salinas man remained the village's elder, but even in a situation such as this, he found himself relying more often on his son's advice and deferring to his opinion.

"It makes no sense," he agreed.

People in the village of Guadalupe Victoria heard the early morning shooting. It was such a volume of gunfire that those who heard it knew some terrible thing must have happened. But by the time a sufficient group of riders could be gotten together, armed and mounted, there was nothing left to find other than bodies.

Four men of the Alvarez family were among the dead, including the boy who'd gone off to be a prizefighter in Juárez but now worked for Señor Guerrero. The other three dead men from the Alvarez family were his cousins, local boys still. Four other local boys were also among those killed, all friends of the Alvarez cousins. Confusing and worrying, the local boys appeared to have donned crude costumes to make themselves appear like Apache. Black rags to give them an appearance of long hair like the Apache men wore. Loose britches and moccasin boots. Some of them were even armed with bows and arrows.

Why would they dress in such a way? Why would they attack their own cousin and Señor Guerrero who was nothing but a friend to the village of Guadalupe Victoria?

Señor Salinas chose not to speculate.

"Were these Alvarez brothers bandidos?" Señor Salinas asked his son.

"Not that I've ever heard of," Nando answered.

They were a few years younger than Nando Salinas. He thought Nando had run around with them some, but he certainly knew them. All of the Alvarez boys had worked for Señor Salinas at one time or another.

"Whatever has happened here is bad business," Señor Salinas said. "To venture a guess at what happened or what motivated it is to get more involved than I care to be."

"Si," his son told him. "We do not need to get involved. Just send word to Palomas that Guerrero has been killed in an ambush. Someone will notify Señor Arellano in Juárez."

Señor Salinas nodded his head.

"And say nothing about these disguises from the local men?" Señor Salinas asked.

Nando shook his head.

"We should bury them before any inquest can be made."

"Señorita Rosales and the two Americans she was with," Señor Salinas said. "What has happened to them?"

"That is an interesting question," Nando asked, looking off into the desert as if maybe he would see the answer on the horizon. "I think perhaps we should not try too hard to find the answer to that question."

They sent some of the men from the village back to fetch a wagon in which to collect the dead, and Señor Salinas sent Nando and another man north to Puerto Palomas. Someone there needed to be told that Guerrero and two of his men were dead. Señor Salinas was hesitant to send his own son. Perhaps there were bandits or Apache raiders on the road somewhere. But Señor Salinas trusted Nando to have the discretion to carry the message and to deliver it in a way that it would not come back hard on the people of Guadalupe Victoria.

Señor Salinas had known the Alvarez family all his life. He'd known these dead boys all their lives. The family had lost four sons this day. The evidence looked bad for them. Perhaps they brought disaster upon themselves. But Señor Salinas decided that if he could avoid more trouble for that family, he would do it. He ordered the ridiculous costumes to be removed before the bodies were taken back to the village.

And that would be the end of that.

Nando would say that it appeared there had been an Apache attack, or possibly bandidos. Such things were common enough on this road. They happened sometimes two or three times in a year, though other years passed without a single attack.

"You must tell them that when Señor Guerrero stayed last night at our house he had Señorita Rosales and her two companions with him. Tell them that they were all welcomed as guests at our home."

"I will tell them, papi," Nando said.

"I CAN'T TELL IF we're just riding through an old dry wash or if we've come upon a trail," Duvall said.

"We better hope it's an arroyo," Pablo said. "Because if it's a trail, it probably leads straight to an Apache camp, hombre. Ain't nobody else riding trails through these hills."

Duvall scoffed.

"Look here, par'ner," he said. "The way things are going, I'd just about welcome a band of Apaches. I've had it up to here with Mexicans."

Pablo chuckled and shot a deliberate look at Marisol.

"Tell me that again?" he said.

Duvall shrugged and winked at Marisol.

"Some Mexicans, anyhow."

Marisol smiled, but she hardly felt any humor.

They'd gone a mile or so north along the road after the attack, but Duvall and Pablo both decided it was too much risk to encounter anyone along that road with all those dead bodies there behind them. So they cut west, leaving the road and following the desert to the broken, hilly ground west of the road.

At the tops of hills, mounted on three horses and pulling two spare horses, they looked like the Colossus of Rhodes, waving their presence to any fellow travelers. So Duvall led them down into the low spots between the hills, and very quickly they found themselves walking their horses along what seemed to be a deliberate trail, but maybe it was just the natural flow of the little bit of water this desert got over the centuries.

The sun stayed below the hills on their right shoulders for a while, but then it climbed higher into the sky, and it wasn't long into the morning before they started to feel the heat of it pressing down on them. The arroyo, or the trail, took them generally north which was the right direction. Duvall figured they were less than forty miles to the border. That would be a tough day's ride – especially in the heat of the day – but they might break during the hottest part of the afternoon, switch horses, and then cross the border after dark.

Marisol kept her thoughts to herself as they went.

She watched how Duvall and Pablo focused on survival. Moving north toward the border. Staying off the road. Riding down among the hills and not across the tops of ridges. Worried about who they might encounter even in this rugged land where it seemed so unlikely that they would encounter anyone.

"I need a drink of water," Marisol announced.

Though she had her own canteen hanging from Fabiola's saddle horn, Duvall did not hesitate. He grabbed up his own canteen, pulled the cork free, and stepped Pecas Gris over near to her, holding out the canteen where she could reach it.

Marisol nodded at him as she took the canteen and drank the water. It was warm. She would have liked cool water, but of course it was warm.

"How soon will we cross the border?" Marisol asked.

Duvall frowned at the sky.

"Not until after dark," he said. "We'll have to give these hosses a rest in the hot hours of the afternoon. When dusk comes, we'll saddle 'em up and ride. Maybe ride through the night. I figure sometime not long after dark we'll get across the border. But we want to be far enough across the border that if Arellano decides to make an excursion over the border he won't find us."

"He won't be afraid to go far across the border," Marisol said. "If he thinks you have his gold, he will gladly go as far as he has to across the border to get it back."

"Uh-huh," Duvall said. "I reckon I don't blame him. But the farther across the border we get, the less chance he's got anyone to help him. Here, everywhere we go he has men who owe allegiance to him. Palomas, Guadalupe Victoria – it don't matter what village we're in, we're covered in folks who work for Arellano. Once we're across the border, we've left that behind."

"I hope so," Marisol said.

"Are you okay?" Duvall asked her.

"Si. Of course. Why wouldn't I be?"

"That was a lot this morning," Duvall said. "A lot of shooting, a lot of people killed. It was terrifying thinking that Apache was coming up out of the desert at us."

Marisol nodded.

"It was all of that," she agreed.

"We were lucky to get out of it. When Pablo shot Alvarez, I was a mite worried." Duvall chuckled and shot at glance in Pablo's direction, but he was off a respectful distance, giving the two of them their first bit of privacy since the gunfight that morning.

"Is he dangerous for us to be with?" Marisol said.

Duvall chuckled.

"Hell, I suppose anymore we're all a little dangerous."

"I just want to get across the border and get settled somewhere," Marisol said. "I'm ready to start my life with you."

"And that's where we're headed," Duvall said. "We're going to do it. Just like we planned. We're going to get me a little place with a few cows and you're going to open up a cantina just like that one you had down in Santa Catalina. It'll be just like we talked about."

One arroyo led to another and that one to yet another. Duvall thought they were still traveling north, but maybe they'd cut a little northwest following this arroyo, and maybe they'd come some ways northeast following that arroyo.

When the sun was at its apex and the horses were wet with sweat, Duvall looked for a place to stop. A row of cottonwoods down along a ravine, or a big juniper bush that cast a bit of a shadow. He'd have settled even for a bit of greasewood that they might cut loose and hold over their heads to block some of the sun. But he found no vegetation, so they had to settle for a low spot where the wind seemed to blow steady.

Before they unsaddled the horses, Duvall walked to the top of a tall hill to have a look around at their surroundings and to watch the backtrail to be sure they weren't being followed.

He saw no dust cloud on the horizon from pursuing riders. Nothing in any direction that pointed to human habitation.

To the north, far off in the distance, Duvall saw mountain peaks. He couldn't name them. But he knew they were in the United States, and that gave him hope. They were getting close. Their morning and early afternoon trek through these arroyos had brought them closer to their goal of crossing the border. If they could just get across that border alive, Duvall felt certain they would make it home.

9

Néstor Lozano and Guillermo Gomez were eating their dinner when Nando Salinas rode into Guerrero's compound at Palomas.

It was Sanchez, Guerrero's lieutenant, who ushered Nando into the dining room.

"This is Nando Salinas," Sanchez said in a grave tone. "His father runs a village south of here, Guadalupe Victoria."

Lozano shrugged to indicate he did not know the village. He had on his red coat, laundered now thanks to Sanchez, and he looked like a matador. He was freshly shaved and had even gotten a haircut during the day, waiting for Guerrero to show up. Though no one would have ever accused Néstor Lozano of being a handsome man, he looked as good now as he could. The bright red coat, the shaved face, the indifference, he possessed an air of arrogance. Nevertheless, Sanchez's heavy attitude caught Lozano's attention.

"Tell Señor Lozano what you have told me," Sanchez said.

Nando Salinas narrowed his eyes at he looked at Lozano.

"Yesterday, Señor Guerrero came to our hacienda in Guadalupe Victoria," Nando said. "He had with him two of his men, Soto and Alvarez, and three others."

"What others?" Lozano said, putting his hands on the table and standing up.

"Two Americans, a gringo and a Mexican from America," Nando said. "And a woman. Señorita Rosales. She is a niece of Señor Arellano."

"Where are they now?" Lozano asked, pounding a fist on the table. "Are they still in the village?"

"They left before the sun rose this morning," Nando said with a frown and a shrug. "I did not even know they had left. But around the time of sunup, we heard shooting."

Lozano's face was drawn. Angry. He knew whatever story Nando had to tell was going to infuriate him, and he was already infuriated in expectation of it.

"Tell me!" Lozano banged his fist on the table again.

"Bandidos, maybe. Maybe Apache. We found a horse shot through the neck with an arrow. Maybe Apache."

Nando Salinas wasn't much of a liar. He had no interest in the politics of being in Señor Arellano's organization. He did not need to rise above Guadalupe Victoria. He had no ambition to move in the service of Señor Arellano to Palomas or Ascensión or Juárez. He was happy with what he had in life. A ranchero, a woman who loved him that his wife didn't know about, and a wife who didn't ask too many questions when he came home late. His father's home would one day be his, and for the time the home he had was perfectly suitable. He had good horses and good friends and all the cervezas he could drink. What more did he need?

So when it came time to tell a lie, Nando Salinas made a poor job of it.

"Some local boys rode out with them. Some of them cousins to Alvarez. I don't know why they were there. But they were attacked on the road."

Lozano pushed his hands off the table and stood erect now, biting his lip. He shot a furious glance at Guillermo Gomez.

"Spit it out," Gomez said. He found that he, too, was growing angry with the man's poor attempt at dissimulating whatever had occurred. "Tell us what happened before we whip you."

"They were attacked," Nando frowned and shrugged, as if that explained everything.

"And what happened?" Gomez said, now standing up himself.

"They were all killed. The local boys were killed. Alvarez and Soto and Señor Guerrero."

Lozano swore an angry oath.

"What of the señorita? Marisol. And the gringo?"

"They were not there on the road," Nando said. "We do not know. Maybe they escaped the attack. Maybe they were taken as hostages? We do not know."

Lozano spun himself in a circle.

"Did you try to track them?" he demanded, his tone incredulous.

"There were no tracks to follow," Nando said.

"A band of Apache came out of the desert and attacked a dozen or more people on the road and three of them either escaped or were taken as hostages, and you're telling me there were no tracks to follow? Or is that there was no one competent to follow the tracks?"

"There were no tracks that I saw," Nando said, bristling a little at the insult. "My father stayed at the site of the attack as they collected the bodies. He might have made a more thorough search. We thought it was more important that I come here with speed to report what had happened."

"Were the horses stolen?" Lozano asked.

Nando blinked at him.

"Not all of them," Nando said, trying to remember which horses were there and which ones were not. Nando had helped to stall the horses the previous night when Guerrero first rode into the Salinas hacienda. "I think the horses of the señorita and her two companions were taken. And possibly two spare horses they traveled with."

Lozano fumed.

"The gringo escaped again," he said. "If they were attacked by Apache, the horses would have been stolen."

"Maybe bandidos," Nando suggested.

"It was not bandidos!" Lozano shouted. He glared at the man for a long time, but he said nothing else. Then finally he turned from Nando Salinas and looked at Gomez, who by now had returned to his seat at the table.

"If this man had time to ride here to make his report, then Marisol and the gringo have had time to ride to the border," Lozano said. "Maybe they have already crossed."

"Si," Gomez agreed.

"They did not come by way of the road," Nando interjected. "I am certain of that. We encountered travelers who had seen no one come up from Guadalupe Victoria. If they came north, they would have had to come through the desert. It is no easy ride. Very hot today, and some of that is rugged country."

Lozano waved a dismissive hand at Nando Salinas.

"If I have questions for you, I will ask them. Otherwise, do not speak. I am appalled at your incompetency in this matter."

Nando winced. He didn't care for the insults, but he also knew better than to make an enemy out of Lozano. He knew that Lozano was a powerful man within Señor Arellano's organization, and that meant he was a man who could make trouble for the Salinas family.

"If they do not come through Palomas, where will they go?" Lozano said to Gomez.

Gomez shrugged. He knew nothing of this part of the country.

"May I?" Nando said.

"Yes! Speak!" Lozano shouted. "What is it?"

"Palomas is the only village on the border for fifty miles in any direction. If they survived the attack and are seeking to cross the border, this is the only place where they could do that. It is fifty miles from here to Juárez. To the west, there is nothing but desert. To the north? Nothing but desert. If they need supplies – food or water, fresh horses, anything – the would have to come here or go through Juárez to the east."

Lozano nodded his head, thinking about what the gringo might do.

"They will not risk coming to Palomas. They killed people here and will fear that they might be recognized. They will cross the border in the desert and then they will go east to El Paso."

Guillermo Gomez frowned and shook his head.

"I do not think they will go to El Paso unless they are desperate for food or water. I think they will make for the east and try to get north, away from El Paso and Juárez. Marisol is very smart, she will know that her father may have people on both sides of the border there who could recognize her."

"Mesilla," Lozano said. "If we are going to catch them, it will have to be in Mesilla."

DUVALL DREW THE REINS up and whispered a command to Pecas Gris.

"Whoa. All right, boy."

Then he threw a leg over the horse's rump and dropped down from his saddle.

Everything at the moment was miserable. Duvall felt the grime of days on the trail in the desert. Sweat from days frozen at the nights. His head pounded from the beating he'd taken that morning, and his hair was matted with blood. His clothes felt heavy with dirt. His legs and back and inner thighs ached. His lips were cracked and he could taste salt all the time. He could feel the sand in his mouth. His eyes were dry and burned.

Behind him, Marisol and Pablo also dismounted.

It was still early in the evening, just after sundown, and a little light still lingered in the sky from the west.

They drew a bath for Marisol last night at the Salinas hacienda in Guadalupe Victoria, and Duvall wished now they'd given him and Pablo a bath, too. But they hadn't, and now he was just a crusty old saddle tramp with thousands of dollars worth of gold bars and coins in his saddlebags. He grinned to himself at the thought of it. He'd been worse things in his life.

"That's Palomas," Duvall whispered to the other two, not taking his eyes off the lights flickering on the horizon.

"Nothing else it could be," Pablo whispered back. "Except for Juárez, there ain't another village on the border for two hundred miles."

Duvall didn't know if that was true, and he didn't know how Pablo knew. But he did think it had to be Palomas. He sure didn't expect that arroyo they rode through to dump them out in the desert so near to the village, but he was glad it did. They wouldn't have to wonder now when or if they had crossed the border. They wouldn't wander lost in the desert. At least, probably not.

"What do you figure, Pablo? Fifty miles to El Paso?"

"About that, yeah."

"If we cut east, and just keep going east and maybe a little north, we'll run into the Rio Grande."

"It's a long ways without water, hombre," Pablo said. "Horses need feed and rest. Maybe I should ride into Palomas and see if I can get some water, buy some feed. Nobody will recognize me from the other night. You and the señorita did all the shooting. Nobody paid any attention to me. I bet I could get in there and get out without anyone knowing. Hell, if you want to try it, I could take the horses to the livery and get a room at the hotel. You and Señorita Rosales could sneak in the back door."

Duvall didn't say anything for several moments. His mind raced, weighing the risk of trying to sneak into the village. Pablo could take the horses to the livery – but the hostler had already seen their horses, just a few days ago. He certainly might recognize Pablo, but he would surely recognize the horses. No hostler ever forgot a horse after just a couple of days. But a night's sleep at a hotel? A hot meal? Maybe they could even sneak a bath? The village held the promise of comfort that tempted heavily. What good was all this gold if they couldn't spend it? Just one of these gold coins could buy them and the horses a night of comfort.

But at last he shook his head.

"That's how we get our necks stretched, amigo," Duvall said. "We go into that village and we'll never come out alive. We'll skirt around the edge of it, get across the border, and point ourselves east toward the Rio Grande. Two more days, and we'll have water and food enough."

Pablo lifted his canteen from where it hung on his saddle horn and gave it a shake. The noise of the sloshing suggested it was only about half-full.

"I don't know about you, but I don't see myself making it two days in the desert. There's a well over by the placita and a couple of water troughs. We can wash up a little bit, water the horses, fill our canteens. If we wait a couple of hours, the village will be quiet. I bet we could get in and get out without anyone even seeing us."

Duvall shook his own canteen. He didn't have much more water than Pablo.

"It's a risk," Duvall said. "Marisol?"

"If you think it is necessary," she said, and shrugged her shoulders. "Riding into the desert without water is also a risk."

"All right. We'll ride up close to the village. Marisol and I will wait for you. You go in and see if you can find a store open. Buy some feed for the horses. Go and fill your canteen and water your hoss. Have a look around without drawing any attention to yourself. If you think it's safe, come back and get us."

Pablo nodded his head.

They walked the horses now. All three of them needed to stretch their legs, and even though the sun was below the horizon, there was no point in making too large a profile with all of them mounted. They were a large enough object in the desert as it was with five horses and three people.

Skirting along to the west side of the village of Puerto Palomas, Duvall could see the church's twin turrets glowing white there beside the plaza. They were about a hundred yards off from the nearest building, which looked like a little house with an adobe wall around it, and maybe another two hundred yards from the church. Pablo could ride almost a straight line directly to the well in the plaza.

"If you run into trouble, you just come on at the gallop and give me a shout," Duvall said. "I'll have my rifle ready."

"I'm hoping it ain't gonna come to that," Pablo said, stepping into the stirrup.

Duvall and Marisol watched Pablo ride toward the town. Only a few yards out, and he started to disappear into the darkness. That light in the western sky wasn't showing anymore, and the sliver of moonlight didn't do much to illuminate him as the distance grew.

"I hope he makes it out without being seen," Marisol said.

"I do, too," Duvall said. He pointed to the north. "I could just about throw a rock from here and get it across the border. I'd hate to have this whole thing come to an end now."

Duvall ripped a page from his prayerbook and rolled himself a smoke. The minutes ticked by. Five became ten. Ten became thirty. Duvall carried a pocket watch that kept time when he remembered to keep it wound, but even squinting at it, he couldn't see the hands in the poor light. Still, he checked it several times.

"How long has it been?" Marisol asked the third time he checked it.

Duvall laughed.

"I have no idea. I can't see a danged thing."

Marisol smiled and put out a hand to touch his shoulder.

"I suppose it should be some consolation to us that we haven't heard any shooting," she said.

"I just wish he would hurry up," Duvall said.

The horses wanted to wander and graze. Duvall had dropped a ground tie for Pecas Gris, but he had to keep walking over to pull the horse back over to him. Marisol had to pull Fabiola back a few times. Duvall held the lead ropes of the two spare horses, but they were both pretty good about staying put. After a while, Marisol let the pony go and she sat on the desert floor while the pony walked around looking for anything to nibble. But the pony didn't stray far from Marisol, coming back over to nuzzle her hat a couple of times so that Marisol had to push her away.

"An hour?" Duvall said after more time had passed.

"Maybe so," Marisol said. "It's impossible to tell."

"Maybe longer than an hour," Duvall said.

He had the Yellow Boy rifle tucked inside his arm, holding it casually. But something to the east caught his attention, and Duvall took the rifle in both hands and leveled it at whatever he saw approaching. Marisol pushed herself up from the ground and brushed her hands off. She walked over to Fabiola and took up the lead rope again.

"What is it?" she whispered, squinting at the darkness and then seeing movement.

"I'm hoping it's Pablo," Duvall said.

The movement started to take shape, and Marisol could see it was a horse and rider approaching. But she wasn't sure until she saw Duvall lower the rifle.

"It's okay," Duvall said. "It's Pablo."

"How can you tell?" Marisol asked.

"You ride with a man long enough, you begin to recognize him. The way he carries himself in the saddle. Pablo always sits a little rounded in the shoulders, like he's hunched forward. Watch him in the daylight, you'll see it."

A minute later, and Pablo was within view.

"It's clear, hombre," Pablo hissed at the darkness as he came near. He held up his canteen and shook it, and it sounded full now.

"If it's clear, how come you're whispering?" Duvall asked.

"I don't know. I guess 'cause I don't want anyone to hear us," Pablo said. "Let's get the horses together and hurry up."

"What took you so long?" Duvall asked, cinching the saddle on the freckled gray.

"Took a bit to find a store that was open, but I did buy four sacks of feed. Here, put these on the spare horses."

The feed sacks were small, but it would be enough to get these horses through the desert. They were tied in pairs and easy enough to lay over the saddles the horses already wore. For good measure, Duvall tucked them under a strap to make sure they didn't fall off.

All three of the riders climbed into their saddles.

"There are people out," Pablo said. "That saloon where you shot Rodrigues and them other two? There's a goodly sized crowd there outside of the saloon. But the troughs and the well are the far side of the plaza. What I'm thinking is, you and the señorita hold up on the street away from the plaza while I take the two spare horses and water them. Then I'll come back out, and you and the señorita can take your horses."

"Sure," Duvall said. They were a block down from the church. A store of some kind, now closed, separated them from the church. Duvall couldn't see the saloon, but there were noises – an occasional shout or laughter; Duvall thought he could hear music.

As they approached the plaza, there beside a tall adobe wall surrounding a little casa, Duvall and Marisol reined up. They stayed in their saddles, waiting as Pablo led the two spare horses. As soon as he crossed the plaza, he was out of sight.

"Is this okay?" Marisol whispered, and her voice sounded tight, worried. Duvall twisted in the saddle to look at her. He'd been watching Pablo, but Marisol's tone caught his attention. In the little bit of light that came from the nearby homes, Duvall could see that her face was drawn in concern.

"It's okay," Duvall said. "We're nearly out of this."

"I have this terrible thought."

Duvall chuckled.

"We don't need nothing but good thoughts right now," he said.

"What if it took him so long because he was caught?" Marisol said. "What if he was caught and he's leading us into a trap so he can get away?"

"What?" Duvall asked, incredulous at the idea.

"Maybe he told whoever caught him that he could bring us if they'd let him go. I mean, we're the two who killed people here in Palomas. Pablo wouldn't be in any trouble, anyway."

Duvall scoffed at the notion and shook his head.

"Huh-uh. Pablo wouldn't do that. Him and me are pals. Have been for years. If you trust me, you can trust Pablo. That's how close we are, and that ain't no joke."

Marisol nodded. Her face softened some in the soft glow.

Still, now she had Duvall thinking. Wondering.

A short while later, Pablo led the two horses back across the plaza toward them.

"The bay didn't want to drink, but he finally decided to," Pablo said.

Duvall nodded. "He'll be glad he did. We'll be right back."

"Si. I'm going to go on down the street, ride into the desert just a bit," Pablo said. "I'll wait for you there instead of here."

Duvall shot a look at Marisol. He bit his lip and then shrugged.

"Yeah. Okay, amigo. We'll meet you out in the desert."

Duvall clicked his tongue and Pecas Gris jogged out into the street toward the plaza. Marisol followed him. His eyes surveyed the plaza. It was hard to see all the way across it because of the planted trees, but he didn't see anyone in the plaza. But then he noticed a man up at the gazebo, standing off to one side. And Duvall saw some other people, sitting on a bench. He reached for his converted Colt in his holster when he realized the man standing up had a rifle in his hands.

He was just turning to tell Marisol to ride away when he heard the strum of a guitar. He looked back to the gazebo and realized the man standing there had a guitar, not a rifle.

"Damned gold," Duvall swore. "It's got me all twisted up. I ain't trusting my friends and I'm getting spooked by a guitarrista."

"STAY WITH THE HOSSES?" Duvall said.

"Si," Marisol nodded her head. She had hold now of both lead ropes. Fabiola and Pecas Gris both drank from the trough, though the pony kept picking up her head to look around.

Duvall glanced at the saloon all the way across the plaza from them. He could see people out, but the atmosphere around them gave him the impression of happy drunkenness. Nobody cared about a couple of riders watering their horses at a trough. At the gazebo, the man with the guitar continued to entertain the small group with him. They also didn't care about Duvall and Marisol.

He slipped Marisol's canteen over his shoulder to hang with his and then took a spare canteen that was already empty. It had been Emster's or Liller's canteen, taken with the horses.

He slid the Yellow Boy rifle from its scabbard on Pecas Gris's saddle.

"Don't want to get caught at the well without my rifle," he grinned and gave Marisol a wink.

The troughs were conveniently close to the well. It was just over in the plaza. The troughs were across the road that ran at the north end of the plaza, up near the boardwalk in front of a supply store. This may even have been the same store where Pablo got the feed. It was closed now, but Duvall had seen a clerk inside, working late by the light of a lantern.

Duvall popped the cork on the spare canteen when he got to the well. He brought up the bucket and poured water into the canteen. One bucket filled the first canteen, but so much of the water also spilled back into the well that Duvall figured he might need to bring the bucket up three or four times to fill all three canteens. He put the cork back in the top of the first canteen and looked around, checking over his shoulders, putting his eyes on Marisol, and giving a deliberate, lingering look at the people outside the saloon.

The folks in the gazebo didn't worry him. If they cared about the two riders, they would have started paying attention to them long ago.

But the ones outside the saloon – drunks were unpredictable. A drunken man could wander this way and, just for the hell of it, pick a fight with a man filling canteens at the well. Or a drunken man might see a woman by herself and decide to give her a try. He might become belligerent if she rejected him and cause any sort of trouble.

But also, if they were in that saloon tonight, there was a good chance they were in that saloon the night Duvall shot Rodrigues and Liller and when Marisol shot Emster. They might recognize him.

With his long hair and scraggly beard, and being a gringo in Mexico, Duvall knew he was an easy man to recognize.

So he left his eyes on that crowd outside of the saloon. He couldn't see faces from this distance, but he could see the shapes of the people, he could read their body language. A woman outside the saloon had the attention of most of the men. She wore a colorful dress, and she was probably sufficient to keep any wandering drunk from coming this way. But there were other pockets of men, too. Two over there. Four or five over there. Any of those groups might break free of the saloon and head this way.

If they did, Duvall would take what water he had and they'd leave fast.

Duvall glanced over his shoulder. Both horses had their heads down at the trough.

Good. When they started into the desert, it would be on horses that had all had a good drink, and that was a blessing. The horses must have sensed from the riders that they were about to embark on a journey through a waterless desert. Duvall couldn't remember the last time he'd had a string of horses that all willingly drank when he needed them to.

He started hauling up the bucket to fill the next canteen.

MARISOL STOOD WITH THE horses. They drank like they were desperate for the water, especially the freckled gray.

Pecas Gris. She smiled to think that Duvall had given his horse a Spanish name. Though his translation was very poor. Freckles Gray, he had named his horse. He probably meant to name the horse Pecoso Gris. Even so, she thought it was sweet.

She wanted this to be over. Wherever they were going, she wanted to be there.

But it wasn't necessarily that Marisol wanted to escape the dangers or the rigors of the desert. She wanted to get on with their lives together.

These last few days had brought violence into her life like she'd never known. But if anything, the violence and the difficulties had only sharpened her vision of the love she felt for this man.

In their flight through the desert, and their capture by Señor Guerrero, she had seen repeated over and over the same character-istics that first drew her to Tomás Duvall. He was protective of her. Even in the worst moments, his first thought went to her safety. But it wasn't solely that he thought of her. She felt safe. When those men this morning came out of the desert and attacked them in the darkness, did not Tomás grab her and hold her tight? Was she not safe in his arms? And he fought courageously. His confidence in himself was not misplaced. He knew the man he was, knew his own capabilities. He was not quick to violence, but when it came to him, he did not shy away from it.

He was violent against the violence.

But to her, he was sweet and tender. And isn't that what her mother always said to her? Find a man who will love you, not one who loves himself. Find a man who will protect you and be there with you.

Her mother learned lessons the hard way. A prostutita in Juárez, lucky to be adored by Señor Manuel Arellano Hermosillio who would pay for her but would not love her, who would buy her whatever she wanted, but would not be there with her. And when she fell pregnant with his child, he put her up in Santa Catalina – gave her a home and a cantina to own. Her mother lived a better life than she'd ever had any reason to expect, but Marisol knew that her mother always ached for the tender affection of a man, for the partnership of a marriage to a man who would love her and only her.

As a girl, Marisol witnessed that ache in her mother's heart.

A woman needs a man just like a man needs a woman. Marisol believed this. If any woman ever found herself in a position where she did not need a man, it was her own mother. A successful cantina, a community of people who treated her well, even if some of them resented her wealth. Marisol's mother was a joyful woman who loved her daughter and built a decent life where there was so much opportunity for it to go a different way. Yet still, she ached for that partnership. She ached for a man to love her. Her mother had raised her to never need a man. She found men who could teach Marisol to ride and to shoot. She herself taught Marisol to cook so that one day she could run the cantina. She taught Marisol to grow fruits and vegetables in her garden. She taught her daughter to read and write and to speak English.

Marisol's mother taught her so many things so that she would never have to rely on a man, but a lesson she didn't know she was teaching her daughter was the lesson of loneliness.

And when she died, did she not die of a broken heart? Marisol believed so.

Dangers on a journey to a new country? Difficulties on a ride through the desert?

She could face these things because she had found what eluded her mother. She had found a man who would be her partner in life.

Whatever, together.

That was the bargain they made back in Santa Catalina, and Marisol meant it with every bit of her being.

While the horses drank, she turned and watched Duvall at the well.

His hair spilled out from below his hat, long and straight. Strands got caught in his mustache and beard. He looked like a wild man wandering in the desert, sweat and blood matted in his hair, a while film of salt left from his sweat crusted on his forehead and neck. Marisol even laughed a little at herself for falling in love with such a scroungy stray.

She watched as he plucked his hat from his head, cupped his hands, and started splashing water on his face and scrubbing his hands across his forehead and his fingers through his beard. Then he bent over and dumped some of the water over the back of his head. She winced for him as the water hit the cuts where he'd been struck by those men who attacked them in the desert.

Soon, she thought. Soon we'll be out of all of this.

"Marisol?" The voice came from the darkness near the buildings behind her.

Her heart froze. Even before she looked over to the source, she recognized the voice of Guillermo Gomez.

She turned and saw Gomez reaching for his holstered revolver. He'd come down the street leading up to the plaza, and she'd never seen him. He wasn't even looking at her as she spun around. Instead, he was searching the area around them, looking for her companions. She saw the moment his eyes lit on Duvall. Now the revolver was out, the hammer cocked.

Gomez looked at her, his face stern in the pale light. He had that revolver down by his side, but he stretched out his other hand, holding it out to her.

"Come," he said. "I can get you out of this, if you'll come with me. There's still time to save yourself, Marisol."

Hadn't she fed him a hundred times in her cantina? More like a thousand times. She'd known him for years. He'd always been a kind man until Néstor Lozano came to Santa Catalina and ordered Gomez to do unkind things. Poor Guillermo, no backbone to stand up to a tyrant.

"Come with me," Gomez pleaded. "You do not have to die."

10

Néstor Lozano swayed a bit as he stood, so he leaned against the counter inside the saloon. Even in the dim light of the hanging lamps, he could see the stain from the blood on the floor in the middle of the saloon. Right there in that space, less than a week ago, the gringo had murdered a man. And out the back door, he had murdered another man. And there in the doorway of the front door, Marisol Rosaloes had shot a man in the back and killed him. Killed him for the gringo.

Lozano threw back the last of the mescal in his glass and slammed the glass down hard on the counter so that it fell on its side and rolled in a half circle.

"I came to Santa Catalina believing my life was made," Lozano said.

He spoke to no one in particular. Four of his men who had ridden with him for the last few weeks were there, drinking cervezas and listening to him. Gomez had gone to be sure that the new horses would be ready in the morning. They were changing mounts in Palomas because at sunup they would ride hard for Mesilla. Across the border to the biggest town in southern New Mexico. Without a doubt, the gringo and Marisol would make for Mesilla. It was the only place they could go.

"I was an important man now," Lozano said. "A village and a territory to run on behalf of Señor Manuel Arellano Hermosillio.

A woman who would be my wife. Marisol Rosales. A beautiful woman! Señor Arellano's own daughter!"

He was drunk, and his men knew it. Sober, Lozano never would have said out loud that Marisol was Señor Arellano's daughter.

"And now I am a fool in Señor Arellano's eyes."

Lozano looked around. He caught the eye of the man behind the bar.

"Another mescal!" he called to the man. And he looked around for his glass, but his eyes took a moment to focus. He found it and picked it up and waved the glass at the bartender. Then he turned back to his men. His eyes could not find any of their faces, just blurs where their heads should have been. And he laughed, because he knew that's all any of them were to Señor Arellano – himself included.

"But I could have been something more. I could have been his son-in-law. How far I would have risen! Santa Catalina would have just been a stepping stone. Maybe I would have been a general when Señor Arellano became El Presidente!"

Even drunk, Lozano knew he'd said too much there. Now he was talking about treason, and implicating his boss.

He swayed and laughed.

"Now I am the fool. The clown. All because of this damned gringo!"

The bartender set down the glass of mescal just as Lozano slapped his hand against the counter. The result, his hand knocked the glass and the glass spilled.

"Fill it!" Lozano shouted at the man's face.

Word had spread across Palomas that Señor Guerrero was killed in a morning raid on the road up from Guadalupe Victoria, and no one dared to cross Lozano now. He was, without question, the highest ranking man in Palomas at the moment. For all anyone knew, Señor Arellano would see fit to make Lozano the permanent replacement for Guerrero. Who wanted to already be at odds with the man if that happened? So the bartender just filled the glass again, and this time he set it down just out of reach of Lozano.

"That gringo has stolen my woman and stolen the gold and stolen my prospects for the future," Lozano said. "But I can get it all back. Every bit of it can be mine again. I can be redeemed in the eyes of Señor Arellano."

He bent toward the blurred faces of his men. He smiled at them, pointing at them and wagging his finger.

"How do I get it all back?" he asked, his eyes moving irrespective of each other. "How do I get back the name of Néstor Lozano?"

He leaned back, found the mescal, and took a healthy drink. He swayed on his feet and put out a hand to steady himself.

"I will tell you how I get back the name of Néstor Lozano."

He stopped now. Swayed. Looked around at blurs. Waited. Nearly forgot what he was saying. And then he remembered.

"Kill the gringo!"

The men started laughing and cheering, and several others in the saloon took up the call. Most had stopped paying any attention to the drunken man, but they'd all drank enough that they could take up a cheer. And besides, hadn't their fathers and grandfathers fought the gringos to humiliation? Guadalupe Hidalgo. Gold in California. Wouldn't any of them be happy to kill a gringo in the name of their fathers and grandfathers?

Lozano laughed and slapped someone on the back.

"Kill the gringo!" he shouted again, and several others shouted it back to him.

And then they heard the shot from across the plaza. And then another shot, and another. Someone outside, across the plaza from the saloon, was shooting like it was the war all over again.

Duvall had the canteens slung over his shoulder. He toted the Yellow Boy rifle in his right hand, and he carried his hat in his left.

He started back toward Marisol and the horses, but his view of her was slightly obstructed by the planted trees that circled the plaza. Something looked not quite right, but he wasn't sure what it was.

He stepped past the trees and frowned. It looked to him like Marisol was talking to someone. Then he saw the shadow standing away from her, a man whose face he could not make out from this far away.

"Qué pasa?" Duvall said at the darkness.

The man turned toward him and swung his arm up. Duvall saw it all in an instant. Guillermo Gomez, Lozano's lieutenant from Santa Catalina. Gomez, who was there the day Duvall met Marisol when she was accosted on the road. The man she was traveling with, an elderly neighbor, murdered. Gomez and two of Lozano's soldiers. Duvall had killed those two and Gomez had fled.

In his hand, a revolver.

Gomez swung the revolver in Duvall's direction, the action seemed more like throwing the gun than shooting it. But shoot it he did. A wild shot from the hip. Duvall with these heavy canteens hanging from his shoulder. He dropped the hat and grabbed the rifle in both hands. His fingers jacked the lever, chambering a round.

The rifle bellowed.

Gomez withered at the return shot, though it was no better aimed than his own. Duvall shrugging the canteens back onto his shoulder, firing from the hip the same as Gomez.

Duvall dropped the lever again, brought it up with a snap. Squeezed the trigger without even trying to place it.

Gomez fumbled with the revolver, trying to draw back the hammer. He got it, and threw the revolver up again. The revolver clapped and Duvall's rifle barked a third time, both shooting almost at the same moment.

Gomez retreated, falling back into the shadows. Duvall advanced, but now he couldn't even see the man. He fired a fourth shot, but he was shooting at the darkness now.

"Go!" Duvall shouted to Marisol.

She was frozen on the spot. But now she broke from her trance and swung herself up onto the piebald pony's back like a champion rider. Fabiola didn't need to be told to move quickly. The pony got skittish the moment the shooting started.

"Vamos!" Marisol called to her mount. And the pony was at the gallop. Marisol ducked as they went under the branches of trees and cut across the plaza, following in the direction where Pablo had been.

"Pecas!" Duvall shouted at the horse. "Come here, you danged hoss!"

But as good as the gelding was, he wouldn't come like a dog.

A flash and bang from the shadows, and Duvall thought he could hear that bullet snap past him. He directed the rifle toward the spot where he'd seen the flash and squeezed the trigger. He heard a shout. Maybe he'd snatched some blind good luck and hit Gomez, or maybe the man had jumped clear and stubbed his toe. Duvall thought he saw movement again, and he worked the action on the rifle and fired another shot.

Pecas Gris took one last drink, dribbled water down into the horse trough, and lazily looked back at Duvall. The ol' hoss had seen enough shooting that a gunfight in the street of a Mexican border village didn't even rouse his interest.

"Come on, you ol' rascal!" Duvall shouted, back-stepping now and seizing his hat from the ground.

He dashed forward now. Twenty paces to grab the reins and step into the stirrup.

Now, for some reason, Pecas Gris decided to get worked up. He danced a circle, leaving Duvall hopping on one foot as he tried to gain the saddle with one foot already in the stirrup. The danged canteens felt like fifty-pound sacks of potatoes weighing his shoulder down.

"Hang on," Duvall called to the horse. "Let me get aboard."

He had the rifle in one hand, the reins in the other, and he was shrugging to keep the canteens from falling off his shoulder.

Pecas Gris decided to run now, and Duvall just managed to throw a leg over the horse's back side.

Cussing and trying to slide himself into the saddle, all he could do was hang on. He hadn't yet got his other foot in the stirrup as he had to pull hard on the reins to keep Pecas Gris from running him right into a branch.

He heard a gun bark from behind him, but the shot didn't find its target.

Now they were bolting through the plaza, Duvall still unable to get himself situated.

He saw the crowd coming out of the saloon. Dozens of people. And among them, he saw the red coat that he recognized as the one Néstor Lozano wore.

Pecas Gris was making right for the opposite side of the plaza, right toward the crowd emptying from the saloon.

Now, at last, Duvall's right foot found the stirrup. The canteens bounced against his sore side – the one where he'd been shot just a few weeks back when they ambushed the wagon loaded with gold.

Duvall used his knee, pressing it into Pecas's shoulder, turning the horse hard toward the street where Marisol had disappeared.

But she hadn't disappeared. She'd reached the street and reined up, waiting for him.

"Tomás!" she shouted, encouraging him forward.

Duvall raised the rifle above his head.

"Go! Keep moving!" Duvall shouted at her.

Marisol wheeled the pony. Duvall was nearly on her heels now.

One last shot rang out behind him as the two of them rode into the street and toward the darkness of the desert.

11

GUILLERMO GOMEZ TOLD A story a bit more generous to him than the actual truth.

In the version he told to Néstor Lozano, he came upon Marisol and the gringo and did not know it was them until the gringo fired the first shot.

"I drew my pistola and returned fire," Gomez said. "But the gringo kept shooting, and then the two of them rode away."

He had to tell the story twice. That night, with Lozano drunk, and the next morning when Lozano was sober and did not remember the details of what had happened.

The second time Gomez told the story, they were already mounted and riding through the desert in pursuit of the gringo.

Whether Lozano believed the story or not, he accepted it with only a small reprimand.

"You could have ended this whole thing if you'd shot him when you had the chance," Lozano grumbled.

But he'd said something similar in the night, immediately after the encounter, and Gomez had an answer when the sun came up.

"They're on horseback," Gomez said. "They do not have one million dollars of gold with them on horseback. We must take the gringo alive to find out what he has done with the gold, or Señor Arellano will never see his gold again."

This made Lozano think.

"Si. It is true," he said. "They must have hidden the gold, or someone else has it and is taking it across the border. All I have thought all these days was to catch him and kill him. But you are right, Guillermo. We must not kill the gringo. We must capture the gringo. If he will not tell us where to find the gold, then we will turn him over to Señor Arellano. Then it will be up to him to get his own gold back in whatever way he sees fit."

Lozano passed the word to his men. The same men he'd had cheering at the thought of killing the gringo in the saloon the night before, now he had to tell them that under no circumstances were they to kill the man.

"He must be taken alive," Lozano told them.

Lozano and Gomez now rode with a dozen men. They'd picked up a couple of men in Juárez, and some of Guerrero's men rode with them now, in addition to those who'd come with them from Santa Catalina.

That morning, while Lozano still slept off his abuses of the night before, Gomez rode west of Palomas into the desert, following in the tracks of Marisol Rosales and the gringo. He wanted to see if it was worthwhile to track them through the desert. The tracks were evident in the crusty desert surface. They'd ridden hard from the town at a gallop, and somewhere outside of town they joined other riders. Gomez counted at least four separate tracks and thought there could be as many as seven. It was difficult to tell for certain. The horses rode close together.

The spread of the kicked-up sand told Gomez that they'd fled the town with a recklessness, though he could not hardly blame them.

They crossed the border at a gallop and continued that pace for a hundred yards or more. They risked a horse stumbling, stepping in a hole, losing its footing on the greasewood brush.

Gomez reached the point where they decided they'd ridden far enough into the desert and slowed their pace. Now, with the tracks less mixed, he decided it was four or five riders, not more than that.

They'd gone north across the border for at least a mile. That's as far as Gomez went before turning back, expecting that by now Lozano would be awake and eager to get moving. When he returned to the Guerrero hacienda where they had stayed since arriving at Palomas, Gomez found Lozano awake and the men preparing to leave.

"We can track them through the desert," Gomez said. "Even if they kept moving through the night, I believe we can catch them."

At first, Lozano insisted that it was better to ride east toward Juárez and then follow the Rio Grande valley into New Mexico Territory. Lozano thought that if they made for Mesilla by way of good roads they would move faster and be in Mesilla waiting for their prey. But Gomez pushed to pursue through the desert.

"Better to catch them in the desert away from everyone than to find ourselves in a gunfight in an American town," Gomez advised. Lozano seldom listened to anyone else's opinion, and maybe it was because he was still feeling the effects of his heavy drinking, but this morning he relented.

So now the two men led their small army of a dozen gunfighters across the border and into the New Mexican desert.

It was no different than the Mexican desert. The desert did not care about arbitrary borders conceived by politicians, and the law in the American desert was the same as the law in the Mexican desert. It was a law of survival.

So they crossed the border, following the tracks of the gringo and Señor Arellano's daughter.

12

PABLO MADE UP THE fire using a couple of dead juniper bushes like standing skeletons in the desert. He kicked at the dry branches and they fell and broke with almost no effort.

"Don't get too comfortable," Duvall warned Marisol as she spread out a blanket. "We'll have to kick that fire down and move when we're done cooking on it."

"Why do we have to move?" Pablo said. "We've crossed the border. We're safe."

Duvall nodded his head over his shoulder to the northwest at a crop of mountains that had stood on the horizon over their left shoulders. Duvall reckoned them to be about twenty miles to the north. These were the mountains he'd seen down in Mexico that marked for him how close they were to New Mexico Territory. A row of six or seven jagged peaks.

"Anywhere there's mountains like that, you better believe there's a band of Apache that'd be happy to take your scalp," Duvall said. "You think about them Apache on the Jornado del Muerto that killed Chuck. Ones just like them are in that mountain range, and it ain't so far away they couldn't be here anytime they wanted. If there's some roaming past and they smell your campfire, we're as good as dead."

Marisol's eyes grew wide as she turned to look at the mountains herself.

"Do you really think there might be Apache?" she said.

Apache were as feared in Mexico as they were in the United States. For a group of travelers, the word itself struck a chill that reached all the way to the bone.

"I don't think it. I know it."

Duvall didn't mind scaring both of them. He was plenty scared himself, and if they felt a little fear maybe they'd both keep a good watch on the horizon. The worst thing would be having Apache sneak up on them.

"We can move after we cook the beans," Pablo agreed.

"I'll put the blanket up for now," Marisol said.

It was too hot for a fire, anyway, Duvall thought. He'd rather be hungry than dead. But he couldn't expect Pablo and Marisol not to eat. So they could make a fire, cook the beans and then ride on a ways and find a spot to make a camp for the afternoon.

"We ain't making much progress," Duvall said.

He took his prayerbook from his pocket and his tobacco pouch from his saddlebag. Wind was blowing hot across the desert, and it would be hell to try to smoke a cigarette, but he was feeling a gnawing at the back of his jaw and needed a smoke.

"You hold still," Duvall told Pecas Gris, creasing the paper to drop and spreading out a pinch of tobacco. "You're my windbreak."

"Si," Pablo said. "It's hard to make progress when it's too hot to ride during the day and too dark to ride during the night."

"Ain't that the truth," Duvall said.

No road through the desert meant it was too dangerous to do anything more than walk the horses in the dark, picking their way along through the greasewood, trying to stay on as straight a course as possible. They didn't have stump holes to worry about, but the bunch grass and greasewood was plentiful here, and a rider not paying attention in the dark could walk his horse right into it and get tripped up.

Duvall watched Pablo struggle to try to get the fire lit. He'd twisted some bunch grass together as kindling, but the wind took away his matches as soon as he struck them, and when he finally got one to stay lit, the wind knocked the fire off the twisted grass. He cussed some and tried again. This time the grass lit, but the wind pressed the flame down and the wood wouldn't catch. Frustrated, Pablo stood up and walked away from it for a moment.

"Anyway, at least we ain't got to worry about no more Mexicans trailing us," he said.

Pablo used his knife to harvest a fresh batch of grass and twisted it up. Then he went back to the fire he'd built but couldn't get to light and tried again. After wasting four matches, Duvall stepped over and kneeled down beside him.

"Watch this," Duvall said.

He struck a patch and immediately cupped it in the same hand he held the match in, just like he did with his cigarettes. Then he held the twisted grass in his other hand, the cigarette between his teeth, and when it caught fire, he pushed it up near the sticks Pablo had broken, using his body to block the wind. In a few moments, they had the sticks burning, and Duvall fed that fire with increasingly bigger sticks.

It took a few minutes to get a good fire that he knew would last, but now Pablo was feeding bigger branches onto the fire.

"Let them burn a little and you'll have coals enough to warm up some beans," Duvall told him.

Marisol sat on her saddle that Duvall had laid down on a tuft of bunch grass to keep it from getting sand stuck all over the underside of it. She had her hat off, tucking into the band a little yellow wildflower she'd picked, and her black hair was blowing wild in the wind.

"It's funny how pretty the desert can be," she said, sweeping her hand at a wide swath of wildflowers in bloom.

Duvall grunted as he sat on the ground beside her. He strained to pull off one of his boots and dumped sandy gravel out of it. Then he pulled it back on and repeated the process with the other boot.

"I swear, I don't believe I'll ever get all these pebbles out of my boots or all this sand out of my underdrawers. Traveling through the open desert ain't a pleasure."

Marisol ran her tongue over her white teeth.

"Si. It's the sand in my teeth that is annoying me. And the sand that blows into my shirt and sticks to me."

Duvall grinned and nodded his head to her.

"Sticks to you under your shirt, huh?" he said. "I reckon I've never wanted to be a grain of sand so bad in all my life."

Marisol blushed and slapped a playful hand against Duvall's shoulder.

"Tomás!" she chastised. "Do not be rude."

But the grin on her face told a different story.

"How far do you think?"

"To Las Vegas?" Duvall said, squinting his eyes and looking northward. "We still have to go the length of the Jornado del Muerto. I reckon we ain't got nothing less than two-hundred and fifty miles. Maybe closer to three hundred."

"No," Marisol said. "Just to a town where we can bathe and spend a night in a bed."

Duvall nodded.

"The question is what town can we go to and feel safe. Mesilla? That ain't but maybe another twenty or twenty-five miles. Maybe thirty, but not more than that. But are we safe in Mesilla? Is it far enough north of the border that them boys who work for your daddy ain't gonna ride up there and find us? If not Mesilla, we're probably all right in Leasburg up by Fort Selden. I don't reckon any Mexicans want to risk starting a war by opening fire that close to an army fort."

"Pablo thinks they will not come this far," Marisol said. "He says we're safe from them here."

"I don't know," Duvall said. "I think we're safe at Fort Selden. But here? There ain't nothing to stop them from following us into the desert, killing me and Pablo, and taking you back to your father."

"If they kill you, they'll have to kill me," Marisol said defiantly. "I won't go back."

Duvall frowned at her.

"We'll just have to see to it that it don't come to that," he said.

Pablo called to them.

"Beans are ready. I cooked them with the last of the jerky."

"We'll be in Mesilla this time tomorrow," Duvall said.

"You said earlier, the Jornado del Muerto," Marisol said. "The Journey of Death? Is that the trail we take?"

"Yep. That's the one. It's the desert section on the old Spanish highway that runs from Mexico City up into Colorado. All that was Spanish land before my country fought your country back in the '40s."

"Is it really so bad?" Marisol asked. "To be called the Journey of Death?"

Duvall gave a small shrug and glanced at Pablo.

"It's a rough trail. Ain't a lot of water for nigh on a hundred miles. And you never know when there might be Apache moving about."

Marisol gave a faint smile.

"And this is the trail we have in front of us?" she asked.

Duvall nodded his head. "When we cross over the Rio Grande."

Pablo gave a small chuckle.

"It's funny. When we started out on this – what's it been? Two months ago? I had a pit in my stomach about the Jornado del Muerto. Now? It doesn't even worry me."

"Is that because you found out that it wasn't so bad or because everything else you've done has been worse?" Marisol asked.

"Si. Everything else has been so much worse," Pablo said.

They ate and rested and rested the horses. They waited for dusk when they could saddle the horses and ride without worrying that they would exhaust the horses. Even with two spare horses, and Pablo and Duvall switching out, the heat was a lot for all of them. But Duvall and Marisol and Pablo found that their own exhaustion, caused by nights of walking to spare the horses, won out this day over the heat and the broiling sun. Until today, they'd found the desert too hot for sleep. But now they slept.

It was Pecas Gris that snorted the alert, and Duvall's eyes came open fast.

"Pablo. Wake up," Duvall said. "Help me saddle the horses."

"What's wrong?" Pablo asked, stretching and yawning.

"Someone's coming."

OUT ON THE HORIZON to the northeast stood some tall hills. It looked like rough country up there. And rough country meant places to hide, natural breastworks that might offer some protection in gunfight.

"We'll make for those hills," Duvall said, pointing ahead.

Five miles, maybe? Maybe a little more than that.

Rough country was hell on a man traveling from one point to another, but it was perfect for the man in flight. Among the hills they could out-pace the riders in pursuit. Among the hills they could lose the riders trailing them. Among the hills they could hide from the riders behind them. If necessary, among the hills they could dig into a defensive position up on high ground and stage an ambush. Maybe in that way they could level the odds. Two men dug in with a vantage over a canyon could easily fight off eight or ten men or maybe even more.

When Pecas snorted and woke Duvall, he jumped to his feet and searched the horizon. The urgency in the snort gave him an immediate sense of danger, and he wasn't wrong. Behind them, he saw a cloud of dust hanging low on the horizon. It had to be a lot of riders to kick up that much dust. Two or three or maybe even four riders would have left no sign. The dust would have blown away with the wind.

They had saddled those horses fast and ridden out before that cloud of dust had taken shape.

"Apache?" Pablo asked.

Duvall shrugged.

"Could be. More likely it's that feller Lozano that works for the man we stole the gold from," Duvall said.

They rode at the gallop for a short distance, but the sun was still not yet down below the horizon, and the horses could only keep up that pace for a little while before they slowed to an easy lope. But the sun was low enough that it illuminated that dust cloud, and when Duvall twisted around to check the backtrail, he wasn't sure that even at a gallop they had done much to distance themselves from their pursuers. He reckoned them to be maybe three miles back, or maybe less than that.

They neared the first of those tall hills, and Duvall realized these hills must have been small, ancient volcanoes – cone-shaped, red slopes growing blacker toward the tops. The hills were clustered, and as the northern horizon opened up ahead of them, Duvall could see that they stretched on into the distance. Maybe a hundred similar hills, or maybe more than that.

Duvall led them down into a deep arroyo, its sides like craggy escarpments, sharp rock all covered over in greasewood or juniper, prickly pear or cholla. The bed of the arroyo was loose sand, easy enough to track through if their pursuers followed them down into the arroyo.

They slowed the horses here. They had no choice. The narrow, curving arroyo didn't lend itself to anything more than a walk.

Duvall led the way with Marisol behind him and Pablo in the back leading both of the spare horses. Five horses left a helluva trail to follow, Duvall thought.

The dark gray rock of the arroyo's walls looked almost like blocks. No question that this was lava rock. Duvall had seen it in the massive malpais up at the north end of the Jornado del Muerto and he'd seen it around the ancient volcanoes in the north of the territory. He suspected the cone-shaped hills probably had bowls at the tops where lava had once blown free. Terrible country for riding horses with all the loose rock, but good country for hiding or staging an ambush.

"Are they still behind us?" Marisol asked, her breathing heavy from the long lope across the desert.

Duvall twisted around, but down in the arroyo there was nothing to see. The arroyo was too deep and too much vegetation grew up at the top.

"We've just got to assume that they are," Duvall said.

The arroyo cut along the base of one of these big hills, curving around to the east side so that they were now in a canyon between two of the hills. On the east side of the first hill, they were plunged now in shadow, and the sky above was growing dim.

"It'll be dark soon, and this ain't country where we can move at night," Duvall said. "We need to find a place to hole up."

But the sides of the arroyo were high on both banks, six to ten feet on either side, and black with lava rock. They could climb out, but they wouldn't be able to get the horses over the sides. So they were at the mercy of the arroyo, following its sandy path wherever it took them, until at last the embankments fell away and the trio of riders found themselves in a plain, maybe a mile and a half to two miles wide, with these low hills around them on every side.

The horses' hooves clinked against the black rock, as the horses maneuvered their feet into the sand to avoid the loose, unwieldy rocks. Duvall worried about their footing. Nothing would bring this to a rapid finale like an accident with one of the horses.

"Best to dismount here," he said.

Duvall scanned the landscape, seeking some refuge, some inspiration. Somewhere behind them, and maybe not far behind them, a group of riders large enough to kick up a dust cloud, was coming after them. Whether it was Lozano or Apache, the result would surely be the same.

The sun was just kissing the horizon off to the west, but it was blocked now by the hill they'd come around. Everything here between the two hills was cast in shadow. And as Duvall surveyed the land around them, he knew time was running thin. Pablo knew it, too.

"If those were Apache behind us, they could pop up out of that arroyo any moment," Pablo said. "I don't know what you're thinking, hombre, but you'd best get on with it in a hurry."

"What's that?" Duvall asked, pointing to what looked to be a black slope clinging to the side of the hill a couple hundred yards beyond them.

"What do you mean?" Pablo asked. "It's a hill."

"Not the hill. Look how that patch there is blacker than the rest."

"Shadows," Pablo dismissed.

"I don't think so," Duvall said. He glanced at Marisol. Took a look at the arroyo they'd ridden through. "Follow me."

They led the horses down into an dry wash where they found a sandy bed for better footing for the horses, but they didn't bother to mount. Duvall had taken one of the spares now, and led Pecas and the spare horse. Pablo had his horse and the other spare. Marisol led the pony. They went quickly. This dry wash didn't have the same tall banks. If riders were behind them, they'd come out of that other arroyo and see them right off. Then it would be a fight. Neither Pablo nor Duvall had a gun in their hands – both of them tugging on lead ropes.

"Yeah," Duvall said, looking at that black slope. It was just exactly what he thought it was, and it became clearer for the other two as they neared it.

Back when these hills were active volcanoes, Duvall couldn't guess how many hundreds or thousands of years ago that had been, lava had flowed down over the rim and off the side of this one in front of them, and it had cut away part of that ridge. Then it had flowed down, making this dry wash. Or maybe rain had done. Rain after rain, rains over centuries. Duvall didn't know. He was fascinated by the landscape and the visible evidence of a time when the earth and the rains cut and shaped, washed away and built new again. But these were mysteries, unknowable to him. The evidence led to conclusions that defied his imagination, but he'd seen the mysteries a thousand times in rocks and slopes and hills and sandy bottoms.

He had to assume that whatever mystery occurred here had been directed by the hand of the Almighty, the all-knowing Almighty, who foresaw a time when three fugitives on the run from Apache or Mexicans would need a place to hide out.

The box canyon cut by water or lava was about thirty yards deep with maybe ten yards separating the ridge from the hillside. The bottom was sandy enough, though mixed with the clinking rocks that could trip up a horse. And near the back of the box canyon, a little outcropping.

"Take the horses to the back there," Duvall told Marisol. "You stay behind them rocks. It won't be big enough to hide the horses, but if trouble comes, you'll be protected from any flying lead."

Duvall slipped his Yellow Boy from its scabbard and took a spare box of shells from the saddlebag. Pablo helped Marisol lead the horses to the back.

"Señorita, you keep that Smith & Wesson in your hand," Pablo told her with a nod to the gun she had tucked into a saddle strap. "If they find us here and get past us, you'll have to use it. If it's Apache, you'll want to use it on yourself."

Marisol nodded.

"Si. You don't need to explain it to me, Pablo. I understand."

Duvall pressed himself close to the rocky wall of the canyon. His fingers moved without benefit of sight, but he was practiced at creasing the paper, holding it between his fingers and sprinkling tobacco onto the paper. He could do it in the dark.

The sun went down an hour ago. Their pursuers never appeared from the arroyo.

Now Duvall hugged the rock and struck a match against its rough basalt surface. The match hissed and spit and flared, and as it turned to flame, Duvall brought it up close to his face, lighting the cigarette. He blew out a cloud of smoke that extinguished the flame and dropped the match into the sand at his feet. He leaned a shoulder against the rough surface of the canyon wall.

"What do you think, hombre?"

"I don't know, par'ner," Duvall said. "Ain't seen nobody. Ain't heard nobody. Maybe whoever we saw back behind us didn't have no interest in us."

"Si. That's what I'm wondering now," Pablo said. "Maybe we didn't even see anybody. Maybe it was a dust devil."

Duvall chuckled.

"It warn't no dust devil. I think I know the difference between a dust devil and a pack of riders."

Duvall drew on his cigarette. The orange fire on the tip glowed bright for a moment, almost illuminating his face. Pablo spit some dust from his mouth.

"You reckon we're about twenty-five miles or thirty miles from Mesilla?" Pablo asked.

"About that."

"Let's move on," Pablo suggested.

Duvall grunted and his cigarette glowed bright again. Pablo waited. He could see the exhale of smoke blow past.

"I don't know, Pablo," Duvall said. "This ground, all littered with rocks. A hoss could take a spill."

"Walk them out through the arroyo," Pablo said.

Duvall drew on the cigarette again, and Pablo saw the orange glow drop down to the ground and then snuff out as Duvall pressed a boot down on it.

"Stay here a minute," Duvall said.

The stars and slight sliver of a moon gave just enough light that Pablo could see Duvall's form take shape as he stepped away from the rock. He walked slowly to the mouth of the box canyon. Pablo could hear the clinking as Duvall stepped onto a pile of loose basalt rock. Duvall whispered a curse, and forced a smile from Pablo.

"Watch your step, hombre," Pablo whispered into the darkness.

"I can't see my feet," Duvall muttered back to him.

More clinking rocks and cursing, and then silence. Pablo couldn't hear the footsteps and lost sight of any movement. So he waited. Moments stretched to minutes. Minutes ticked by. Then, from behind him, Pablo heard Marisol's voice call softly.

"Tomás?"

"No," Pablo whispered back. "It's me. Duvall's done walked off into the dark."

"Where has he gone?" Marisol said, and her form came into view – a hand pressed against the rock wall of the canyon, her arm outstretched. He could see her hat, but her face was as dark as the canyon wall.

"I suggested we go on now, tonight. Walk the horses out of here. Make for Mesilla as fast as we can. We ain't seen nor heard nothing of whoever was behind us, and I think Duvall agreed with me that maybe whoever we seen didn't know we was there."

"I don't think so," Marisol said quietly. "I am sure that was Néstor Lozano behind us."

"All the more reason for us to get to Mesilla," Pablo said. "If we can move in the dark, maybe we can leave them behind."

The two of them stood quietly for a long while. Pablo had to look for her shape against the rock to even know that she was still there with him. Behind them, at the back of the canyon, the horses sometimes moved. A shoe striking a rock. A soft neigh. A shuffling in the sand. Quiet noises that seemed louder than they were in the stillness and the dark.

And then came a sound from in front of them. A clinking of rocks. Whispered curses.

"It's me," Duvall said. He didn't shout the announcement, but he spoke freely and not at a whisper. "Don't shoot me."

"What did you find?" Pablo asked.

"I don't think they followed us up through that arroyo we come through," Duvall said. "But I found them. They're east of us, in front of us now. Probably a mile up yonder. They rode around these hills, to the south of them, and they made their camp east of the hills."

"In front of us?" Pablo repeated, immediately understanding the danger that created.

Duvall was closer now when he spoke, and Pablo saw the moonlight flash against the brass receiver of the Yellow Boy.

"Yep. Which means we're going to have to sit tight right here for at least the day tomorrow, let them get on up ahead where they won't see us behind them."

Again, Pablo saw the problems.

"We can't do that, Duvall. These horses are going to need water and feed."

"Yep."

"We're going to need water," Pablo said.

"Yep."

"Can we go a different way?" Marisol asked.

"Not much," Duvall said. "First light, we could push north through these hills, let them keep going east. Then we could turn east when we get a few miles to the north. But we'll always have to worry that they're going to be between us and Mesilla. They see us, and all they have to do is turn around and come at us. We can't turn back now. Three more days in this desert and these hosses'll be dead. And if we go to riding them too hard, they'll be dead in two."

"Can we sneak past 'em?" Pablo asked.

"I don't see how we have any choice but to try," Duvall said.

At the back of the canyon, Duvall struck a match. Then he struck a second. And then a third. He used the brief moments of light to get his bearings. He could work in the dark. Anybody who'd ever worked cattle could work in the dark. But he had to know what he was doing first. In the light of the matches, Duvall marked in his mind where he could find some dry sticks and grass. Now he set about breaking up those sticks, ripping some of that dry grass from the sandy and rocky soil. A little ways from the horses, he made up a small stack of grass and sticks. He struck another match and got a small fire going.

"They won't see it," Duvall said confidently. "They're all the way around the other side of this hill."

He found some more sticks to feed into the fire and pretty soon had sufficient light to see by, and then he and Pablo saddled the horses. They made sure all the gear was secure and that nothing was going to shift and rattle or clang. They led the horses out of the box canyon, and Duvall went back to kick sand on the fire.

As Pablo had suggested, they followed the path of the arroyo. It wound around the base of the hill, but its sandy bottom showed in the dim light from the stars and moon.

They moved quietly, Duvall leading two of the horses and Pablo leading the other two. Marisol had the lead rope on her pony.

"THEM BOYS UP AT that campsite are afraid of the dark," Duvall said.

"Si. I don't blame them," Pablo said.

The fire glowed bright out on the horizon. Whoever was out there had built a beacon in the desert. Not because they wanted to summon anyone, but because they wanted to see if anyone was coming. Duvall understood the fear that could compel a man to make such a terrible mistake, but that sort of fear had to be overcome. The best hope a man had of surviving a night in the desert was to not let anyone know he was there. But these men, these ones were announcing their presence.

"We know one thing for certain," Duvall said.

"What's that?" Pablo asked.

"They ain't Apache. No Mescalero I ever seen is going to light up a fire like that."

"Néstor Lozano," Marisol said. "It's surely him."

"I expect you're right."

They spoke in whispers even though they were giving that campfire and the men around it a plenty wide berth. The three of them were mounted now. They'd come out of the arroyo and away from the hill, and Duvall decided as long as they kept the horses to a walk it didn't matter much if they walked or rode. They were away now from most of the loose rock that could trip up a horse.

Duvall was on one of the spare horses, He'd pushed Pecas Gris out in front of him because he knew he could trust his horse to stay with them and not bolt. The Yellow Boy rested across his lap, a hand on the receiver, ready to drag it up and put it to use if the situation required.

But so far, so good.

The horses had been calm and silent, their footfalls finding sand with each step. Not that a clinking rock could be heard from the glowing camp on the horizon. It was hard to judge at night, but Duvall reckoned that camp to be a good four hundred yards off their right shoulders. They'd already come up even with it and passed it by. Another hour, even at just a walk, and the campfire would be gone from view and those men around it – regardless of who they were – would be a distant problem.

"We won't linger too long when we get to Mesilla," Duvall said. "We'll put the hosses in a livery, get them fed and watered and rested. Get ourselves a bath and a night in a hotel room, and then we'll ride out for Leasburg and Fort Selden."

They went on another fifty feet or so, Duvall feeling safer now, feeling like they'd passed the threat. Still there were hours of darkness ahead of them, plenty of time to put miles between them and the men at that campsite.

Then one of the horses snorted a warning, and it was loud – loud enough that Duvall looked back sharply to see if anyone at the camp had heard. Though he was too distant and it was too dark to see anything. The horse, it was the spare horse without a rider, scuffled its feet and gave a loud scream – this one surely would have been heard in the campsite – and the other horses became agitated.

"Quiet that hoss," Duvall hissed a Pablo, but in the thin light he could see Pablo struggling, pulling the lead rope.

That's when the wolves attacked.

They must have thought that last horse in the pack was the weak one, for the wolves undoubtedly chose that horse. Duvall figured he and Pablo and Marisol must have smelled so much like the earth that the wolves didn't know there were humans about. Or maybe they were so hungry that they didn't care.

Whatever it was, Duvall saw the shadow of a wolf leaping at the spare horse, trying to get at its legs to bring it down. Pablo saw it too, and panicked and turned loose of the horse's lead.

Now, all around in the darkness, they could hear the snarling growls of a pack of wolves.

In the front of the group of riders, Pecas Gris made a sudden and fearful run, taking flight to escape the wolves. Before Duvall could do more than hold on, his mount charged in Pecas's wake, a headlong and reckless gallop without fear of greasewood or rock, hole or boulder. The horses knew only to escape.

Marisol's pony fled, too, and Pablo's horse.

The four of them were sprinting across the desert.

That spare horse, the target of the wolves, it made its own headlong dash, but it ran for the campfire. The wolves pursued, and even as the wind rushed past his ears and he tried desperately to bring his horse under control, Duvall could hear the panicked screams of the spare horse and the angry cries of the pursuing wolves.

And then he heard the rifle shots. One or two at first, but then several rifles firing at once. Firing wildly into the darkness of the desert. Not like thunder, for thunder never comes so fast upon itself.

Rifle crack after rifle crack, some so rapid that they overlapped each other. And though they couldn't make out any words, they could hear men shouting and wolves barking and the screams of a horse whose only hope was to run faster than the demons nipping at his heels.

13

GUILLERMO GOMEZ HEARD THE cry of the horse and grabbed his rifle.

He and a man called Eduardo had the watch that hour, and Guillermo had just put a few more sticks of juniper on the fire. There were no logs in the desert, so to keep the fire burning bright, they had to constantly feed it. The pile of wood they'd collected just before sunset had rapidly diminished already, and Gomez worried that they wouldn't have sufficient wood to keep the fire burning through the night.

The fire was Lozano's idea. Guillermo advised against it. He knew a fire only invited attention and that Apache could be in this desert. What worried him were those low hills nearby. Hills like those could collect water and be a place where Apache might camp. But Lozano insisted it would be better to see them coming. Lozano was from Juárez and did not know how to survive in the desert, Guillermo decided. But he was also an angry man, and a mean man, and it did no good to argue against him.

"What was that?" Eduardo said.

"A horse," Guillermo answered, straining his ears. But then he did not need to strain them further, for the sounds came plain now. A horse screaming, dogs snarling and barking.

"What is going on?" Eduardo asked, and the fire showed the fear in his eyes.

Their own remuda became suddenly restless, pulling against their tethers, snorting and dancing nervous dances on their lead ropes.

Guillermo raised his rifle. The others were waking now, asking what was going on. Lozano demanded to know.

"Wolves are attacking a horse."

"What horse?" Lozano asked, jumping from his blanket and snatching up his rifle.

"They're coming at us!" someone shouted, and indeed, Guillermo could hear that the horse was charging toward the camp and the wolves were coming behind it. He still could see no movement in the darkness, but he could hear the direction and he now raised his rifle and fired a shot. Eduardo answered that shot with one of his own, and in moments, every man in the camp was firing wild shots into the darkness.

It came as something of a shock, with a dozen men firing roughly in the direction of the fleeing horse, when the horse bounded through the campsite.

Two wolves launched themselves at Eduardo, and the man let out a tremendous scream as one wolf caught him at the ankle and another took him by the wrist. The wolves, their jaws locked in, dragged him in separate directions.

Guillermo turned his rifle on one of the wolves and fired a shot into the dog's side. Another of the men used his rifle as a club and battered the other wolf.

Eduardo's screams were drowned out by the gunfire, though, as the rest of the men in the camp turned their rifles and revolvers onto the pack of wolves. More than a dozen of them, maybe as surprised as the men to find themselves in a sudden pitched battle. The wolves began to scatter in the presence of gunfire. Their prey forgotten.

Eduardo rolled on the ground, screaming. His arm and leg mangled by the dogs.

Some of the other men fired more shots into the darkness, hoping to scare off the wolves.

Lozano had been asleep and awoke to chaos, and his mood reflected it.

"Someone go and get that horse!" Lozano shouted at the men still pointing their rifles in the direction from which the wolves had come and then retreated.

Eduardo screamed.

Lozano turned his rifle on Eduardo, firing a shot into the man's face that silenced the screaming. The other men saw it.

"Get that horse!" Lozano shouted at none of them in particular. Then he turned on Guillermo Gomez.

"Where did that horse come from?" Lozano asked.

Guillermo pointed.

"Off in that direction," he said. "It was saddled. Perhaps the wolves killed the rider?"

Three of the men raced into the darkness of the desert, trailing behind the horse that had fled through their camp and started all this.

"When we lost the tracks this afternoon," Lozano said. "They went into those hills and avoided us."

"Si," Guillermo agreed. "It seems like they did. And they tried to come past us in the dark."

"Tried?" Lozano snapped. "The succeeded. They did come past us in the dark."

"Maybe not," Guillermo shrugged. "That horse had no rider. Maybe the wolves got them, or at least got one of them."

Lozano fumed. He stamped his feet and swore under his breath. He told one of the men to drag Eduardo's body out of the camp. There was nothing left to do now but wait for the men who'd gone after the horse to return. Lozano debated with Guillermo if they should saddle their horses and try to go after the gringo and Marisol in the dark, but Guillermo finally persuaded him against it.

"If the wolves got one of them, we will need to wait until daylight to make a search," Guillermo said. "Maybe the wolves got all of them and there is no one left to pursue."

No one made any effort to return to their blankets. The two men who dragged Eduardo's body away returned, both of them watching over their shoulders as they came back.

"Did you take him far away?" Guillermo asked. "Those wolves will return to the body. If you didn't take him far enough and those wolves come back into the camp, it could be your bodies getting dragged into the desert next."

The two men gave each other sheepish looks.

"Make a torch," Guillermo said. "Take someone with you who is armed. Get that body way away from our camp."

Guillermo Gomez had never been the sort to get angry with his men like this, but he could have shot those two men. He knew they'd been too scared to carry the body very far. But they were only inviting the wolves to come back by leaving the body too near the camp.

Four of the men went together, including the two who first went. Two took rifles and held torches. While they were still gone, the three men who went after the horse returned. The horse had calmed from its scare and was plenty docile, now.

They emptied the saddlebags there by the fire where they could see. Three boxes of ammunition. Matches. A paper sack of tobacco, obviously bought somewhere in Mexico because the printing was in Spanish. A shirt and a pair of drawers folded up. The usual sorts of things a man travels with. But no food and an empty canteen strapped to the saddle horn. A small silver flask that was empty but smelled of whiskey, and when they turned it in the light they could see the initials engraved on the flask: "PL."

"This was a spare horse," Lozano decided. "It carried the empty canteen and the empty flask, the unopened sack of tobacco. And there is no gold in the saddlebags."

"What do you think that means?" Guillermo asked, though he already knew what conclusion Lozano would reach.

"It means there is no body that the wolves devoured. The wolves attacked a riderless horse in the dark and the horse fled into our camp. Our chance at catching the gringo just rode past us while you were on watch."

Guillermo stiffened. He'd feared that Lozano would blame him. But how was he to know that riders were slipping past them in this vast, dark desert? It was hardly his fault. He'd foolishly thought that perhaps he could get through this night without the fault being laid at his feet. But Lozano's temper – of course this would come back to him.

"I was doing my duty," Guillermo said defiantly. "I was alert. But the desert is wide and the darkness is complete. How was I to see them and know that they were passing us by?"

Lozano's hand shot across Guillermo's face. A stinging rebuke.

"You be careful, Guillermo. I have come to question your commitment when it comes to Marisol Rosales. You have known her many years. No?"

"Si. Many years."

"When I sent you to stop her from going with the old man to Juárez, you failed to bring her back to me."

"The gringo intervened," Guillermo said quickly.

Lozano's hand snapped across Guillermo's cheek a second time.

"Si. Si. The gringo," Lozano said angrily. "But you have continued to fail me when it comes to Señorita Rosales. And what happened on the street in Palomas? How did you come face-to-face with the gringo and fail to kill him? I am beginning to question your resolve.

Maybe you are in love with her and unwilling to do the hard things with her."

Guillermo said nothing, deciding it was better to leave the accusations unchallenged. Néstor Lozano would believe what he wanted to believe, no matter what Guillermo said in his own defense. And to a point, wasn't it true? What man in Santa Catalina was there who did not love Marisol Rosales, at least a little bit? Beautiful, and with such a happy spirit. Of course he loved her. And did he hesitate to deal with her? Perhaps there was truth in Lozano's accusations.

Lozano went on: "But you had better remember that you work for Señor Manuel Arellano Hermosillio. She and this gringo have stolen his gold, and we are here to recover it, no matter what. And I believe before we are done, we will have to kill Señorita Rosales. If you are not the man to do that job, then perhaps you should saddle your horse and ride back home now."

"I will do what I must do," Guillermo muttered.

"I will do what I must do," Lozano spat back. "You will do what your are told."

"Si. I will do what I am told."

THE HOTEL WAS A long, white-washed adobe building with the doors to each room opening onto the street. Just a single story.

Outside, a long line of heavy wood beams running the length of the building held up the awning to offer shade outside the rooms. The doors were painted a bright, sky blue. Eight of them along the side of the building leading into eight rooms. It was Mesilla, so the rooms were not fancy. A bed was all any of them needed, and a bath, and the baths were outside in the yard behind the hotel. Eight baths, one of each of the rooms, though the baths were also available for rent by anyone, even if they were not guests of the hotel.

White sheets hung in a grid pattern, separating each of the tubs and giving bathers privacy. Two of the baths were reserved for women only.

"We are lucky we rode into town at dawn," Marisol said as she undressed behind a sheet.

"Why so?" Duvall asked.

"We get fresh water in the baths. By afternoon, I'm sure the tubs are filled with mud."

"Huh," Duvall said, stepping into his tub. "It's never dawned on me to get to the bath early in the day. But you're right. I can see the bottom of the tub."

Marisol giggled.

Duvall scrubbed because the desert dust didn't come off easily. Weeks of it caked on him. Behind his ears, in his nostrils, in the corners of his eyes. Behind his knees, around his ankles, and down in the crack of his ass. How the trail dust found the crack of his ass he'd never understand, but after a long ride, it was always there in quantities.

The water was not particularly warm, but the morning sun coming down over the tops of the grid of sheets made the coolness of the water plenty pleasant.

The Yellow Boy sat propped against the tub. His saddlebags, heavy with gold bars, were draped on a small stool beside the tub. Pablo kept his saddlebags with him at his bath, too.

As the sun rose and the trio rode into Mesilla, there was no sign of pursuit on the desert horizon.

"They'll be coming," Duvall said. "They'll be here before dark."

"We'll ride out at dusk?" Pablo asked. "Be gone from Mesilla before they even get settled here?"

Duvall dunked his head under water and went to work on his hair with the soap. So much salt from his own sweat, and dust from the trail. His hair was matted and stiff, and he had to keep working the soap just to get his fingers through it. But already he was beginning to feel refreshed. Little cuts here and there all over his body, along with the big gashes left by the assault on the road north of Guadalupe Victoria – they all stung against the soap, but intuitively, Duvall felt healing with the sting. Like pouring whiskey into a wound. It hurt, but it also healed.

"I don't know, Pablo," Duvall said honestly. "The hosses need a rest. We've used them hard for weeks. A couple of days in a livery wouldn't hurt them none. And we've got a long and rough road ahead of us still. A hundred miles on the Jornado del Muerto."

"You said we couldn't stay here long," Marisol reminded him.

"I know it. And we can't. But we're in America now. We're out of Mexico, and we're nearly beyond the reach of Señor Arellano. Maybe we're already beyond his reach. Lozano and them others? They'd be risking a response from the army if they tried anything here, and they know that. Hell, they may not even follow us all the way into the city."

Marisol made a noise and Duvall chuckled.

"What's that mean?" he asked, wishing he could see her face past the sheet.

"I know Señor Arellano. He is a prideful man and his pride will not allow him to give up easily. But it is also so much money, Tomás. You yourself said we would not be safe in Mesilla. We are too near the border."

"The hosses need rest," Duvall said.

"Si. The horses do need rest," Pablo agreed. "But we are also too near the border. We can rest the horses in Leasburg. There beside Fort Selden where there are soldiers everywhere. We have had our baths. The horses are getting fed and watered now. Let us rest this morning, and then let's leave this afternoon. We can spend a couple of days in Leasburg, under the safety of the army."

Duvall sighed heavily but did not answer. The water was chilly when he first got in, but now he found himself getting accustomed to it. He could have put his head back on the edge of the tub and slept right there in the bath.

"I'm worried that if we don't give them a rest, the hosses don't make it to Leasburg. Or if they do, they don't make it beyond Leasburg. That run in the desert last night was hard on all of them. They've been going for days, and we're down to just the one spare hoss."

But Duvall knew it was more than that. They'd taken two rooms in the hotel. Duvall and Pablo intended to share a room and Marisol would have privacy. But even sharing a room with Pablo, a bundling board between them on the bed, Duvall knew he needed the sleep a bed and a room could offer. He'd not slept more than two or three hours at a time in the desert, and that was sleep he snatched on a bed of sand with rock and bunch grass below him and the sun overhead cooking him. He'd dozed in the saddle at night some, but that wasn't sleep.

"I don't even know if it's the right decision," Duvall admitted. "But I'm so tired, I can't even remember to put one foot in front of the other. So let's finish our baths and let's get to our rooms and get some sleep. We'll see later what's best to do."

Luis Basurto handed his brother a cerveza and sat down across the table from him. He drew a heavy breath. Armando was his younger brother, very smart but also very rash.

"Let me hear your confession," Luis said.

Armando took a drink from the beer and looked around. They were alone, sitting at a table outside a cantina on Mesilla's square. They had a view of the hotel from where they sat. Javier and Ricardo were nearer the hotel and out of sight. The gringo, Señor Arellano's niece – or so he called her – and another man had come into town earlier in the day. Now the four men in Señor Arellano's employ watched them.

"This will not be easy for you to hear," Armando said. "But before you react, remember that what's done is done and there is no changing what has already happened. All we need now is to figure out what we do next."

Luis Basurto rubbed the hair on his cheeks. He wore a trimmed beard and a suit, and even here in the dirty town of Mesilla, after a two-day ride and days with only a single change of clothes, he somehow managed to still look clean and dignified, like he could be on his way to argue in a courtroom in front of a judge.

"What have you done, Armando?"

Armando looked very much the opposite from his older brother. He wore a pair of britches that looked like he'd worn them for three days straight, which he had. His shirt was wrinkled and his coat bore the dust from the trail, even though they'd not been on the trail for days. Armando's beard was not trimmed like his brother's. He'd shaved before they left for Mesilla, so it was short whiskers on his cheeks and chin, but he knew he had a scruffy look. He looked like he would be at home with Javier and Ricardo – gunmen and fighters, more comfortable with a knife than with a fountain pen. But even Luis had to admit his younger brother was the better lawyer. Armando had a sharper mind and a firmer grasp of the law. But Armando was also reckless and needed Luis to guide him away from mistakes.

"When we had just finished studying the law in Ciudad de México, you remember what we did next?"

"Si. Of course, I remember. Señor Arellano sent us here to los Estados Unidos," Luis said.

Armando nodded his head. It was important to him that Luis remember very clearly.

Luis and Armando Basurto grew up in Juárez, raised by their mother. Their father had been killed by a man in a knife fight in a Juárez saloon. But the man whose life their father saved that night, he never forgot the debt he owed to the Basurto family.

The boys with their mother lived comfortably – more comfortably than most – because their father had saved the life of Señor Manuel Arellano Hermosillio. And Señor Arellano had treated them almost as well as he did his own sons. He provided for them, and with their mother, he saw to it that the brothers received an education. Both brothers studied law in Mexico's capital city, and shortly after, they both spent two years in los Estados Unidos. That had been almost a decade ago, just after the Confederate States lost their war for independence.

Señor Arellano sent them to the United States to see the aftermath of the war. They traveled to Philadelphia and then to Washington D.C. They went into the Confederate States, to Richmond and Savannah. They met military and political leaders from both sides. They visited the military governors of the defeated states to learn how to quell ongoing rebellions. They drank whiskey with politicians who talked of both subjugation and reconciliation.

Even in those days, Señor Arellano was interested in what revolution looked like and wanted to see what lessons could be learned.

"Si," Armando said. "And what lesson did we learn in los Estados Unidos?"

Luis nodded his head, remembering.

"War is a hard business," he said.

"Si. That war devastated the country. Even the Northern States reeled with the loss of life and property."

"Very expensive and very wasteful," Luis agreed.

"And the people suffered," Armando said.

"Si."

"Do you remember – a year ago – Señor Arellano called us into his study at his Juárez hacienda?"

"I remember," Luis said. "He said there were men who wanted to make him El Presidente. They were talking of revolución. Generals in the Mexican army had come to him."

"Si," Armando said. "If Señor Arellano brought the money and the guns, they would make him the ruler of the nation."

Luis grinned as he recalled that meeting with their benefactor and employer.

"We tried to tell him. War is not good for anyone, the victors or the beaten."

"Si. We tried to tell him. We tried to dissuade him. But his heart was set on power." Armando took a drink from his cerveza and looked down to the road where the hotel was. The gringo and Señor Arellano's daughter and the other man had gone into their rooms after their baths, but they had not come out. "When I saw that his heart could not be moved, I came up with my own plan."

Luis clenched his jaw and gave his brother a severe look.

"What have you done, Armando? Tell me now."

"Do you remember Rodrigues?" Armando asked.

"Your friend from when you were young," Luis said. "Señor Arellano killed his cousin. Si?"

"Si. Yes. Rodrigues's cousin was the lover of one of Señor Arellano's daughters. Señor Arellano did not approve, and he had the cousin killed and then banished Rodrigues so that he did not have to worry about Rodrigues trying to get revenge."

Luis nodded his head.

"I remember all of this. What did you do, Armando?"

"When Señor Arellano told us about the gold shipment, I went to El Paso and spoke to Rodrigues."

"No," Luis said, shaking his head. "You did not! You did not help to steal Señor Arellano's gold!"

"Keep your voice down," Armando said, looking around the cantina and the street. He nodded his head slowly, his eyes on his brother, a look of guilt on his face. "We saw what a civil war can do to a nation. Devastation and hunger, death. And what if Señor Arellano's side lost the war? We would be murdered for rebels."

Luis shook his head in disbelief.

"After all that man has done for us? How could you betray him like this?"

"It was so much gold," Armando said. "I worked out a plan with Rodrigues. To steal the gold. He was to recruit some gringos and set them up to take the blame. He had two men with him who he trusted. They would steal the gold. The gringos would take the blame. And then you and I could go and meet them here in los Estados Unidos. The plan was a good plan."

"Where is Rodrigues?"

Armando grinned at his brother.

"I am supposed to meet him here in Mesilla. This is why I went Santa Catalina, to be sure the gold shipment was successfully taken. With Señor Arellano in Santa Catalina, panicked because of the stolen gold, I came back to Juárez to get you and to cross the border. But what luck that Néstor Lozano sent us here to wait!"

Armando's grin grew to a smile.

"You see, brother, the whole affair has worked perfectly."

"And the gringo in the hotel?" Luis said.

Armando nodded his head.

"I recognize him. Before the gold left Juárez, I met with Rodrigues to be certain everything was going according to plan and to confirm that the gold would be shipped. The gringo was there."

"Does he know you?" Luis asked.

"He does not know me. We did not meet, and Rodrigues would not have told him my name. None of them were to know my name. But surely he will recognize me."

"This is all so foolish," Luis said, shaking his head. "What have you gotten into? What have you done? You will get us both killed."

"No, no. Don't you see? If the gringo is here in Mesilla, it means Rodrigues is somewhere nearby. He sent the gringo to get me. Which means the gold is also near. We have done it! You and I are rich. And Rodrigues, too."

Luis took a healthy drink from his beer. He wore a look of disbelief.

"Armando. You should have said something to me before you did all this."

"You would have tried to talk me out of it," Armando said.

"Si. Of course I would have!"

"But how much better that I did it, and we are now rich men in America."

Luis said nothing. He wasn't sure it was better. Señor Arellano would never forgive this, and he would never stop coming after them. The gold was valued at nearly one million dollars. At last, Luis let out a heavy breath and closed his eyes.

"You have killed us Armando."

"It will be fine," Armando said. "But I need you to get Javier and Ricardo away so that I can go and see the gringo. I cannot do this with them watching. They are loyal to Señor Arellano."

"How am I to get them away?"

"Tell them we will take over the watch," Armando said. "Tell them to go and eat. Say to them that we will have a long night and they should eat and sleep now. When they are gone, I will go and see the gringo and find out what message he has from Rodrigues."

14

JORGE ROUNDED UP WHAT few cattle he could find. Only a handful survived the winter, but that was more than Hazel thought would be found.

"I will take them to Señor Callahan," Jorge said. "He will buy them."

"Ben Callahan is the man who sold those cattle to my husband. He won't care to buy these back."

"No," Jorge said, shaking his head and looking at Maria for help. "He will buy them. He may not pay a high price. They are underfed and very poorly looking, but he will buy them."

"You keep whatever you can get for them," Hazel said and she glanced at the table where there were fresh fruits and vegetables, cheese wrapped in cloth and smoked meat. "You have been so good to me. I would have been worse off than those cows if you hadn't taken care of me."

The baby, asleep in the bassinet, made a noise. Hazel blinked sleep away from her eyes and held her breath to see if the baby was waking or would stay down. Jorge smiled.

"No. They are your cattle. I will bring to you whatever we can get Señor Callahan to pay. It is fair. Maria and me, we are happy to help a little bit."

"But it isn't a little bit," Hazel said. And if she weren't so exhausted, she could have cried at the kindness of this couple. It was not, by any means, a little bit they had done for her. Jorge had done work around the house. He had brought food. He had rounded up those cattle. He was seeing to their sale. Maria, almost daily, came to hold the baby and give Hazel a chance to sleep or to cook or to clean. Hazel honestly did not know what she would have done had it not been for their kindness. And she desperately wanted to repay them, but she had nothing of any value she could give.

"You have been to town?" Hazel asked.

"Si."

"And no letter for me?"

Jorge shook his head sadly.

He did not know what sort of relationship the young woman had with her family. Did she come west to get away from them? Many young women did. Maybe they would offer her no assistance to come home. This could not go on forever, though. Jorge had already talked to Maria about it. He didn't mind helping for a few weeks – whether Hazel was a widow or just the unhappy victim of an inconstant man – Jorge believed it was his Christian duty to help her however he could. But there had to be limits. This could not go on indefinitely.

"They will send me money to get me and the baby home," Hazel said confidently. "And when they do, I will insist that you take something for all you've done for me."

"Si, si," Jorge said, patting her hand. "We will see about that when it comes time for that. For now, what can I do to help you here?"

Hazel looked at the empty water pail, and Jorge followed her eyes. He smiled and nodded, took up the pail and walked it out of the cabin to the well.

Maria stood up now and she took the woman's hand that her husband had just let go.

"You look so tired," Maria said.

Hazel laughed.

"I feel so tired," she confessed. "The baby had an upset tummy last night and cried for a very long time."

Maria nodded her head.

"Oh, I remember those sleepless nights," she said. "They seem like they will go on forever, but it is only a short time. And then they are gone."

"I won't miss them when they are gone," Hazel said.

"No," Maria laughed. "No, you will not miss them when they are gone. But you will miss how small your baby is, and how sweet she smells."

"She does smell sweet," Hazel said.

"You go and rest now. When the baby wakes, I will take her for a little while. Jorge is going to look over your garden and see how it is coming along. He saw some loose posts on your paddock that he is going to fix. We will stay long enough that you can get some sleep."

"Thank you so much," Hazel said, and her eyes were already beginning to droop.

"You will hear from your parents soon," Maria said. "It takes a letter so long to make the travel."

Hazel climbed up into the loft where she and her husband had made their bed. A strong breeze came through from the cabin's open windows. It took nothing for Hazel to get to her dreams of returning to Chicago.

15

THE KNOCK ON THE door was so soft and quiet that Pablo Peña didn't even think as he opened the door. He was sure it was Marisol. He didn't even have a gun in his hand when he opened the door.

"He's still asleep," Pablo said as he opened the door.

But it was not Marisol. Instead, a man he did not know, a rough looking Mexican, pushed him aside and stepped into the hotel room.

"Wake him up," the stranger said in English. "Hurry, now. We do not have much time."

Pablo gawked at the man. He looked down to see if the man had a gun in his hand, but both hands were empty.

"Duvall?" Pablo said tentatively. "Hey, Duvall. Wake up, hombre."

"Wake him up," the stranger said again, urgency in his voice.

Pablo stepped over to the bed and grabbed Duvall's ankle, hanging out of the blanket, and he gave Duvall's leg a shake.

"Yo. Amigo. I need you to wake up."

"Huh?" Duvall asked, sitting up. He blinked at Pablo. Daylight came from around the curtains, and Duvall wondered at first if he'd slept through the night. He blinked again and his eyes began to focus, and he saw that Pablo looked pale in the dim light of the hotel room, and Pablo was looking at the door. Even before he looked himself, Duvall's heart skipped a beat. That was a look of fear on Pablo's face.

Duvall had seen the man before. Just once, in a smoky and dark saloon in Juárez.

"Do you recognize me?" the stranger asked. "You saw me once in Juárez"

"I do. You're Rodrigues's amigo."

"Si. Rodrigues and I were friends from when we were children."

"I seen you more than once, though. I also saw you at the cabin in the mountains down by Santa Catalina."

The stranger nodded.

"Si. That is right. When the others were arrested in Santa Catalina."

Duvall swung himself out of the bed now. He'd looked, quicker than Pablo had, and knew the man was unarmed. He didn't know how Rodrigues's amigo had turned up here, standing in his hotel room in Mesilla, but the man didn't appear to have come to kill him. So Duvall could guess why he was here.

Duvall pulled his britches on and put on a shirt. He pulled up his suspenders over his shoulders and then buttoned the shirt. None of the men spoke. Rodrigues's amigo seemed content to wait while Duvall got dressed. But when Duvall sat back onto the bed to put on his socks and boots, the man started getting jittery.

"You must hurry," he said. "There are men here who are not friends."

Duvall narrowed his eyes at the man.

"But you're a friend."

"Si. You know that I am. You saw me in the saloon in Juárez and at the cabin at Santa Catalina. Where is Rodrigues? What message do you have from him?"

Duvall cut his eyes at Pablo and gave a small shake of his head, just to make certain that Pablo didn't say anything foolish. Now was not a time to confess that they'd killed Rodrigues.

"What's your name, par'ner?" Duvall said.

"Armando Basurto. And your name?"

"Tommy," Duvall said, though no one regularly called him that. "My name is Tommy."

Duvall took a breath, wondering if he could feign his way out of this.

"You say there are men here who are not friendly?" Duvall said. "How many?"

Armando seemed frustrated, but he answered the question.

"Néstor Lozano sent me here with my brother and two other men. He is leading the effort to recover the gold for Señor Arellano. He had us watching Mesilla for the men who took the gold. For you. And you have with you Señor Arellano's daughter – the Rosales girl from Santa Catalina. You should not have brought her."

Duvall shrugged.

"Well, we did bring her. Can't change that now. What about your brother? Can we trust him?"

"Si. Of course we can trust him. He is my brother."

"He knows about the gold?"

"I told him today," Armando said. "But he understands he has no choice now but to go with me."

"So there's two other men in Mesilla who pose a threat?" Duvall said.

"Si. Two for now. But others will come. Lozano anticipated that you would come through Mesilla."

Duvall glanced at Pablo again, both of them thinking the same thing – Lozano would be here sooner than Armando Basurto expected.

"What do you want to know, Armando?" Duvall said.

"Where is Rodrigues? Why did he not come here himself to meet me?"

"Rodrigues was delayed in Palomas," Duvall said. "He sent me on ahead to meet with you and let you know."

"Palomas?" Armando said. "Lozano sent riders to Palomas."

"He knows he has to be careful."

There was a long delay as Armando accepted what Duvall told him. He seemed to be thinking it over, and Duvall worried that he'd made a misstep somewhere.

"Where is the gold?" Armando asked.

"They buried the gold," Duvall said. "In the desert, north of Palomas. On this side of the border. The gold is in New Mexico Territory, but it was too dangerous to try to hold on to so much gold. So they buried it."

Duvall stepped over to his saddlebags sitting beside his holstered Colt on the dresser at the foot of the bed. He stepped past Pablo. He reached into a saddlebag and felt his fingers land on one of the heavy gold bars. Then he reached deeper until he got to the sack of coins. He slipped his hand inside and withdrew a single twenty-dollar piece. He held that up and showed it to Armando Basurto.

"Rodrigues sent this for you."

Duvall flipped the coin at Armando and he caught it. He smiled looking at it, holding it up where he could see it better. Then he chuckled.

"He could have sent a gold bar instead of just a coin," Armando laughed.

Duvall smiled and nodded his head.

"So you're going to take me to Palomas?" Armando asked.

Duvall glanced a Pablo again.

"Si. That's right," Pablo said, seizing on an opportunity. "But not tonight. Our horses need rest. They need to eat and drink water. It's been a long journey for the horses. Tomorrow at dusk we'll start back for Palomas, and we'll take you to Rodrigues and the gold."

Armando nodded his head, but something seemed to be gnawing at him. For a moment, Duvall worried that the lies were about to catch them.

"Rodrigues should not have stayed in Palomas. He was safer to come here. We talked about that. The most important thing, once he had the gold, was to get out of Mexico. Señor Arellano's reach in Mexico is too long. Palomas is not safe for him."

"What about these other two who are with you?" Duvall asked, changing the subject quickly. "How will you get rid of them?"

Armando thought about this for several moments. Then he said, "I have an idea that I think will work. We will tell them to ride back to Juárez to tell Señor Arellano's man there that you are here. He will get together men to bring here to get you. It will take them two days to ride to Juárez. It will take another two days for Señor Arellano's men to get back. But that is not enough time for us to get to Palomas, get the gold, and then get back here before they arrive."

"We don't have to come back to Mesilla," Duvall said, encouraging Armando. Duvall wasn't going back to Palomas – he just needed those other two away. "Send them to Juárez. That's the right idea. Get them away. When we come back from Palomas, we'll just avoid Mesilla."

"Si," Armando said, nodding his head. "I will talk to my brother. We will send them away to Juárez. I will come back later to let you know. But between now and then, do not leave your rooms. Do not leave until we have gotten rid of them."

Armando Basurto cracked open the door of the hotel room and looked both ways down the street. Then he hurried out the door.

Neither Pablo nor Duvall said anything for several moments, the two of them stood their ground looking at the closed door.

"Hombre?" Pablo said. "What now?"

Duvall nodded his head.

"First, I need to get over to Marisol and let her know what's going on," Duvall said.

"We should be together," Pablo agreed.

"That was good thinking to tell him we couldn't go before tomorrow," Duvall said. "Now we've got to figure out how we get out of town with Armando Basurto watching us."

"And his brother," Pablo said. "And maybe two others."

"And we've got to get out of here before Lozano shows up. If Lozano talks to them and the Basurto brothers find out Rodrigues is dead, the next knock on that door is going to be followed by gunshots."

"Gracias a Dios," Guillermo Gomez muttered as the shimmering on the horizon began to take shape. He could see trees and low buildings. They were coming up to Mesilla, and none too soon. Those trees meant the water of the Rio Grande in front of them, and it was all Gomez could do not to kick his horse into a gallop to dash for the water. His canteen had run dry that morning, and his lips and tongue felt like the sand they were riding across.

"Mesilla," Néstor Lozano said, and while he expressed no gratitude, Guillermo could hear the relief in his voice.

Even the horses seemed to appreciate that succor lay on the horizon. They quickened their gaits. No more than a fast walk, but faster than it had been.

"When we get to Mesilla, take two of the men and go find Luis and Armando," Lozano said. "I will go with the others to take the horses to the livery, and then we will scour the village for the gringo."

"The men need to rest," Guillermo said, looking over his shoulder.

There were hard feelings among the men. They had traveled a rough trail through the desert without sufficient water. None of them had said a word, but Guillermo understood the unspoken grievance. These men who rode under Lozano's command had witnessed him execute an injured comrade. That man attacked by the wolf last night, he did not need to die. Unless the wolf was rabid, and it probably was not because it was hunting with a pack, his injuries did not need to cost him his life. He could have been treated. It would have meant the loss of two more men who would have had to turn back to Palomas or taken the injured man to Juárez. But losing the injured men and two men to escort him to a doctor was better than to have a man die.

But the injured man did not just die. Lozano killed him. And for no reason but to shut him up.

Si. These men had hard feelings. They did not trust the man who rode in command of them, and Guillermo Gomez did not trust him either.

"The men can rest when we have the gringo in our custody," Lozano snarled.

"The horses need rest," Guillermo said.

"I just said to you that I intend to take the horses to the livery," Lozano snapped at him.

"Si. But if we must ride on –" Guillermo started, but Lozano cut him off.

"If we must ride on and the horses are not fit to go farther, then I will sell these and buy new horses. The only thing that matters now is catching the gringo and recovering Señor Arellano's gold. Do you understand me, Guillermo? If you are unable to set your mind to that singular purpose, then maybe you should go home to Santa Catalina. Maybe you can work there for the laundress and clean the clothes of better men who do their duty."

Guillermo winced.

"I am only thinking of the men," Guillermo said. "They need food and water."

"And they shall have food and water!" Lozano said. He dragged hard on the reins and spun his horse around to face the men. "You shall have food and water. You shall have rest. But now, we must catch that gringo. Nothing else matters. This bastard stole from Señor Arellano! That is no different than if he stole from you and your families. What he took from Señor Arellano, he also took from the mouths of your children and your wives, your sisters, and your mothers. If you are not men enough to do your duty, then turn back now."

Guillermo shook his head at the sudden outburst. None of those men would ride back, even if they no longer wished to follow Lozano. On the horizon ahead of them was water and rest and food.

Lozano sneered at them for some moments, and then he nodded his head.

"Let me hear no grumbling," he said. "You have had your chance to leave."

He wheeled his horse back around and broke into a trot. Guillermo cast a lingering look at the men. Three or four of them looked at him with pleading eyes, as if he could do something about Lozano.

Guillermo just sighed and shrugged his shoulders at the men.

"Do your duty," he said weakly.

The men followed Lozano across the bridge spanning the Rio Grande and into the village. Several dozen adobe buildings. Little homes and storefronts, cafes and warehouses. Scattered among them, a few pecan trees and other recently planted shade trees.

Guillermo took two men with him and set off to find the Basurto brothers whom Lozano had sent to Mesilla to watch for the men who stole Señor Arellano's gold.

It was late in the afternoon. Not yet dusk, though, so they walked the streets in the hottest part of the day.

"First we will find a cantina where we can drink and eat," Guillermo told the men. He was confident Lozano would be tied up with the horses for some time and was not afraid that they would be caught and accused of loafing.

"If he does not get us killed by American soldiers, he will drive us into the ground," one of the men grumbled.

"I understand you are unhappy with Señor Lozano. But he is Señor Arellano's trusted man. We must do as he tells us. You enjoy the wages you receive from Señor Arellano. No?"

"Si. We are paid well."

"Si," Guillermo said. "Then we will earn our wages without complaint."

Guillermo felt a bit revived and not as harshly disposed toward Lozano when they had finished eating, and he thought the other two did also. He would have liked a bath to knock away the grime from the trail. And a decent night's sleep would have helped. But food and a cerveza made a difference.

Refreshed, at least a little, the three men resumed their hunt for the Basurto brothers. They walked slowly through the streets of Mesilla, hoping the men would be easy to find. There were plenty of Spanish speakers in Mesilla, Americans of Mexican descent. And he saw people who looked like they would keep their mouths shut, Guillermo asked them.

"I am looking for four Mexicans. They have been here several days but are strangers to Mesilla."

Most of the people waved him away, but finally one old man – old enough to have been born a Mexican before the border shifted over him – nodded his head.

"Si. I have seen these men." The man gave Guillermo a suspicious look. "These men you speak of, they have spent days watching the liveries. But now they watch the hotel near the plaza."

Guillermo's eyes grew wide.

"The hotel?" he said.

"Si," the old man said, nodding his head. He narrowed his eyes. "It is like they have watched the liveries waiting for someone to arrive in Mesilla, but now, because they watch the hotel, I think whoever they waited for must be here now."

Guillermo handed the man a coin.

"Si. Gracias, señor. Where is the plaza?"

The old man pointed down the street. "Two blocks, and then turn to the right. You will see the hotel across from the plaza."

Guillermo's took quick steps. Whatever the food had done to revive him, the thought that his quarry might now be within reach revived him even more.

Do not kill the gringo. That had been his own advice to Lozano, and Lozano took the advice and made it an order. But after the incident on the street in Palomas – and the way Lozano had used that incident to accuse Guillermo – he half wanted to kill the gringo the moment he saw him.

Luis Basurto ran down the street, side-stepping horses and wagons, pushing past children and women. When he reached the plaza, Luis was out of breath. He bent over and grabbed his knees and tried to slow his breathing enough to speak.

"What is the matter, Luis?" Armando said, straightening up in his seat and frowning at his brother.

Armando sat on a bench under a willow tree at the edge of the plaza where he could see the hotel, though he saw little need to watch it now.

Luis wiped his mouth on his sleeve.

"Did you get Ricardo and Javier on the road to Juárez?"

Luis shook his head. Armando looked around, half expecting to see the two gunfighters somewhere nearby.

"What is wrong? Tell me."

"Néstor," Luis said, and drew another breath. "Lozano."

Armando stood up quickly. "He's here?"

Luis nodded his head. Caught his breath a little more.

"At the livery. I saw him riding into town just as Javier and Ricardo left."

Armando nodded his head, trying to think quickly.

"Did Javier and Ricardo see Néstor?"

Luis shrugged.

"No. I don't know. Maybe? They had just started south on the road to El Paso. They certainly were in sight. When I saw that it was Lozano, I just ran to you. If they saw Lozano and turned back, I don't know."

Armando frowned.

"But Lozano was coming up the road from Juárez?"

"No," Luis said. "He came on the road west of Mesilla, from the Rio Grande bridge. The same way the gringo and Señorita Rosales came into town this morning."

"That is odd," Armando said. He looked down the road and saw no sign of Lozano. But they might have only minutes before Lozano was here, in the square. "I must go and warn the gringo. They've got to leave the hotel. I will arrange to meet them later tonight when we know better what to do. You go and delay Lozano. Do not let him come to the plaza or the hotel."

"What do I say to him?" Luis asked.

Armando thought about it for only a moment.

"You must assume that he saw Javier and Ricardo and that he already knows that two of the men who stole Señor Arellano's gold are here with Señorita Rosales. So do not try to lie to him about it or he will be suspicious. Tell him what we told Javier and Ricardo.

Tell him that the two men are here with the woman. Tell him that I am watching the hotel to make certain that they do not leave. Tell him that we have them trapped. What is important is that he does not think it is urgent for him to come here. Delay him. Get me ten minutes, or twenty if you can. Now go, Luis. Hurry."

"Armando," Luis said. "If that gringo tells Lozano you were involved, Señor Arellano will kill you for weeks."

Armando nodded his head.

"This is not something I do not know," he said.

"If it looks as if Lozano is going to catch them, you will have to kill them."

"Si. I know this. Now, hurry. Delay him as long as possible. His men have been on a long ride. Invite them to rest, to stop and eat – whatever it will take to slow them down."

Luis nodded.

"I will do my best."

Luis turned and started to jog. He made it about thirty yards before he pressed his fingers into his side and slowed to a long-strided walk. Armando, though, ran as fast as he could across the plaza and toward the hotel.

He knocked hurriedly on the door to the room where he had spoken earlier with the gringo, but this time when the door cracked open, he was met with the barrel of a Colt revolver and Tommy's suspicious glare.

"There is a new development. We are all in danger. Let me in, quickly." Armando pushed his way into the room as the gringo lifted the Colt away from his face. "A man who works for Señor Arellano, his name is Néstor Lozano. He has just ridden into Mesilla."

Marisol Rosales was also in the room now. Armando had met her when she was a child and he was traveling with Señor Arellano to Santa Catalina. He doubted if she remembered him, but he suspected from the expression on her face that she did not trust him.

"I know Lozano from Santa Catalina," the gringo said.

"Then you know he is a serious man. A killer. All we can do is delay him now. We cannot stop him. You must leave this room now. Go somewhere and hide. He will come to the hotel looking for you. You must not be here. And later, I will meet you with my brother and we will go to Rodrigues in Palomas."

Already the gringo and the Mexican were grabbing up their saddlebags.

The expression on Marisol's face had not changed. She watched Armando as he spoke and as the other two began gathering their belongings.

"My brother will do what he can to delay Lozano, but we must assume he already knows you are in the hotel. Get your things and get out of Mesilla. Tonight, at midnight, meet me and my brother at the bridge crossing over the Rio Grande."

The gringo slung two saddlebags over his shoulder and lifted his rifle.

"Tonight at midnight. The Rio Grande bridge," Tommy said. "We'll be there."

Armando took a heavy breath and pulled open the door to the room. He stepped outside and looked up the road both ways. He left the door standing open and stepped far enough into the street to see the plaza.

"It is clear. Lozano is not here. Go. Now! Hurry."

The three fugitives dashed out the door, hurrying along the block away from the direction of the livery.

Armando pulled the door closed and walked back to his bench in the plaza to wait for his brother and Lozano to arrive.

16

Duvall carried his rifle in one hand and held Marisol's hand in his other as they dashed down the road, past the adobe storefronts, the horses lashed to hitching posts, the children playing in the street. Their flight drew some curious glances.

When they were several blocks from the hotel, Duvall stopped running. But he kept going at a quick pace and turned to another block as soon as he could. They passed a school where a few young children were playing in the yard. The buildings on the street went from stores to homes. Many of them were surrounded by high adobe walls or fences made of willow sticks. In a vacant lot between two houses, Duvall at last stopped.

"You okay?" he said to Marisol, still holding her hand.

"I don't know," she said. Her face was flushed and her chest rose and fell with heavy breathing. Her dark eyes were moist with worry. "I cannot think."

Duvall nodded his head and smiled to her. He pulled her sombrero away from her forehead and planted a kiss there.

"Not much longer," he said. "I'm going to get us out of this and away from Lozano. I promise you that. Just stick with me a little while longer."

"I can handle whatever comes as long as we're together," Marisol said. "Just as we promised."

Duvall squeezed her hand and turned his attention to Pablo.

"Par'ner? We got a damn bad job that needs to be done."

Pablo offered a wry smile.

"Si. I know."

"They don't know your face," Duvall said. "If I thought I could do it, I'd go myself."

Pablo shrugged his shoulders.

"Is okay," he said. "I know it needs to be me."

"What job?" Marisol asked, a confused look on her face as she shifted her gaze from one man to the other.

"Somebody has to get the horses," Pablo said. "We ain't making it up the Jornado del Muerto on foot."

"Might be better to wait for dark," Duvall said.

Pablo frowned.

"No. We need to move as soon as possible. The minute Armando finds out that Rodrigues is dead, he'll tell Lozano where to find us."

"Maybe," Duvall said. "But at this point, he can't say anything to Lozano without revealing that he was partnered up with Rodrigues. Our friend Armando has bigger things to worry about than us."

"Until we don't show up at the bridge at midnight," Pablo laughed. "When he realizes that the gold is gone, we're going to become his only concern."

"So go get the horses," Duvall said. "But watch your back."

"Si. I'll watch my back. Where will I meet you when I have the horses?"

"We're going to make our way to the river," Duvall said. "There's brush enough in the bosque that we can hide if we see someone coming. We're just going to keep walking north along the river until you catch up to us. We've probably got about two hours before dusk. I'd like to see you before then."

Pablo nodded his head.

"If I ain't caught up to you by dusk, you can guess I ain't coming," Pablo said. "If they catch me, I'll tell them you headed for Palomas to get the gold."

Duvall winced.

"Don't talk like that," he said. "They ain't gonna catch you because they won't recognize you. It's me they know, and Marisol. And it's us they're looking for. Ain't none of 'em laid eyes on you."

Pablo slid the saddlebags down from his shoulder.

"Take this," Pablo said. "There's gold in my saddlebag. Give me that extra one that ain't got gold in it. If they do catch me, there ain't no sense in them getting some of the gold back, too."

Duvall traded saddlebags with him. This was Liller's gear that came off his horse. Or Emster's. Or Rodrigues's. Duvall had lost track of which horse was which at this point.

"Take some gold coins so you can pay the hostler and so you've got some money if you need it."

Pablo hit his pocket and they could hear the jangle of coins there.

"I like having a little walking money," he grinned. "Eighty dollars in gold in my pocket."

They watched Pablo as he went back the other way, armed with a Smith & Wesson Model 3 and a Winchester Yellow Boy rifle. He was working his way around the outskirts of the town, well away from the plaza and the hotel where Lozano would be looking for him. When he'd gone a block or so south, Duvall looked at Marisol.

"He'll be back. They don't know him."

"Are you trying to convince me, or yourself?" Marisol asked.

"Maybe both of us," Duvall admitted. "We've got to walk a ways. Are you okay to do that?"

"I'm fine."

"Are you scared?" Duvall said.

"A little."

"Me, too. But it's going to be okay."

The pair set off on foot in the opposite direction from the way Pablo went. They soon found themselves beyond the town. A line of trees to their left marked the Rio Grande, and they walked through desert grass and greasewood brush toward the river. The road north to Leasburg and Fort Selden followed the river, never more than a hundred yards east of the Rio Grande's banks.

"Beyond Fort Selden is the Jornado del Muerto," Duvall told Marisol. "It's part of the old highway that ran into the mountains when all this was part of Mexico. It's about a hundred miles of desert with not much water, boxed in my mountains to the east and west. That's a rough go up through there. In Leasburg, we'll have to buy a wagon. We can't make that trip without taking supplies. Water, especially."

"It cannot be worse than the desert from Palomas to Mesilla," Marisol said, licking her lips that were still cracked and sore.

"Maybe it ain't worse, but it's about twice as long. And there's always a chance we'll encounter Apache. But I don't think Lozano will follow us beyond Fort Selden. No matter how much he wants to get that gold back, he's not going to be prepared to make that trip. He'll have to turn back, and then we'll be free."

GUILLERMO GOMEZ AND THE two men with him struggled to keep up with the fleeing trio without also being seen.

It had been pure chance. Guillermo and the other two were walking along a boardwalk in Mesilla when the gringo, holding Marisol's hand, ran past. They were out in the street. The gringo, Marisol, and a Mexican. For a moment, Guillermo couldn't believe it. They'd just finished eating in a cantina and had wandered outside to begin their search for the gringo – And there he was! Charging past like a raging bull.

"That is them!" Guillermo said to the other two. "Come on!"

They pushed their way past people on the boardwalk, though the street was not so crowded. Men, and even women, shot angry looks at them, and some made snide comments. But Guillermo also understood that three armed Mexicans who stank of days in the hot sun and now sweated sand were intimidating to these Anglos in los Estados Unidos. A sneer was enough to back down anyone who looked eager to start trouble with him.

The three men pursued their prey past storefronts.

They ran past a school where children played in the yard.

Then they were in among homes. And then, up ahead of them, Guillermo saw just in time that the gringo and Marisol and the other man had stopped running and were talking. Guillermo led the other two men behind an adobe wall, and they watched and waited.

And then the three broke up. The Mexican started back the way they'd gone. He walked right past Guillermo without ever seeing him. And then the gringo and Marisol started walking the other direction – out of town.

"Let's go," Guillermo said. "Stay with me."

He made the decision without thought, but even as the decision was made, Guillermo wondered what was behind it.

Fear? Had he not been afraid on the street of Palomas, exchanging gunfire with the gringo?

Did fear not run his entire life? Was he not afraid of Néstor Lozano? Did he not accept all the abuse – the demeaning comments, the tirades, the smacks across the face – out of fear?

Or maybe it was love.

Whatever hidden sentiments might exist within him, Guillermo made his decision and started out of the alley as soon as he saw that the gringo and Marisol had turned and started away from Mesilla. It did not matter to him that Lozano would be livid. Any decision he made would have been the wrong one for Señor Lozano. Whatever choice Guillermo made was bound to bring down Lozano's wrath.

"ARE YOU WORRIED?" MARISOL said.

"A little," Duvall said, drawing on his cigarette. His eyes stayed on the road to the south. As soon as it started to get dark, Duvall made the decision to step into the bosque. They found a place where willows and brush hid them from the road, and there they waited. Dusk, that period of twilight, sometimes it seems to last forever, and sometimes it seems to be gone in a blink. Duvall had noticed this phenomenon before. He'd reasoned that the length of dusk depended upon when a person realized that it was dusk. Catch it in the beginning, and dusk ticks by slowly. But realize that dusk is on you when it's half over, and it seems to go from dusk to dark so fast.

Tonight, it was an eternity.

"What if he doesn't come?" Marisol asked.

Duvall sighed. He drew on the cigarette again. Blew the smoke out. Coughed a bit to clear his throat. Dropped the last of the cigarette into the dirt and stepped on it.

"He'll come," Duvall said.

"They might have caught him."

Duvall nodded.

"He'll come." Duvall craned his neck to try to see farther down the road to the south, looking back toward Mesilla. He watched the road for several moments. "Anything could have happened. Maybe when he got to the livery, Lozano's people were still there. Maybe he had to wait. Maybe he had to ride south or east of the town to avoid Lozano, and it's just taking longer than he expected. Anything."

"Si," Marisol said, and she put a hand on Duvall's shoulder.

They did not speak for a long while, and the sun set. They had only the smallest remnant of light left surrounding them, just that light reflecting from the sky from the sun now below the horizon.

"I've got to go back for Pablo," Duvall said.

"I think I should say no. I think I should say it is too dangerous. Lozano is there with all his men. But I think if I say that, you will not listen to me."

"I ain't got no choice," Duvall said. "Coming down here to Mexico, I lost all my pals but Pablo. He's the only one I got left. I can't leave him if there's a chance I can save him. Beside, my hoss is still in Mesilla. I ain't leavin' Pecas Gris down yonder in a livery."

Marisol said nothing, and Duvall knew she was already resigned to the thought that he would go back to Mesilla.

"My trouble is, what do I do with you."

"You take me with you," Marisol said, and she frowned at him as if taking her with him was obvious.

"I can't do that," Duvall said. "It's too dangerous for that."

"No," Marisol said. "I'll not stay here in the brush and wait hours for you to come back, not knowing what is happening to you. It is hard enough waiting for Pablo. It would drive me mad to wait for you and to not know if you were caught or killed. You cannot leave me here to not know. And what do I do if you never come back? Do I go back to Mesilla and turn myself over to Néstor Lozano and hope for mercy from my father? And if he is gone? Do I go to Mesilla and prostitute myself for the rest of my life so that I can buy food to survive?"

Duvall winced at that and shook his head.

"I'll leave the gold with you."

But Marisol shook her head.

"No, Tomás. Did we not make a pact? A vow to each other? Whatever comes, we face it together. That is the promise you made to me. I will go with you to Mesilla, and we will find Pablo together."

Duvall sighed. He started to argue, but Marisol placed her fingertips against his lips and shushed him.

"Have I not shown to you that I am as capable as anyone? When that man stood in the doorway of the saloon in Palomas and your bullets were all spent, did I not shoot him down? I have earned your trust, Tomás. I have earned the right to go with you."

Duvall sighed again.

"Yeah. All right. I reckon a woman can point a gun and squeeze a trigger as well as a man. But if I tell you to run, you've got to run. And if I tell you to stay close to me, you've got to stay close to me."

"Si," Marisol said, and in the waning light he saw the smile on her face. "Si. I will stay close to you, Tomás."

When she said his name like that, she made Duvall feel funny inside.

17

PABLO PEÑA FELT THE butt of the rifle crash into his back and immediately understood his mistake.

He'd left Duvall and worked his way around the outskirts of Mesilla, sticking close to adobe walls and trees and anything else that would allow him to go unnoticed and to stop periodically and have a look around. He just wanted to make sure he wasn't going to walk into a crowd of Mexicans who were looking for him.

Then he turned down a narrow street, walking along between two long, windowless adobe buildings. Maybe warehouses of some kind. He heard the heavy footsteps coming rapidly behind him, but he didn't have time to turn before the rifle butt smashed into his back and knocked him face first into the ground. He dropped the rifle on his way to the ground, but he had presence of mind to grab the grip of his revolver. But to no use. Immediately, a knee was on the back of his neck, pinning his face in the dirt, and a hand seized his wrist so that even if he could have twisted around, he couldn't get that gun free.

And then came the rifle butt like a sledgehammer to the back of his head. Once. Twice.

In Spanish, an angry voice said, "Do not try to get free. Cooperate with me, and you may live to see the dawn."

They snatched him up off the ground. Hands holding him fast. They disarmed him – revolver and knife. They punched him several times in the gut, doubling him over. One of the slapped his ear. There were three of them, but one of them did all the talking.

"I am Guillermo Gomez. I am a lieutenant for Néstor Lozano and we both work for Señor Manuel Arellano Hermosillio."

"I've never heard of any of you," Pablo said, and his own voice sounded weak to him.

"We saw you with the gringo and the señorita. You are a fool to lie to me. I know who you are. Now tell me, where is the gold?"

Pablo spit blood into the dirt and realized his nose was bleeding heavily.

"I don't know anything about any gold," Pablo said.

That slap across the face and ear again. It stung like the devil.

"You tell me what I want to know, or this will go much worse for you. The gold. I know you do not have it. Tell where it is."

"A man called Rodrigues has it," Pablo said, reasoning that the lie had worked well before so he might as well try it again. "He buried it in the desert north of Puerto Palomas."

Gomez shook his head, looking angry.

"Do not be a fool. Do not play children's games with me. I know that Rodrigues is dead. I know that you and the gringo killed Rodrigues and two other men. I know that you did not bury the gold in the desert."

Pablo took a breath.

"The truth is, I never had the gold. Rodrigues had it. He buried it, but I don't know where. That's why we killed him."

Pablo watched the reaction on the man's face. He didn't know if Pablo was telling the truth, but he knew what Pablo said was plausible. He took a step back while the other two continued to hold Pablo against the adobe wall of the building. He rubbed his chin. He narrowed his eyes in menacing fashion.

"Si. Maybe. But if that is true, it will not go well for you when I take you to Néstor Lozano. The only advantage you have that will allow you to bargain for your life is the stolen gold. If you do not have it, he will kill you. If you know where it is, you would be wise to tell me now."

Pablo tried to shrug, but the other two men held him fast.

"I told you the truth," Pablo said. "I don't have the gold. I never had the gold. Rodrigues had it, and he hid it."

Guillermo Gomez took a heavy breath.

"That is unfortunate for you."

Gomez picked up Pablo's rifle and leaned it against the building several feet away from where the two men held Pablo.

"Where is the gringo going?" Gomez asked.

"I don't know," Pablo said. "We parted ways. No gold to divvy up, no reason for us to keep on together."

Gomez shook his head.

"I do not believe you. And if you lie to me about the one thing, why should I think you are not lying to me about the other?"

Without warning, Gomez threw a fist into Pablo's gut and doubled him over. He went over with so much force that one of the two men holding him lost his grip. Feeling himself half-free, Pablo made an attempt to break away. He threw a wild punch at the man whose grip stayed fast, but Gomez was on him quickly, two quick punches and a knee to the groin, and Pablo was back on the ground, dripping blood onto the dirt. Gomez gave him a kick to the ribs.

"You are meeting the gringo later. Where are you meeting him?"

Pablo didn't answer. That kick to the ribs had knocked the breath out of him. He pushed his face into the road. Tears were in his eyes, and he didn't want these men to see him cry. But they dragged him to his feet and slammed him against the wall, and Gomez was in his face again.

"Tell me where you are meeting the gringo."

"I'm meeting him at the Rio Grande bridge west of town," Pablo said. "We're meeting at midnight."

Gomez curled his lip. Staring hard at Pablo's face, trying to decide if the man was lying to him or not.

Then he looked at the other two men.

"We cannot take him through the streets like this," Gomez said, motioning to the blood and dirt on Pablo's face. "We need to find a place to hide him while I go and get Señor Lozano."

The two men continued to hold Pablo, and Gomez grabbed Pablo's rifle and gunbelt and walked to the back of the building and disappeared around the corner. Several moments later, he returned and motioned to the men. Pablo didn't have much fight left in him, and the two men holding him were both strong. They easily wrestled him down the street to the back of the building.

"Bring him in here and hold him here," Gomez said, and he pushed open a door.

Inside, the building was very dim. The only light was that coming from the open door. The building was long and open. Pablo was right to guess it was a warehouse. Stacks of crates reaching seven feet tall filled much of the room, but they were different sized crates. Some were tall and wide, others shallow. Goods that had come up from El Paso, maybe. Pablo didn't know, nor did he much care.

The two men dragged him up against one of the exterior walls, behind some stacked crates, and pushed him to the ground.

"If he tries to move or get away, break his legs," Guillermo Gomez said to the two men. "I will return shortly with Señor Lozano, and then we will see if he wants to continue telling lies."

ARMANDO BASURTO MERELY SHRUGGED his shoulders when Lozano found the hotel rooms empty.

"I don't know how they could have gotten away," Armando said with an innocent look to Luis. "We were watching the hotel rooms. They must have known we were watching them."

Néstor Lozano was enraged, and Armando suspected that part of his fury came from the fact that there was nothing he could do or say to the Basurto brothers. These other men, in a tirade Lozano could take a riding crop to them or bash their skulls with a rifle. What were they going to do? They were his men as sure as if he owned them, and if they complained or argued or tried to walk away, he could shoot them without fear of repercussion. But not the same with the Basurto brothers. They were trusted advisers to Señor Arellano, and much higher up the pecking order. If Lozano laid a hand on either Luis or Armando, he would find his throat cut in an alley in Juárez within an hour of Señor Arellano finding out about it.

At least for now.

If Armando's treachery was exposed, he and Luis both would face much worse than a cut throat.

The men were gathered outside the street in front of the hotel, and though it was a side street off the plaza, they were drawing curious looks from passersby on the main road. More than a dozen heavily armed Mexicans, most of them looking like they'd just fought the Apache in the desert, gathered outside a couple of hotel rooms, occupying the entirety of the street.

"We should go and find someplace to talk," Luis said, evidently following the same line of thinking as his younger brother. "People are beginning to stare."

"I don't give a damn what people are doing," Lozano bit back at him. "You had the gringo! How could you let him go?"

Armando held up his hands.

"This is not what we do," Armando said. "We are attorneys. The law is our business, not watching outlaws."

"I sent Javier and Ricardo with you for that very reason," Lozano said.

"And we were sending Javier and Ricardo back to you in Juárez with a message that the thieves were here," Luis said. "What else were we supposed to do. Armando? Did you watch the hotel?"

"Si. I watched it," Armando said.

"There you are," Luis said, as if that was an explanation. "Now. Let's calm down and figure out how we can find them. They can't have gotten far."

Lozano clenched his jaw and looked around at his men. Javier and Ricardo cut short their journey to Juárez almost before it began. They'd only just left the livery when Lozano and his men appeared on the horizon. Thinking at first that it might be the rest of the thieves they'd come to Mesilla to watch out for, they turned around and rode back to the livery. Then they realized it was their boss. So now they were back in Mesilla.

So far, though, no one had become suspicious of Armando. Nothing he had done – except allowing the escape of the two men and the woman – had tipped his hand. And letting the gringo and Marisol Rosales escape, it was easy for men like Lozano to accept that a lawyer had done such a thing through ineptitude rather than malice. Armando just had to keep suspicion off himself until midnight. Then he and Luis would meet up with the gringo at the bridge, and from there they would go to Rodrigues and the gold.

"Si," Lozano said. "They cannot be far. Ricardo and Javier – the two of you have been here for several days in Mesilla. You know the town. Si?"

Both men acknowledged that they knew their way around.

"Take two men apiece and split up, search the town. Where would the gringo hide? Go and find him. We will wait for you in the placita."

Luis nodded.

"Si. That is right. Search the town. Do something other than stand around here drawing attention," Luis said.

The men divided up as Lozano instructed them to, and those left – including the Basurto brothers – made their way to the plaza.

There had been no time for Armando to speak to Luis outside of the hearing of the others. Luis had no idea what had happened to the gringo and the Rosales woman. He'd held his breath when Lozano's men kicked in the doors of the hotel rooms.

"What kind of law is there here?" Lozano said to Luis.

"A marshal and a couple of his deputies," Luis said. "They are not much to look at. The marshal spends more time eating at his desk than he does enforcing laws."

"Good," Lozano said. "We will take over this town until we find the gringo."

Even with the other men gone with Ricardo and Javier, Luis and Armando and Lozano and his remaining men still made up a group of eight, and they seemed like a very conspicuous group in the plaza. They went to the gazebo at the center of the plaza where they could sit on benches in the shade. Armando was aware of the way people on the streets were looking at them and whispering behind hands about them. Armed foreigners, rough-looking men. There were enough here of Spanish descent that they might have blended in if there had been two or three of them. He'd not once felt conspicuous when it was just him and Luis with Javier and Ricardo. But now they drew so much attention. It could not be long before Lozano got to meet the marshal.

"This is all a disaster," Lozano said. "They have buried the gold in the desert."

"But you do not know where?" Armando asked.

"I have no idea. Somewhere between here and Santa Catalina is all I know. And the outlaws who stole Señor Arellano's gold are all dead, except these three we are chasing."

"What do you mean they are all dead?" Armando said, and though he tried to hide the urgency in his voice, he thought his tone had betrayed all of his treachery. Lozano, though, took no notice.

"Some are dead at our hands," Lozano said. "We caught two of them down near Santa Catalina and killed them. The rest are murdered at Palomas by their own."

"Murdered at Palomas?" Armando said, passing a concerned look to Luis. "What do you mean?"

"Three men, two gringos and a Mexican, were killed in Palomas by the gringo. Señorita Rosales shot and killed one of them. The gringo killed the other two."

"Who were they?" Armando asked.

Lozano shook his head dismissively.

"Outlaws. Thieves. And one of them was a traitor," Lozano said.

"A traitor?" Armando swallowed.

"A man by the name of Rodrigues who worked for Señor Arellano. I think I met him before, but I am not sure."

"And where is Rodrigues now?" Luis asked, his voice cracking.

Lozano gave Luis Basurto a quizzical look.

"He is dead in Palomas, as I just said," Lozano said.

"Killed by the gringo?" Armando said.

"Si. I just have said that," Lozano said. "Now, only the gringo and Marisol Rosales and the Mexican with them know where the gold is buried. A million dollars of Señor Arellano's gold is buried in the desert, and only three people left alive know where to find it. I can only assume the gringo decided he would not share the gold with his compatriots and killed them in Palomas. I am only sorry that I did not get to kill the traitor Rodrigues myself. I would have been well-pleased to deliver his head in a sack to Señor Arellano. But the gold is the most important thing. We must take the gringo alive so that we can find the gold. Otherwise, it is lost forever."

Armando felt the dryness in his throat.

"I am going for a cerveza," he said.

"I will come with you," his brother said. "If that is all right with you, Señor Lozano?"

Lozano waved a hand.

"Si. Go. Drink your cervezas. Your work here in Mesilla is done. Whatever happens now will be my work."

"Is it true, do you think?" Luis said. "Rodrigues is really dead?"

"How else would Lozano know his name?" Armando said. He stared off into the plaza beyond his brother, unable to bring himself now to look Luis in the eyes.

They spoke in hushed voices even though they stood outside in the courtyard in front of the cantina and were alone there.

"Oh, Armando. What have you done? What have you brought down upon us?"

Armando clenched his teeth.

"It is too late to worry about that," Armando said. "We must deal with what is in front of us."

"Did you talk to them? The gringo?"

"Si. When you took Javier and Ricardo to the livery, I went to see them. And then I went to warn them when you came back to tell me that Lozano was riding into town. They escaped the hotel because I warned them. We agreed to meet at the bridge over the Rio Grande at midnight."

"Do you think the gringo will be there?" Luis asked.

"Of course he will not be there," Armando snapped. "He killed Rodrigues. He has no intention to meet us. He lied to me when I spoke to him in the hotel. He said Rodrigues was waiting for us in Palomas."

"So what is in front of us?" Luis asked. "Other than Señor Arellano's wrath?"

"We have two choices," Armando said. "We find this gringo before Lozano and make him tell us where the gold is. We can offer to partner with him. We can offer to protect him from Lozano. Once we have the gold we kill him. Or we don't kill him. We can make a deal to split the gold and wish him a fond farewell when he has his share and we have our share."

"If he killed Rodrigues, he will not hesitate to kill us," Luis said.

Armando shrugged.

"Maybe or maybe not. Right now, he needs us to escape from Lozano."

"How can we help him escape from Lozano?" Luis said.

"Our other choice is to kill him now and forget the gold."

Luis nodded his head.

"Give up the gold to avoid being exposed as traitors and facing Señor Arellano," Luis said. "Or trust the gringo who killed Rodrigues to get the gold and spend the rest of our lives fleeing Señor Arellano."

Armando grinned.

"We would flee in comfort," he said.

Luis shook his head. But then a determined look came across Armando's face.

"We will trust the gringo," Armando said. "I planned too much, worked too hard, to lose that gold now. I did all of this, set all of this in motion, so that you and I would never have to live through the insanity of a civil war. We will get the gold. If that means we have to trust the gringo, then we will trust him. And when we have the gold, if we do not want to trust him any longer, then we will kill him."

"He has already lied to you once," Luis said. "He told you Rodrigues was waiting for you in Palomas."

"Si, but that was before Lozano was here. Now we have to find him before Lozano does."

Luis stood up and took a drink of his cerveza, walking over to the edge of the cantina's courtyard. The sun was down below the horizon, now. The plaza was bathed in the soft light of the gloaming. And then Luis Basurto's attention was drawn to something new.

"It may be too late for that," Luis said. "Lozano may have already found him."

Armando craned his neck to look past Luis, and he saw one of Lozano's men coming into the plaza, not quite at a jog, but certainly at a hurried pace.

"This is it, Armando," Luis said. "The whole thing is about to come down around us. You should have never orchestrated all this, brother. You should have talked to me first. I would have talked you out of it."

Armando took a last drink of his beer and stood up from the table. He stepped over to Luis and put a hand on his shoulder.

"No," he said. "This will all come out fine. Trust me. There is still opportunity for us to get the gold and avoid Señor Arellano's war. Now come on, let's go see what they have found."

Luis released a heavy breath.

"It will be all right," Armando said, patting Luis' shoulder. "You will see. There will still be a way to get out of this. But just in case, my hand will be on my revolver."

18

THE RIO GRANDE WEST of Mesilla was not overly deep, but it was a wide river.

The bridge spanning the river here was built under contract from the Butterfield Mail company which managed an important stage station at Mesilla during its brief existence. A bridge being cheaper to maintain than a ferry crossing, it was of timber construction and had trestles at intervals of about five feet to support its span of the river. For some years after the war, the bridge was maintained by the soldiers at Fort Fillmore in Mesilla, though they were now gone, too.

West of the bridge, the road evaporated into the desert. At some point there must have been a road going west into Arizona Territory and California, but Duvall had seen no evidence that the road had ever been there. He suspected the bridge was little-used, now. But it was sturdily constructed, wide enough for a stagecoach or a wagon, and convenient for those few who lived near Mesilla west of the Rio Grande. Duvall figured it had also been convenient for the soldiers from the fort who made occasional excursions into the desert chasing after the Apache.

He and Marisol approached the bridge from the north, keeping close to trees and brush along the riverbank. About a half hour before midnight, Duvall found a spot among the trees for Marisol to hide. He rolled a smoke and then a little before midnight approached the bridge.

A few minutes later, he saw a man coming at him along the road to Mesilla. There wasn't much light to see by. A little moonlight, and what the stars provided, but in the dark he saw no other shapes. It looked like maybe Armando Basurto had come alone.

"I wasn't sure you would show up here," Duvall said. "Or, if you did show up, that it would be just you."

"Oh, do you mean you thought I would bring Señor Lozano and his gunfighters after I discovered that Rodrigues is dead and that you killed him?"

"I thought there was a chance that might dispose you toward vengeance."

"Si. And it does. I have thought that perhaps my best course of action is to kill you. Prevent you from telling Lozano of my involvement in the plot to steal the gold. But this is business. Si, Tommy?"

"That's right. Business."

"And when men are partners in business, sometimes they must do things that anger their partners. Si? So tell me, why did you kill Rodrigues?"

"He cut us out," Duvall said. "He cut us out, set my friends up to take the fall, and he killed two of my pals."

Armando Basurto chuckled.

"So, you are one of those?"

"You know that was his plan?"

"I knew that there were some who would be led like sheep to the slaughter to help cover his escape with the gold. It was a good plan. He made it to Palomas."

"That's right. He made it to Palomas. And he'd have been across the border if I hadn't caught him there."

"Where is the gold?"

"Like I told you, Rodrigues buried it."

"You know where?" Armando asked, his voice heavy with greed.

"I know where," Duvall said. Then added, "Roughly. I know what village he buried it in. But my pal Pablo knows exactly where it's buried. He saw the spot and told me where. I can find it."

"What village?" Armando asked.

"Nope," Duvall said. "No, sir. That's as much as I tell you."

"You will need me now," Armando said. "If you plan to get that gold, you will need my help."

"That's right. I need you, and you need me. We have to partner up, and if we're going to do that, we're going to have to build trust between us. But we both need Pablo. Did they kill him?"

"No. They are holding him. They plan to deliver him to Señor Arellano. But they want you, especially, and will not turn back to Mexico until they have you."

"Uh-huh. So how do we get Pablo free?"

"Lozano and his lieutenant rode into Mesilla, eleven men with them," Armando said. "Add to that Javier and Ricardo who were with me, and he has thirteen men, plus himself and Guillermo Gomez. If you want to free your friend, you'll have to kill those fifteen men. My brother and I are no help in that. We are advocates. Lawyers. We are not gunfighters."

"What about Javier and Ricardo? You said they were with you. Can we trust them?"

"No. They are loyal to Señor Arellano and will do what Lozano tells them to do."

"There's got to be another way," Duvall said. "Some way to get Pablo away free from them."

"Maybe. If I can help you get your friend free, I have shown that I can be trusted?"

"We got Pablo out of this, and I'll take you to the gold," Duvall said.

"And we split the gold?" Armando asked.

Duvall didn't give a damn about that gold. And he had no intention to stick a toe into Mexico ever again. But he needed Armando Basurto to believe him and to believe that they had a common interest.

"We split it. Half for you and your brother. Half for me and Pablo."

"Si. That is acceptable to me."

Duvall figured that was better than acceptable. Unless Rodrigues intended to do to Emster and Liller what they'd done to Duvall's pals, there was no way half of that money was going to the Basurto brothers under the original deal with Rodrigues. At best, it was going to be split five ways. And maybe Rodrigues intended to kill the Basurto brothers and just split it three ways.

"I have an idea about your friend. I anticipated that his freedom would be a condition for us working together, and I have already taken steps in that direction. I convinced Lozano that he should send your friend to Juárez. First thing in the morning, they will leave from the livery. He will be going with a three-man escort. I tried to convince Lozano that he should send only two men, but he would not agree to that. Three men in the escort. If you can deal with Rodrigues and his two friends for revenge, you can deal with three men to save a friend. Si?"

"I'll do what I have to do," Duvall said. "But I need my hoss from the livery."

Armando made a doubtful grunt.

"What's wrong with that?"

"Lozano has two men watching the livery. They figured out that your friend was going there. Lozano sent his lieutenant, Guillermo Gomez, to check. He said he recognized your horse and the señorita's horse. Lozano put two men to watch the livery overnight. If you go to get your horse, those men will stop you."

"Or try to stop me," Duvall said.

"If you kill them, Lozano will know you have gotten your horse. He may change his mind about sending any men to escort your friend to Juárez."

"So the best we've got is that I have to try to save Pablo in the morning on the road to Juárez without a hoss?"

Armando spread his arms.

"It is what I can offer you. You accomplished the ambush of Señor Arellano's gold wagon. You survived Rodrigues's attempt to sacrifice you while he made his escape. And you managed to kill Rodrigues and his two outlaw friends. I suspect you are resourceful enough to save your friend."

"And when I have him?" Duvall asked.

"You will meet with me and my brother, here at the bridge, to-morrow night at midnight, and we will go for the gold together."

"Good," Duvall said. "That's how trust works."

"Si."

Just then, from the trees down by the river where Duvall had left Marisol, there came a muffled yelp. Duvall swung around fast, drawing the converted Colt from its holster. He saw nothing at first, but then he felt the barrel of a revolver in his back.

"This is how trust is ensured," Armando said, and now Duvall saw Marisol and another man coming up from the trees. The man had one arm around Marisol, and Duvall could readily guess that the arm he couldn't see had a gun pressed into her back. "Señorita Rosales will accompany us. We will keep her safe and out of sight from Señor Lozano and his men. But she is our assurance that you will do what you say. Save your friend in the morning, and the three of us will meet you back here tomorrow at midnight. Then all of us will set out together."

Luis Basurto and Marisol were up by the bridge now.

"I'm sorry, Tomás," Marisol said. "I never heard him coming be-hind me."

"It's all right," Duvall said. "I should have been smarter about where I hid you."

"Do not be so sad," Armando said. "We are all partners. Think of it like this – while you go to rescue your friend, Señorita Rosales will be safe with us and away from tomorrow's danger. In twenty-four hours, we will all be reunited, safe and sound. And in a few days, we will all be very rich. And that will conclude our partnership, and we will go our separate ways in good faith."

"If you hurt her, I'll kill you," Duvall swore.

"There is nothing to fear on that account," Armando said. "Look in her belt. My brother has not even taken her gun away, nor will he. She will be set up tonight with a private room. Free to leave if she chooses, but I think you would agree that leaving us would put her in terrible jeopardy. Do not think of her as our captive. She is in the protection of your partners. What do you call it, our group? – Señorita Rosales is part of our outfit. This is how we grow to trust one another."

"I'll be fine, Tomás," Marisol said. She'd stopped struggling now, and Luis Basurto had released her from the hold. "Go and do what you have to do. I'll see you tomorrow."

19

Duvall didn't know the last time he'd trodden so far on his own two feet. Given the choice, he far preferred riding to walking.

With three saddlebags slung over his shoulder and a rifle in hand, he walked through the darkness for several hours, keeping to the outskirts of Mesilla until he came upon the road south to El Paso and Juárez. He didn't know how far south of Mesilla he'd gone. He passed a ranch at some point and considered snooping around, trying to find the barn in the night to sleep there. But he decided against it. He kept walking.

Duvall didn't know exactly what he was looking for, but he would know it when he found it. He needed a piece of ground where he could make an ambush. The trouble was, the ground in the flats along the Rio Grande offered no advantages. No canyon where his prey would be boxed in. No rocks where he might find a place to lay in wait unseen and then fire from a defensive position. No hills or valleys. Everything was just flat.

In the dim moonlight, what he could see were the shapes of trees down along the banks of the river. He could do it there, except he needed to be close to the road. Close enough where he could be sure of at least his first shot. If he could whittle the numbers down to two-to-one with his first shot, maybe he could deal fast enough with the two.

What he kept reminding himself was that he was good at this.

Tommy Duvall had learned so many lessons on this sojourn into Old Mexico.

He'd learned about the value of friendship – a thing he thought he'd understood until all but one of his friends was dead. He'd learned about the value of a good woman who loved him. He'd learned that murder for money was too high a price to pay, no matter how rich it made him. Hell, for that matter, he'd learned that money itself – heaps of gold bars – wasn't worth much at all.

But something else he'd learned about himself: Tommy Duvall learned that he had a talent for killing. He was a straight shot and he didn't cower under fire. He learned that he was fast with his guns, but more important than that, he was fast with his mind. He could think about his next shot even before he'd taken this one.

He wasn't sure how he felt about it, being good at killing, but it had kept him alive so far because he'd been better at killing than the men who were trying to kill him.

He'd have to be good at it in the morning, too.

At last, Tommy found he could go no farther. His feet were busted. His legs were sore. He had no canteen – the canteens were back with the saddles and the horses at the livery. And he was too exhausted to do anymore. So he walked off the road some distance, dropped his belongings, and used the saddlebags full of gold as his pillow.

The first light of sunup woke him. He'd slept sound despite the cold of the night. He woke with a start. His first thought was that he'd slept through the morning and missed when Pablo came by, but he saw how low the sun was on the eastern horizon and knew that they'd not come through here yet.

He took stock of his surroundings – flat land all the way over to the trees that marked the location of the Rio Grande some three hundred yards or more away. Even the trees were pretty diminished here. A river cutting through a desert.

He gathered up his things and started to walk south, and he'd gone probably a mile or more with the sun slowly coming up on his left shoulder when he saw something ahead on the road. At first he thought he was seeing a rider approaching, and he paused long enough to make certain that he had a round chambered in the Yellow Boy. But as the something he saw approaching drew nearer, Duvall realized it was a man pushing a cart.

Duvall studied the man as the two approached each other. He wore a sombrero and a poncho. His head and back were bent with his labor. He'd probably pushed that cart along this road a thousand times. As the man with the cart got nearer, Duvall realized that if this man worked for Lozano, Duvall would be as good as dead. The man was unassuming, but he easily might have had a six-shooter up under that poncho. So Duvall watched the man close as they came within twenty yards of each other. He was ready to move that rifle fast.

But this was no gunfighter working for Néstor Lozano. The man was of Mexican descent. How old he was Duvall couldn't guess. Ancient. His hands and face were weathered. His cart was loaded with alfalfa, probably bound for that ranch Duvall had passed in the night.

Still, Duvall kept the rifle ready. But the man passed by him without reaching for a gun under the poncho.

"Hola," was all he said.

Duvall turned and watched him go. And when the man was twenty yards on, Duvall called to him.

"Hey, old timer. You speak English?"

The man stopped and turned.

"Si," he said, but he made a gesture to indicate he didn't speak much English.

"You taking that alfalfa to sell?" Duvall asked.

"Si."

"How much for the cart?" Duvall asked.

The man looked at his load.

"Three dollars."

"No. Not the just the alfalfa," Duvall said. "I'll pay you forty dollars right now for that cart, the alfalfa, your hat, and your poncho."

The old man laughed, waved a dismissive hand and turned back to his labor.

But Duvall reached into his pocket quickly and pulled out two twenty-dollar pieces of gold. He threw them into the dirt in front of the man.

"Forty dollars," Duvall said. "For three dollars worth of alfalfa, a five-dollar cart, a two-dollar hat, and a poncho so full of holes you should pay me to take it from you. Hell. Sixty dollars so you don't even have to think about it."

He pulled another coin from his pocket and held it out for the man to see.

The old timer, bent in the back, narrowed his eyes. Trying to find the con.

"Sixty dollars, and you can go on back home to wherever you grow that alfalfa, and you can take the rest of the day off. Come back by here tomorrow, and you can get the cart back if you want it."

The old man shook his head, not because he was unwilling to make the deal but because he couldn't understand.

"This twenty-dollars is to help you make a fast decision," Duvall said, waving the gold piece pinched between his fingers. "Be quick or you lose this one."

The old man shrugged.

"Si. Okay."

He bent over and picked up the two gold coins in the dirt. He set his hat on top of the load of alfalfa and then pulled his poncho over his head and put it there, too. He stopped and looked at his belongings and back at Duvall. Then he shrugged, took the offered coin in Duvall's hand, and without another word started back to the south toward home.

DUVALL WAS SWEATING UP under that old man's poncho. He'd taken off his coat and put it under the alfalfa. His hat, too. The woven-straw sombrero was light on his head and didn't feel right. But the brim was wide and would hide his identity when he dropped his head to mimic the old man's labored walk.

The Yellow Boy was tucked into the wagon, hidden beside the alfalfa. But Duvall knew where to find it, and it would be easy to get to quickly.

His britches and shoes might give him away, he knew, but he hoped Lozano's gunmen would ignore him. He'd moved the Colt out of its holster and into his belt so that it sat up higher and would be better hidden by the poncho.

And up ahead, four riders were on the horizon, coming south toward him.

He liked the ground where he was. Nobody behind him, nobody else around except those four riders. So he stopped for a few moments while they were still too far to see him clearly. He took off the sombrero and wiped his forehead. He didn't need sweat dripping down into his eyes.

He took just a moment to study the riders. At a distance, he couldn't discover much about them. One rider out front of the other three. Just the length of a horse. Not far out in front. The other three rode basically abreast of each other. But one of them, the one riding in the middle of the pack, he rode like a man in pain. Sitting heavy in his saddle. Bent. Suffering.

That was Pablo. Beaten by Lozano, no doubt.

Duvall dropped his head now, and he told himself not to pick his head back up until the riders were past him. He rubbed his hands in the loose dirt of the road, spreading it on his hands and wrists. Trying to hide the fact that he was a white man.

Head down, he started pushing the cart. And his constant refrain was an attempt to impose his will on the four riders coming toward him: Don't look at me. Don't even notice me. I'm just an old man delivering a load of alfalfa.

The wheels on the wagon squeaked as they turned. The whole wagon seemed to rattle and clang. Duvall hadn't been aware of it until now. It had been just a constant noise occupying the background of his thoughts. But now he was aware of it. His senses were on alert.

Lozano's gunfighters would hear it, too, and they would hear it when it stopped.

Keep your head down, Duvall told himself. Resist that urge to look up. Don't expose yourself.

The wheels squeaked. The wagon rattled. He could smell the alfalfa. Probably smelled like a well-cooked steak to a horse.

They were close enough now that Duvall could hear the footfalls of the horses. An easy, steady gait on all of them.

From below the brim of the sombrero, Duvall could see the lead horse. It was almost even with the cart. And then something happened that Duvall hadn't thought of – he didn't even realize what was happening at first because his eyes were down, his view obstructed by the sombrero.

But that lead horse, a pretty white horse, it smelled that alfalfa in the cart and went for it.

The man riding the horse cursed and then laughed and pulled the horse away, shouting at it in Spanish.

Duvall quickened his pace. He wanted to get past these men. He'd willed them to not even notice him, but they had all noticed him.

The other horses came even with the cart, but their riders pulled them away.

Behind him, though, Duvall only heard three horses walking.

"Señor!" a man's voice with a heavy Mexican accent said.

"Si?" Duvall answered. He didn't turn around, but he did stop pushing the cart.

"Señor!" the voice called again.

Duvall took a step back, away from the cart so that he would be clear of it. He imagined the men now behind him. Pablo and the two flanking him were still going. Maybe one or both of those two were looking back, but probably not. It was the front man, the man on the white horse, who'd stopped, and Duvall guessed he'd probably turned so that the horse was facing him. No chance of going for the rifle, now. No chance of turning and taking aim and being sure with that first shot.

As he spun, Duvall brushed his left arm over his face, knocking that sombrero off his head. His right hand clutched the Colt hidden under the poncho.

The man on the white horse gave a shout of surprise as Duvall swung the big Colt at him. His thumb clicked the hammer back just as Duvall leveled the Colt. He squeezed the trigger.

His first shot did what it needed to do.

The white horse bucked and reared.

Thumb back on hammer. It was an adjustment of inches. Duvall squeezed the trigger and shot the rider on Pablo's left square in the back.

The third man was twisted around, reaching for his gun, but he saw that he was already beat. His horse, spooked by the sudden bark of the gun pistola, wanted to run, and the man let it. They went at the gallop.

"Hold that hoss right there, Pablo!" Duvall shouted, and Pablo drew hard on the reins to keep his own horse from running, too.

Duvall dashed to the cart and wrenched the Yellow Boy free. At the same time, he dropped the Colt into his holster. He brought the rifle to his shoulder, taking aim down the barrel. He squeezed the trigger and dropped the lever. Squeezed the trigger again. Pretty sure that second shot hit its target, but he worked the action on the rifle and fired off a third shot. The rider flinched that time. That was a definite hit.

A gun barked. The man on the white horse was shot, but he'd recovered enough to get his own gun into the fight. His shot missed, though. Duvall swung the rifle around and paused only long enough to take a quick aim. The man grunted when the bullet smashed him in the chest.

The other rider, shot in the back, was having trouble with his horse, and he gave up. He dropped out of the saddle and stumbled, more hurt maybe than he realized. Duvall worked the lever on the Yellow Boy and put another bullet in the man, and he fell to the ground.

Now Duvall dashed to the man on the white horse. He'd lost his strength. He couldn't raise his revolver, but he also hadn't turned loose of it. Duvall grabbed at the man and dragged him down out of the saddle, and with the rifle pointed at his head, dispatched the man.

He finished off the other one in similar fashion.

He gave no thought to what he'd done. Executing wounded men. It didn't sit right with him when he'd seen Liller and Emster and Rodrigues do it after they'd ambushed a wagon loaded with gold. But he wasn't leaving these men alive to put a bullet in his back.

Duvall mounted the white horse, rifle in hand. The only word he said to Pablo was that he would be back.

He rode in pursuit of that third rider, the one whose horse had run. Duvall thought he'd shot the man twice in the back, maybe three times. But rider and horse had gone on and by now were a couple hundred yards south.

But as Duvall pursued, he saw the horse had slowed and the rider was slumped. When he caught them, maybe a half mile or so south of where he'd staged his ambush, the rider was barely hanging onto consciousness. Duvall took the horse's bridle and pushed the man down out of the saddle. He swung a leg over the back of the horse and used the Colt to finish the man.

Duvall tied a rope around the man's torso, looping it under his arms. He got back on the white horse and dragged the body to the brush by the river. He left the body there, tossing a couple of limbs on top. With some luck, the body wouldn't be seen for days. As little traffic as there was on the road from El Paso to Mesilla, maybe the body would never be found.

Duvall got back on the white horse's saddle and led the other horse back to Pablo, the two dead bodies, and the cart of alfalfa. Only now did he turn his attention to Pablo.

He'd come down off the horse and was half-standing, half-leaning against his mount. He had a hand on the horse's neck, trying to calm him.

Pablo's face was bruised and swollen. He had a cut over his eye.

"You all right, par'ner?" Duvall said.

Pablo grinned at him, but he winced as his cheeks raised, disturbing the cuts and bruises on his face.

"Si," Pablo said. "I've had better days, but I'm all right."

"Can you ride?" Duvall asked. "You looked a little low in the saddle just now."

"Sure I can ride," Pablo said. "Especially if we're riding north. It was riding south to my death that was weighing me down."

"Riding to your death can have that affect on you," Duvall chuckled. "Hopefully, we're all finished with that. I'm going to take these bodies down to the river and dump them."

"Nice trick with the cart and the sombrero," Pablo said. "I didn't even recognize you."

"I did something to give myself away," Duvall said. "The man on this white hoss, he had me figured out."

"Probably your boots," Pablo said. "I ain't never seen a Mexican alfalfa farmer with boots in that good of condition."

Duvall nodded. He tied the other two bodies and dragged them down to the river, the same as he'd done with the first one. It took some time to get it done, but it was better than leaving the bodies where someone might find them and ride into Mesilla and spread word that three men were killed on the road. Lozano would know what had happened. Better that he think Pablo was halfway to El Paso.

When Duvall returned, Pablo gritted his teeth and gave an unnecessary look around.

"Where's Marisol?"

20

"Did you sleep well?" Armando asked.

"I slept fine," Marisol said. Her manner was curt.

The Basurto brothers had taken her back to a little adobe cabin in Mesilla that they'd rented while they stayed in the town. It had just two beds in the cabin, but they had given her one of them, and she'd had a private room to sleep in. Now, Armando and Luis sat at a table eating breakfast, and Armando offered her a plate.

"Where is Lozano?" Marisol asked.

"He and his men slept in another house we rented," Armando said. "But I doubt they are even there now. I am sure they are searching the town looking for the gringo. You love him?"

"I do," Marisol said flatly.

"Señor Arellano must not be happy about that."

"I don't think so. I believe he intended for me to marry Néstor Lozano."

Armando grunted derisively and then chuckled.

"And you did not want to be married to that dog?"

"No," Marisol said, and despite herself, she grinned at him.

"We mean you no harm, señorita. Our only interest is in recovering the gold. We will stick to our word. When we have the gold, we will split it with your gringo and you and his friend, and we will go our separate ways in peace."

Marisol studied his face. She thought she believed him.

She remembered Armando and Luis Basurto from times she had visited her father in Juárez. Maybe she had seen one or both of them in Santa Catalina, also. They were not fighters like so many other men who worked for her father. Instead, they were professional men. Lawyers.

"Why?" Marisol asked. "Why did you do all of this?"

Armando glanced at Luis, as if deciding whether to answer the question. Then he shrugged and began to speak.

"Your father intends to start a war in Mexico. A war that would see him become the president. But wars are expensive and devastate a country. If you survive the fighting you will still face hunger and poverty. And you may not survive the fighting. Especially for us, close advisers to Señor Arellano. If his revolución failed? We would surely be hung right next to him. But even if he won the war, how long before the country recovers from the bloodshed and the destruction of property? I decided I did not want to live in a country torn apart by war. And so I planned to steal his gold that he intended to use to finance the war. It is as simple as that."

"You will hang if he finds out," Marisol said.

"Si. It is a risk. But all things are a risk. I weighed my options and settled on the one that I thought least risky."

"And is it just coincidence that the option you settled on is also the one that makes you very wealthy?" Marisol asked.

Armando laughed and merely shrugged his shoulders.

"We are not fighters, my brother and I," Armando said. "What I want you to understand, and what I want you to convey to the gringo, is that we will not betray him. We want our share of the gold. And we want him to have his share. That is all. There is plenty to go around."

Marisol gave him a half-hearted smile, but she did not respond. Instead, she wondered what Armando would say when the gold was there in front of him. Would he wait for Tomás to turn his back and then shoot him?

"Where is Pablo?" Marisol asked.

"By now? He should be with the gringo. If everything happened the way it was supposed to. Hopefully, we won't know until midnight if the gringo was successful."

Marisol wrinkled her brow.

"What do you mean?"

"I convinced Lozano to send the gringo's amigo to Señor Arellano. With an escort of three men. They left at first light. I told the gringo about this, and I am sure he went to rescue the man."

"Alone?" Marisol asked, alarmed.

"We're not the men to help him," Armando said. "We're lawyers. But I think your gringo can manage all right by himself. He clearly is a man who can handle himself. He killed Rodrigues."

"If they kill Tomás, you'll never see the gold. I do not know where it is."

"Si. I know," Armando said. "But the gringo would not go to get the gold without his friend. So I made a million dollar bet that the gringo could save his amigo and come back for you."

"And if he fails?" Marisol said. "If he doesn't come back? What do you do with me, then?"

Armando shrugged his shoulders.

"If the gringo fails – if he is captured or killed – we will turn you loose. You're on your own at that point. Get away, and if you're caught, don't say a word about us."

Marisol narrowed her eyes.

"If I'm caught, you'll kill me," she said. "You can't risk it to leave me alive because I know too much. The same for Tomás if he is captured."

Armando said nothing.

"It serves no purpose to talk like this," Luis said. "The man will rescue his friend, and he will meet us tonight at the bridge. We will go and get the gold, and that will be the end of it."

"Si," Armando said. "You're right. There is no purpose in guessing what might happen if we fail in some aspect of our plans. We must succeed."

They left Marisol in the house, instructing her not to leave, not even to show her face in a window, and then the two brothers left. Luis promised that they would return soon to give her whatever information they could discover.

"Keep that gun close to you," Luis said. "Just in case."

Marisol ignored the advice to stay away from the windows. From the front window of the house, she could see one of the main roads leading to the town square. She stayed back, just at the edge of a curtain, to avoid being seen but also to see the road. She stood for a long time and watched the people passing by. Three times she saw men whom she believed were Lozano's men. They came past in groups of two or three. None of them walked with any urgency from what she could tell. Nobody ran or hurried as if some important activity occurred. They just walked past out on the main road as people who might be going to supper or going to visit a relative.

Not knowing was the hard part. Not knowing if Lozano's men had found Tomás or discovered that Pablo had been rescued or learned that Tomás had been killed trying to rescue Pablo.

Anything could be happening in the world beyond her curtain and window, and it tortured Marisol not to know.

"TAKE THESE HOSSES ON up to Leasburg. Use some of them gold coins to buy supplies sufficient to get us home. You'll need to buy a wagon. Water – plenty of water, Pablo. Groceries. And, hell, you'd better buy a couple of boxes of bullets in case we run into Apache."

Pablo shook his head.

"I ain't leaving you here alone, Duvall."

"Par'ner, you ain't fit to fight. They done beat the hell out of you. I'm going to get Marisol and we're going to meet you on up the trail. We might be a couple of days behind you."

Duvall didn't know yet how he was going to get free of the Basurto brothers. Some ideas were cooking in the back of his mind, but he didn't have a firm plan. What he did know, though, was what would be necessary once he was free. The Jornado del Muerto was their salvation. A trail so treacherous it was known as the Trail of Death. That was how they would ultimately get free of all these men pursuing them. And he told Pablo exactly what he wanted him to do and where he wanted Pablo to be when they finally managed to shake loose the Basurto brothers.

"And stay clear of Mesilla," Duvall offered one last caution to him. "Cut east toward the mountains, and when you're sure you're clear, head back to the road."

Pablo, already starting off, gave a wave of his hand. He had the horse he was riding and two of the other three horses. Duvall kept the white horse, intending to ride that one back up to Mesilla. He was going to get Pecas Gris and Marisol's piebald from the livery. He didn't yet know how, but he wasn't leaving his horse in Mesilla. He was attached to that horse.

Right away, Pablo left the road and cut out to the east, heading to the line of mountain peaks east of Mesilla. He'd only need to ride a couple of miles that way to avoid the town.

Pablo had his own saddle bag, now. He had his share of the gold that they'd managed to get out of Mexico. The smallest bit of the million dollars they'd stolen, but enough that Pablo could live comfortably for a long time without having to lift a finger too often. Duvall kept his gold. He had it in the back of his mind that he'd give it up if he had to. Hand it over to Armando and Luis Basurto if that would be enough to convince them to let him and Marisol go on north and forget the idea of turning back to Mexico to get the rest of the gold.

If Armando and Luis Basurto couldn't be convinced, Duvall would kill them. He'd already made his mind up on that account, too.

He did not fear riding back into Mesilla, even with Néstor Lozano's men scouring the town for him.

It was no different than coming down here to face three men to rescue Pablo. It didn't scare him to do it.

This was another lesson that Mexico had taught him, and it taught him in the roughest way possible. But the lesson Duvall learned was this: Dying didn't scare him. What scared him was loving something that death could take away from him.

He'd lost all his pals, except Pablo.

He'd lost Billy, who'd been with him since they were boys. Billy, who'd ridden across Texas with him, gone to New Mexico Territory with him when things got too bad in Texas. His best pal.

And now he found himself clinging desperately to a hoss and a woman, so desperately that he'd ride directly into a village where a dozen men were looking to kill him.

Dying didn't scare him, but losing what he loved damn sure did.

Duvall put on the sombrero and poncho, resting his own hat on the saddle horn. It wasn't much of a disguise, but it had bought him the few seconds he needed to beat his opponents once, and maybe it could do the trick one more time.

It was only just now around midday, so Duvall was in no hurry. He still had hours before dark, and hours beyond that before he would meet the Basurto brothers and Marisol at the bridge. But he also didn't want to stay here, anywhere near the bodies. The evidence of a struggle was still on the road. Blood in the dirt. The tracks from where he'd dragged the bodies off through the desert. So he left, but he walked the white horse at an easy pace.

Still at least a couple of miles south of Mesilla, Duvall spotted a cluster of trees standing together. Just four or five of them, and none of them very tall. But they made shade, and that was good enough. So Duvall rode the white horse over into the shade and dismounted. The grass here was poor, but the horse – tied to a branch – pulled leaves from one of the trees. Duvall sat down with his back to one of the trees and rested for a bit. He reloaded the Colt and the Winchester. He searched through the saddlebags on the white horse and found some jerky. There was also a canteen on the horse, so Duvall ate some jerky and drank some water.

Mostly, he tried to keep his mind empty. He didn't want to think too much about what he had to do. He'd laid a plan together and knew better than to think too much about it. He didn't need to start second guessing it now.

Wait for dusk. Ride into Mesilla with the poncho and sombrero. If anyone is watching the livery, maybe they don't notice him. Get Pecas Gris and Fabiola.

But a man can't make his mind empty. Thoughts come unbidden.

Not much more than a month ago, Duvall had come through this way. They'd crossed to the west bank of the Rio Grande, but they'd ridden probably not more than four or five miles from where he sat now.

They'd lost Chuck by then – killed when the Apache attacked on the Jornado del Muerto.

But Richie Hull was still alive. And Bull.

That feller Bassett was still alive then, too, but even after riding the Jornado del Muerto together, Duvall still didn't know much about Bassett. He never got to know him too well until those days they spent together in the hotel in Santa Catalina. They'd shared a room and talked.

Bassett talked about his pregnant wife, his troubles with the cattle that didn't make it through the winter. He needed the money. He was in a desperate situation with a child on the way. Bassett wouldn't live to see his child. He'd never see his wife again.

That was the outlaw's life, and Duvall was never going to live that life again.

Bassett should've never lived it to start with. He had a pregnant wife before he became an outlaw. He should have hired on at Ben Callahan's place.

But that was the trouble with hard lessons. Sometimes a man don't learn a hard lesson until it's too late to do anything about it.

Billy Muggs.

Duvall couldn't think of Billy without feeling sad. He'd always believed that Billy and him would be riding together until they were old men. And now Billy was dead in a grave in Mexico.

"Los Invasores," Duvall muttered to himself.

They'd named their outfit just in time to all get killed off so that no one else would ever even know that name. All but Duvall and Pablo. Los Invasores.

21

Néstor Lozano took up residence at the same hotel where Duvall and Marisol had taken rooms.

During the morning, his men carried a table and chairs out onto the covered boardwalk in front of the room, and Lozano made his headquarters outside in that shade. He kept a couple of men with him to run messages should they need to do that. Guillermo Gomez stayed nearby. The rest of the men scattered through the town of Mesilla in a search for a man who was not there.

But they had new orders, now.

So far as Lozano knew, the Mexican, Pablo Peña was on his way to Señor Arellano. Retrieving the gold was now out of Lozano's hands. Arellano himself could see to it that the gold was recovered. He could do whatever was necessary to force Pablo to confess the location of the gold.

"Kill the gringo," Lozano told his men. "Capture the woman."

The lawyers showed up mid-morning.

"You look like a commander at war, Néstor," Armando said when the Basurto brothers finally joined Lozano.

"I am a commander at war," Lozano said. "If I return to Mexico without the gringo's head and without his niece, how will Señor Arellano receive me? I am fighting a war to keep my position."

"His niece," Armando chuckled derisively. "We all know who Marisol Rosales is and what relation she is to Señor Arellano."

"What is that supposed to mean?" Lozano asked.

"Is she not his daughter, Néstor? Call her what she is."

Lozano waved a dismissive hand at the lawyer.

Lozano did not care for attorneys, generally. Lozano preferred that men settle their differences like men. A fist or a knife or a gun could settle a dispute more decisively and much faster than a fight in the courtrooms where the winner was declared based on who could hire the lawyer who cheated the best. Real men settled disputes with their hands, not like bickering women. But these two, Luis and Armando Basurto, Lozano despised them specifically. They roamed Señor Arellano's hacienda in Juárez as if it were their own. They ate at his table while men like Lozano ate at the bunkhouse table.

But Lozano would be glad to show his value was greater than that of any lawyer.

The Basurto brothers found chairs and placed them in the shade near Lozano's table.

The younger one, Armando, he was relaxed. Smiling. Lounging in his chair. He almost seemed to be enjoying himself. Everything a fiesta for him here. It angered Lozano the way Armando sat around so relaxed. Nothing that happened here would come back on him. He would share none of the responsibility of failure should the gringo escape, even though he was the man who'd last laid eyes on the gringo. He'd had him – he'd seen him and been watching him – and somehow the gringo managed to escape.

"He's a wily man, the gringo," Lozano said. "Guillermo Gomez came face to face with him in Palomas. Did I tell you that? They shot at each other in the street. Still, the gringo managed to get away from my lieutenant. Much the same as he managed to get away from you, Armando."

Armando gave a small shrug.

"Si. He does seem to be slippery. But you will get him, Néstor. I am confident."

Lozano detected in his tone some amusement. The lawyers think they are so smart. Smarter than everyone else. Everyone else exists for their amusement. Lozano would have liked to have slapped that man across the face for his insolence. But he knew better. Like it or not, Lozano knew that the lawyers were protected.

Lozano looked at Luis Basurto. He did not seem so relaxed as his brother. Luis' eyes moved about. He watched whenever Lozano's men approached. He listened intently to their reports. But what struck Lozano more than anything was how Luis Basurto seemed relieved when the men said that they had seen no sign of the gringo. It was almost as if Luis Basurto was hoping the gringo would not be caught.

"Do you think the Mexican can be compelled to talk?" Armando asked.

"Anyone can be made to talk," Lozano said with confidence. "Maybe not in a courtroom, but in the desert where no one will come to save you. That is where men like me get answers to questions."

"Maybe you should have kept the Mexican here," Armando said. "You could have taken him to the desert and gotten your answers. I'm sure Señor Arellano would much prefer to have you bring the gold to him rather than send to him a man who must be tortured."

Lozano slapped his hand on his table and stood up over Armando.

"You are the one who convinced me that I should send the Mexican to Señor Arellano!"

"Si," Armando said. "And I think that is best. You have provided him with the means to recover his gold. All I am saying is that if you brought the gold yourself, that would sit better with him."

Lozano snarled at the man and clapped his hands together. He started pacing about.

"You are no help to me," Lozano muttered. "Do you offer such worthless advice to Señor Arellano? And then a day later tell him that he should not have followed your advice?"

Armando grinned.

"I do not mean to irritate you, Señor Lozano. We are just having a friendly conversation."

Lozano turned on Luis, now.

"And you? What are you so nervous about? If I did not know better, I would swear you are hoping to see me fail. But if I fail here, where does that leave you? What happens to Señor Arellano if we cannot recover the gold?"

Armando stood up and stepped between Lozano and his older brother.

"Calm down, Néstor. No one wants to see you fail – except, of course, the gringo. We have complete faith in you and are certain of your success. Si, Luis?"

"Si," Luis Basurto said, now rising from his chair. "I should go back to the house."

Armando nodded to him.

"Si. That is fine. I will come and get you later. I will stay here and keep Néstor company. We need to be friends again. Eh, Néstor?"

Lozano narrowed his eyes and sneered, but he sat back down in his chair and waited for a new report from his men. But his suspicions were aroused. Something was wrong with Luis Basurto.

"Did you know the man, Rodrigues, who betrayed Señor Arellano?" Lozano said to Armando after some time.

"I might have seen him," Armando said. "But I do not remember him."

Lozano nodded his head.

"There will be an inquisition, I am sure, when Señor Arellano learns that one of his own men betrayed him. But Rodrigues would not have known about the gold. No? He was no one that Señor

Arellano would have taken into his confidence. And he was banished. Driven away from Juárez. So how did he know about the gold?"

Armando shifted his weight in his chair.

"That is a good question, and one that Señor Arellano will want to know the answer to."

"Si. He will want to know the answer. How did a junior man in his organization – one banished many months ago – how did he know about the gold? How did he know about the gold and plan this theft? He had time enough to recruit men and they were there in Santa Catalina, waiting for the gold shipment."

Armando shrugged and said nothing.

"I didn't even know about the gold shipment," Lozano said. He looked over at Guillermo Gomez who was standing not far away, leaning against one of the posts holding up the awning. "Guillermo? Did you know Señor Arellano was sending gold through Santa Catalina?"

"No," Guillermo said. He'd largely ignored Lozano's rants against the Basurto brothers that morning, but now his interest was piqued. "I knew nothing of it."

"Not many people would have been in a position to know. Eh, Armando? Did you know about it?"

Armando looked past Lozano at the bright sun reflecting off the whitewashed adobe of the building across the street from the hotel. It was almost blinding, and it made his eyes water. The brown street, too, was so bright from here in the shade. It was afternoon, now. Armando did not know what time, exactly, but sometime in the afternoon.

"Did you know about the gold, Armando?" Lozano said again. "Tell me, where is your smug grin, now? Where are your little jokes at my expense? Do you not have some remark you want to say that will make me the fool and to amuse everyone at my expense?"

"You are being careless, amigo," Armando said, and his voice sounded dangerous. "I do not know what you are trying to insinuate, but you are being very careless."

Armando stood up now, and as he did, Lozano's hand dropped to the revolver holstered on his hip. Armando cocked his head, but his hands were empty and he had made no threatening movements.

"What is that about?" Armando said. "Are you threatening me, Néstor, or are you scared of me?"

Lozano glanced at Guillermo Gomez who was just watching the two of them. He had not moved.

"I promise that I am not scared of you, Armando," Lozano said.

Armando nodded his head and smiled.

"I am going to check on my brother. I will return shortly."

Armando walked away and Lozano silently watched him go. When he was in the plaza, walking across to the street where his house was, Lozano snapped his fingers at Guillermo Gomez.

"Go watch their house," Lozano said. "Do not let them see you. Take someone with you, and if you see anything suspicious, you report it back to me."

"Si," Guillermo said. "I'll watch them."

"Do not fail, Guillermo. Do not let them slip away from you."

"My brother is a fool," Luis Basurto said, pacing the small parlor of the rented house. "He has killed us both. When Señor Arellano learns of his deception, learns of how Armando has plotted against him, his fury will only be quelled by our deaths."

Marisol had no pity for the man.

She'd come to understand through Luis' rantings that it was Armando who came up with the plan to steal from Señor Arellano. Perhaps Luis was only a hapless victim of his brother's duplicity, but he was going along with it now. And, though Marisol felt a twinge of guilt at her own betrayal, it was still her father who the Basurto brothers betrayed. It was Armando Basurto who set all of this into motion. All the killing fell at his feet.

"I will tell you where the gold is," Marisol said. "You can have it all."

Luis stopped his pacing and looked at her.

"Let me go, and I will tell you where to find it."

He narrowed his eyes.

"It is a trick," he said.

"No trick," Marisol said. "Tomás doesn't even want the gold. He doesn't care about it. We just want to be together, he and I."

"Tomás? The gringo?"

"Si. He doesn't care about the gold. We were trying to leave it behind. We just want to escape and be together. Let me go now, and I will tell you where to find the gold."

Luis shook his head.

"I will not do anything without asking Armando first."

"You are giving him more courtesy than he gave to you. He did not ask you before he betrayed my father. Did he? You make the deal with me."

"You know where to find the gold? Exactly where it is?" Luis asked, and Marisol believed the man was ready to strike a deal.

"Exactly where it is," she said.

Luis took a heavy breath. Indecisive.

"All of the gold," Marisol said. "You and your brother do not even have to split it – or shoot us in the back if that was your plan. You can have it all without a fight. Just let me go."

Luis looked at the gun on Marisol's belt. True to his word, Armando had allowed her to keep it.

"There was no plan to shoot you in the back," Luis said. "Armando struck a deal with the gringo. He would keep his word."

"There was no plan that you knew of," Marisol said. "I believe Armando keeps his plans secret from you."

"Si. Perhaps. Some of them. But he would need me to help to shoot you in the back. No? He is willing to split the gold."

"But there's no need," Marisol said. "Don't you understand? Tomás and I do not want the gold. We just want to be free, to go together."

Luis nodded his head, still thinking.

"But if I let you go, how will you get away? Lozano's men are scouring this town."

"They are looking for Tomás, not for me."

Luis shook his head.

"No. They are looking for both of you. Lozano will not be satisfied to get the gringo and not you. You are part of the prize."

"I can sneak away," Marisol said.

But then she lost her opportunity. The door to the house flung open. Armando Basurto, sweating and breathing heavily, stepped inside and closed the door behind him. He stood for a moment, catching his breath. Then he looked from Marisol on the sofa to Luis, standing in the middle of the parlor where he had been pacing.

"What is going on in here?" Armando asked. But then he waved his hand to keep them from answering. "Nevermind. It is not important. What is important is that Néstor Lozano has figured out that it was us who were working with Rodrigues."

Luis stammered.

Marisol sank into the sofa. Any hope she had of striking a deal was gone now. If Lozano had become an enemy of the Basurto brothers, they would need an ally. Marisol did not have to wonder what man they would think of to turn to.

"We must leave now, while we can," Armando said. "He has no proof, only suspicions. But the longer he sits with his suspicions, the less proof he will need."

Marisol could see Luis Basurto go pale.

"We're not meeting the gringo until midnight."

"Si. I know," Armando said. Marisol had not seen him appear this way before. Frantic. Rushed. Desperate. She did not underestimate the danger she was suddenly in. Armando twice walked to the window to be sure no one was coming at the house. "We'll have to go and hide until then, someplace where they won't find us. We can go to the livery and get our horses and ride out to the bridge. We'll hide in the brush and trees by the river and just wait for the gringo."

"What if he failed?" Luis asked. "What if the gringo did not get his friend? What if Lozano's men killed him? If he's dead, not only do we not get the gold, but now we're exposed."

Armando waved both his hands like he was trapped on the tracks and frantically trying to stop a train that would not stop.

"There's no time to think like that. The gringo is resourceful. He has evaded Lozano. He killed Rodrigues. He will do what he set out to do."

"She knows where the gold is," Luis said.

Armando stopped and stared at Marisol.

"She told you this?"

"She did," Luis said. "Just now, before you came in. She said if I let her go she would tell me where the gold is buried."

Armando started to laugh and shook his head.

"No brother. She tells you the gold is buried in a place. You let her go. She happily goes to Denver or Charleston or San Francisco and you are out in the desert with a shovel looking for gold that was never there. No – we find the gringo. We all go together to get the gold."

22

"THERE'S A MESS OF Mexicans looking for you, son."

The man at the livery looked to be about forty-years-old. He looked like he'd been running this livery back when the Confederates took over Mesilla during the war. He probably had been. He wore a thick beard and had a big round belly that suggested stalling horses had paid pretty well over the years.

"I'm aware," Duvall muttered.

"They recognized your hoss when they rode in," the man said. "Wanted to know if you'd sold me that hoss or just keeping it here."

"What'd you tell them?"

The man chuckled.

"I told them that unless they intended to make me an offer on them hosses, it warn't none of their business."

"That's probably a good thing to tell them," Duvall said. "But you don't want to make these men too angry."

"No, I reckon not. They look like some bad men."

"They're big men down in Old Mexico," Duvall said. "They work for a big man. They're accustomed to throwing their weight around and don't give a rip who gets knocked down."

"I figured that," the man said. "They got two over there across the road been watching my place. I suspect they're watching for you to come in."

"Uh-huh."

"They ain't seem to have recognized you there in that sombrero."

"That was the idea of the sombrero," Duvall grinned at the man, relieved to have found an ally.

"But when I go and fetch that piebald pony and that freckled-gray for you, those men are going to know who you are."

"Likely so," Duvall said.

"You got a plan for what to do when that happens?"

Duvall chuckled.

"Shoot straighter'n 'em?"

"Ha. Well, maybe – if you want – I can help you out."

"How so?" Duvall asked.

"I got a boy in the back. He could get together a string of hosses, include your piebald and the gray. He could walk them down the road apiece. Them fellers won't think nothing except he's exercising some of the hosses."

"That would work, except I need my two saddles and tack" Duvall said.

"Heft one of them saddles over your shoulder and walk out of here with it. He'll put the saddle on another hoss and ride it to lead the string. When he meets you, then you can take both saddles and your two hosses."

Duvall studied the man's face for a moment, looking for any hint of duplicity.

"I don't know what trouble you're in, son," the man said, as if reading Duvall's mind. "But them's Mexicans, and you're American, and I side with my own."

"I'm obliged to you," Duvall said. "I reckon you might just have saved my life. Where can I meet your boy?"

"We keep a second corral about half a mile south of here. You should've passed it on your way into town."

"I saw it."

"Meet him there."

Duvall took Marisol's saddle on his shoulder and walked out of the livery, heading south. He resisted the urge to check over his shoulder to know if those two Mexicans watching the livery were following him. He'd find that out soon enough. But when he reached the corral, he saw no one on the road behind him. The livery sat on the edge of town, and there wasn't much between the livery and the corral to the south. Duvall figured a house near the corral probably belonged to the hostler.

There were already a half dozen horses in the corral. Duvall balanced Marisol's saddle on the top rail of the fence and waited for about half an hour when he saw the string of horses coming down the road. It had gotten dark enough by now that he couldn't even see the boy leading the horses at first. The boy was on foot, but he had Duvall's saddle on the lead horse. They'd not put the saddle on Pecas Gris.

"You the man in the sombrero I'm supposed to give these two horses to?" the boy asked. The boy looked to be about twelve-years-old, too small to do anything about a string of horses that spooked and ran. He had big front teeth that shone in the dying light of the day.

"I'm the one," Duvall said.

While the boy put the other horses in the corral, Duvall tied Pecas Gris and Fabiola to the post. Pecas Gris nuzzled him like the two hadn't seen each other in months. Duvall pushed the freckled-gray's head away, even though it was nice to have been missed, and saddled Marisol's pony. The boy brought Duvall's saddle to him.

"My pa told me to tell you that them two Mexicans is still watching the livery. They didn't follow you out, and I watched to see if they followed me. But they didn't. So you're clear, and good luck to you."

"Tell your pa I appreciate his help," Duvall said.

Once the horses were saddled, Duvall did not linger.

Leading Marisol's pony, he rode out toward the Rio Grande bridge, hoping to get there while he still had some daylight left. He was not going to be caught again by the Basurto brothers arriving ahead of him.

Duvall slid the Winchester Yellow Boy from its scabbard and lowered the lever to lay eyes on the bullet in the chamber. Satisfied, he sat down on a big cottonwood branch that had dropped to the ground, and there he waited for darkness to envelop him.

He'd tied the horses to a cottonwood some distance from the bridge, there where he was waiting. He had hours before midnight, but better to be here early, in the daylight, and know there was no one around and see them when they arrived than to arrive on time and be surprised by a man coming up out of the brush.

Tonight there would be no surprises.

With just half an hour of daylight left, Duvall saw a rider approaching in the distance. A lone man on a horse, and he seemed to be making for the bridge, a good distance beyond Duvall. As the rider drew nearer and still hadn't seen him, Duvall realized it was not a man on a horse at all. Instead, it was a boy. The same boy from the livery. And he had a fishing pole sticking up like a flagless guidon pole. He was riding near the river's bank, just outside of the bosque, and would come very near to Duvall.

Here in the brush and trees, with the sun behind him, Duvall didn't think the rider could see him at all. On purpose, Duvall began moving around, but the boy never seemed to notice him. When the boy was past, and only about thirty yards away, Duvall stepped out of the brush and called to him.

The boy jumped. He'd had no idea Duvall and the horses were right there.

"Hey, mister," the boy said, twisting around in his saddle and reining his horse to a stop. "Where's your sombrero?"

"I traded it back for my hat."

"That one fits you better," the boy said.

"Yep. I reckoned so, too. You about to fish?"

The boy nodded ahead.

"Yeah. From the bridge."

"What do you catch here?"

"Cutthroat trout is the best," the boy answered. "There's bass, too. And catfish, if you like catfish, but pa says they's bottomfeeders and too bony for his liking."

"Your pa ain't wrong," Duvall said. "How late you plan to be here?"

"Just 'til dark."

"You think you can catch something that quick?"

"Been a hot day. Them fish'll be out now that it's dusk. And they'll be up under the bridge where the water stays cool. The trick is to get them in the cool water in the shadow of the bridge where they feel safe and comfortable. They're in that cool water, eating bugs, they ain't on their guard. You try to get them in the water that's hot from the sun, and they're ready for you. But in the cool water them fish are all relaxed, I can take them by surprise. You watch, you'll see me pull three out for supper for my whole family before it's even dark."

"Good luck to you," Duvall said, tugging on the brim of his hat. The boy gave the horse a touch with his heel, and the horse got moving again.

Seeing no one else on the horizon, Duvall decided to step out a ways and watch. The boy took his time. Dismounting and tying off his horse. Baiting his hook. Getting some grass into the bottom of his basket. And then he walked out onto the bridge and dropped his line in the river. It took a couple of tries, but the third time he tried a spot, Duvall saw the tip of the pole dip, and then the boy fighting the fish on the line. He couldn't see what the boy caught from the distance, but he guessed it wasn't a catfish because the boy didn't toss it back.

Duvall wandered back into the bosque to sit with the horses. He unsaddled them, feeling pretty confident now that they were well-hidden and safe.

About dark, the boy rode back past. Duvall didn't doubt that he had three fish in his basket for supper.

Duvall found his prayerbook in his pocket and his tobacco pouch. He rolled a smoke in the dark and then struck a match. The flare of the match seemed so bright.

He whiled the time thinking about how to deal with the Basurto brothers. What seemed best was to kill them. As soon as they arrived, he could gun them down. Anyway he looked at it, that's what seemed best. He'd considered telling them the truth – the gold is buried in the Guadalupe Victoria cemetery, go and get it, but me and Marisol won't be going with you.

Maybe there was some slim chance they would accept that. Duvall doubted it. They would expect him to go, probably planning to shoot him in the back once the gold was dug up. Lawyers. They wouldn't trust him. Cheating and lying was their instinct, and they expected it from everyone else. There was probably a better chance that Lozano would accept the location of the gold and let him go. Then again, Duvall was all but certain that Lozano wanted to kill him more than to get the gold.

"I'm tired of the killing, Pecas," Duvall told the horse. "There's been too much of it. Too many dead over this gold. I'm about convinced that gold is cursed."

He thought about the boy catching the fish. Get them where they're relaxed. That was what the boy said, and he wasn't wrong. But how do you get a couple of Mexican lawyers to relax?

An hour ticked by, and another. The later it grew, the more watchful Duvall became. He hadn't seen anyone else since the boy from the livery had come along to catch his family's supper. Though, if someone was riding past on the road, Duvall probably wouldn't have seen them in the dark. He was still well south of the road. But he would surely hear hooves on the bridge boards.

He struck a match to light a smoke and used the light to look at his watch. It was about eleven o'clock, now. Time was getting close.

Duvall saddled the horses. Working in the dark, though this was far from the first time he'd saddled a horse in the dark.

When the horses were saddled, he took up the rifle and stepped out of the bosque. He kept close to the brush and made his way toward the bridge. When he was near it, he sat down and waited. He wrapped his hand around the gunmetal receiver of his rifle, the only thing that might catch the moonlight and reflect it enough to give him away. He was as invisible down by the bridge now as if he wasn't there at all. And he waited.

23

In the silver light of the moon, Duvall could see the three approaching. They were on foot, leading two horses.

He saw no movement behind them that would suggest they'd been followed. And though he couldn't make out features from this distance, one of the three was a woman. But still, he didn't move. He'd wait until he knew for sure, and he'd keep watching beyond them. But as they neared, there was no doubt left.

"Tomás?" Marisol called into the darkness.

Now Duvall stood up and stepped away from the bosque, coming out into the moon's light where they could see him. Marisol rushed forward, putting her arms around him.

"Safely returned, as promised," Armando Basurto said.

The Basurto brothers stayed back a respectful distance, showing they intended to be no threat. Luis held the horses and Armando took a couple of steps forward. Duvall squeezed Marisol but then subtly moved her around so that she was behind him.

"Where is your friend?" Armando asked.

"He's safe," Duvall said. "They beat him pretty good, and I decided it was better for him to go on. He agreed."

"He does not care for his share of the gold?" Armando asked.

"He trusts me," Duvall said. "He'll get his share if I get mine."

"We need to move quickly," Armando said. "Mesilla is not safe. I believe that Néstor Lozano has come to distrust us."

"We ain't prepared for a ride through the desert," Duvall said. "We don't have supplies for it. We'll need supplies. That means we ride to El Paso. Buy our supplies there."

"No," Luis said, standing back with the horses. "That is not good. Señor Arellano knows too much of what happens in El Paso."

"Only other thing to do is ride north to Leasburg, up there by Fort Selden. We supply there, then cut out across the desert," Duvall said. "That's a hard go."

"Where are we going to?" Armando asked.

Duvall chuckled.

"You think I'm going to tell you that?" he asks. "No, sir. You find out where we're going when we get there. I'm not having you put a bullet in my back as soon as you know where the gold is hidden. All I'll tell you is that Palomas is where we start."

Armando shrugged his shoulders.

"I thought we were building trust," he chuckled. "But that's fine. I understand. We'll go to Palomas, then."

"But not through El Paso," Luis added. "If we must go to this other place, then we will go there."

"Leasburg is north, along the Rio Grande. Only about fifteen or twenty miles. You and your brother make for Leasburg, and we'll meet you there."

Armando laughed.

"We have not built so much trust," he said. "We will go together to Leasburg. From now on, we go together everywhere until we have the gold."

Duvall took a breath. He didn't think they'd go for it, but it was worth a try.

"Where are your horses?" Luis asked.

"In the bosque down yonder," Duvall said.

"Are you ready to ride now to Leasburg?" Armando asked.

"We just need to mount up," Duvall said.

"Then go and get your horses. Señorita Rosales can wait here with us. In the interest of building trust."

"Yep. All right. I'll be right back."

Duvall started to turn but then he stopped. Armando said something, but Duvall raised a hand and shushed him.

"I hear something," Duvall breathed.

He'd been out here in the dark alone for so long, that all the noises of the riverbanks were familiar to him. Now, though, he heard some new sound. And as he listened, he knew what it was.

"A rider's coming," he said, and Duvall raised the Yellow Boy to his shoulder, pointing it into the darkness to the south.

"I don't hear anything," Armando said, but then he did. Clearly they could hear the pounding of hooves, but not a chorus. Just a single rider. And then, a horse and rider appeared in the moonlight, charging directly toward them.

The rider reined up about forty yards from the bridge, probably had Duvall in sight now.

"Hey! Mister. Is that you?"

It was the voice of a child, but also the familiar voice of a confident fisherman. Duvall lowered his rifle.

"Boy? What are you doing out here at this hour? Ain't it past your bedtime?"

"My pa sent me. He told me I'd better come on fast. Them Mexicans all looking for you around town? They come to the livery and are saddling up their hosses."

The boy's tone carried a sense of urgency.

"Just now?"

"Just now. They come about thirty minutes after them two come to get their horses. They was in a hurry, seemed angry. My pa told me to ride out and if you was still here by the bridge to warn you. He thinks they're following them two. When them two came to get their hosses, my pa seen two following them. One of the two ran off, like he was going to get the others. And the other one, he watched which direction they went in."

Duvall looked at Armando.

"Were you followed?"

Armando stammered and gave no real answer.

"Okay son," Duvall said to the boy. "Don't ride back the way you came. Keep on riding that way and go back to the livery the long way. Tell your pa I thank him for sending the warning."

The boy called to his horse and started away at the gallop.

"We've got to move," Duvall said. "Cross the bridge, follow the river north to Leasburg. Marisol and I will meet you there."

"Go and get your horses," Armando said. "We go together."

But now Duvall heard a new noise. It took a moment to be sure because he could still hear the boy's horse leaving. But then he was definitely sure. This was not a single rider, but the thunder of several horses coming fast. Lozano and his men were closing in on them.

"There may not be time for that," Duvall said.

The others heard it, too.

"Armando," Luis said, fear in his voice.

"I hear them," Armando said. "Leasburg, gringo. I will see you there."

"I'll be there," Duvall said, grabbing Marisol by the wrist and leading her south along the bank toward the horses.

The Basurto brothers rushed to get onto their horses. Marisol ran as fast as she could, but Duvall was dragging her. And then he stopped and pulled her into the trees with him, puller her close to him and pressing her face against his so that his lips almost touched her ears.

"Don't make a sound," he said. "No matter what you hear, don't make a sound."

And then the thundering of the horses was louder. Through the branches, Duvall could see them coming like a cavalry charge. The silvery light glinted against the metal on their drawn rifles. Men were shouting in Spanish. Now, rifles cracked. Through the din, Duvall could hear the sound of horses on the bridge. The Basurto brothers were crossing to the west side of the Rio Grande. More shots, and a man screamed.

The unmistakable sound of a splash into the river.

"Come on, now," Duvall whispered. "With me."

They hurried through the darkness, Duvall going first to push branches out of the way. Marisol almost pressed against him she was so close.

The shooting was growing distant. A chase on the other side of the river.

A branch knocked Duvall's hat from his head, and he had to feel around in the darkness to find it. Then they continued to push through.

His face and arms scratched from the branches, he at last heard Pecas Gris ahead of him.

"Quietly, now," Duvall said. "Stay right with me."

He untied the horses from the cottonwood and led them out from the trees, finding the same hole in the brush he'd found to lead them in. Both horses seemed restless and on alert after the charge and the shooting.

At the edge of the trees, Duvall paused just to have a quick look around, but there was nothing to see. Not from here, anyway. Lozano's men had followed the Basurto brothers across the bridge. He saw nothing, but there were shouts that seemed nearer than the shots.

"Quiet now. Some could still be on this side of the river," Duvall said.

They stepped out into the darkness. Duvall held the pony while Marisol stepped up into the saddle. The piebald pony danced a circle, but so quietly she seemed to be on her tip-toes. Duvall swung himself into the saddle and Pecas Gris started to go. Duvall dragged the reins to keep the horse well wide of the bridge, and as they stepped away from the trees, Duvall could see the shapes of men and horses in the middle of the bridge. The men, some of them, were dismounted. It looked like four horses on the bridge and only one man still in the saddle. The others were on foot, their attention seemed to be on the river.

"As quiet as we can, now," Duvall whispered to Marisol.

He brought Pecas Gris to a lope, directing the horse south and east before turning north, giving the bridge a wide berth.

As they drew even with the bridge, probably a hundred yards or so out, there was renewed shouting – urgent shouting – and the crack of a rifle.

"They've seen us," Duvall said. "Ride hard!"

Marisol leapt out in front of him, the pony at a gallop. Pecas Gris followed. Duvall kept the gray from overtaking the pony, but he stayed near to Marisol. Another crack of a rifle, and then another.

They were on the road now, headed back into Mesilla. But Duvall wasn't worried about the town – the danger now was all to the west of the town, at the Rio Grande bridge. There would be pursuit, surely, but Lozano and his men would have to try to track them in the dark.

They reached the town at a lope. The streets of the town were all but empty. A few men lingering on the boardwalk after a night of drinking. At the main road leading north and south out of town, Duvall turned Pecas Gris to the north.

Fifteen or twenty miles to Leasburg and Fort Selden. For the first time in weeks, with Pecas Gris trotting toward the Jornado del Muerto, Duvall felt a sense of relief – like he'd finally escaped the danger.

24

HAZEL COULD NOT SLEEP because the baby would not sleep.

She felt the baby's head again, but she did not believe she had a fever.

Moments like this, in the middle of the night, all alone and uncertain of what to do, that's when Hazel felt his absence the most.

"Your daddy wouldn't know any better than I do what to do with you," Hazel told the baby. "But at least he could be here. At least he could be helping."

She bounced the baby in her arms. She shushed the baby.

"He felt so bad," Hazel said. "He had such high hopes. He thought he could build a place here. A place for us. But all them cows died, and there wasn't nothing left. And your daddy was broke in half. Everything he thought he was building was lost, and we didn't have nothing."

Hazel kissed the baby's forehead. She was so tired she didn't even know what she was saying anymore.

"I don't know what to hope for. Do I hope that wherever he is he's okay? Or do I hope he's dead somewhere?"

Hazel rubbed the baby's back, pressed her head into her own chest and held her tight, wishing she would sleep.

"If he's alive and okay, then that means he ran off on us," Hazel said. "And that would hurt my heart worse than anything. But at least he'd be okay. If he's dead somewhere, well, that would make me sad, but at least I'd know he loved us and tried to come home. And I just keep going back and forth in my heart which one I want to be true."

The baby didn't sleep. Not for a long time.

Finally, Hazel put her down in her bassinet and walked outside. The baby cried, but Hazel needed a moment. The night air was cold. She breathed it deeply, so deep that it hurt. She didn't even feel the tears. Her face was numb. Her eyes were numb.

She'd left the door open, and the cold air was in the house, fighting with the heat from the stove. But the cold air had been the tonic that shushing and rocking had not been.

Hazel resisted her inclination to lie down and sleep while she could.

"I've had no word from home since my last letter," Hazel wrote on a piece of stationery. "I fear perhaps it never arrived. The mail here, like many other things I have taken for granted in the past, is not always reliable. My present condition has grown increasingly trying. We lost all but a few of the cattle to the winter snows. Some weeks ago, my husband left for town in search of employment. He has yet to return, and I fear he may never come back. If you received my last letter, you know your granddaughter was born in the interim. She is the darlingest thing you've ever seen, eyes as bright and blue as the summer sky. But like the summer sky, they can be fast to storm up. It is just us, now. Me and the baby, and little ability to sustain ourselves."

She was careful not to treat her husband too harsh in the letter. She feared he might have fallen to an accident with no one knowing who he was or to whom to deliver the news. Or worse, an accident that no one knew about – a fall from a horse or an attack by some wild beast or hostile tribe. She did not express her fears that maybe he just couldn't stay with her.

She wanted to come home. Perhaps she hadn't expressed it clearly enough in the previous letter, or perhaps that previous letter never arrived.

She had a little bit of money. Neighbors had shown kindness to her and arranged for the sale of what few cattle that were left. Money enough to get through a few weeks more.

If her folks could send some money, she'd take the stage to Great Bend, Kansas. She'd been told that the railroad had been finished that far west. In Great Bend, she would take the train to Chicago. If her folks could send her the money.

She finished off the letter and said a prayer over it. She was done praying for her husband. She felt those prayers had been answered now, one way or the other.

She folded the letter and sealed the envelope and wrote out an address on the envelope, and then she hurried to bed before the baby started to cry again.

25

"WE'VE GONE IN A big circle," Pablo Peña said. "Now back to where we started from."

"It's not a circle," Tommy Duvall said. "This ain't where we started from. We started a hundred miles to the north. We went in a hangman's noose, and we're damned lucky to have escaped it."

"I guess that's right," Pablo said.

"Of course it's right," Duvall said. He was sitting at the campfire, and he picked up a stick from the fire and used it to draw in the air. It's amber end glowed in the fading light of the day. Duvall raised the orange end of his stick into the air.

"We started way up yonder in Las Vegas. We rode a hundred miles down the Jornado del Muerto."

Duvall drew a straight line in the air down. Then he curved his imaginary map into a half circle.

"Then we went down to Santa Catalina. Turned west from Santa Catalina and rode up into Palomas."

He brought the stick back up to close the imaginary circle.

"Then we cut east at an angle through the desert to come back to the southern end of the Jornado del Muerto. Now we're back on the trail of death. We didn't make a circle, Pablo, we rode the shape of a hangman's noose. A lot of good pals got their necks caught in that noose."

"Si," Pablo agreed. "Good amigos, all of them."

"Whatever shape it takes, I'll just be happy when we reach an end to it," Marisol said.

"Soon," Duvall said. "Five days, maybe six, and we'll be back to Las Vegas."

They'd passed by the Point of Rocks on their way south, noting the landmark and knowing it meant they were half a day's ride from Fort Selden. But this was the place where Duvall told Pablo to go and wait for them.

Pablo, the morning after Duvall saved him from torture and execution, had ridden straight to Leasburg. There, he traded a farmer Señor Arellano's three horses that he had with him along with a couple of gold coins for a wagon and a mule team. He bought supplies – a cask of water, flour, jerky, potatoes, feed for the horses, blankets, and a couple of boxes of shells. He bought two lanterns so that he could travel by night. He wasted no time, setting out for the Point of Rocks that same day. He immediately employed his lanterns, driving the mules by night, and arrived at what had all the appearances of a well-used campground below a series of hills that he recognized even in the dark as the southern landmark of the Jornado del Muerto.

Pablo woke the next morning wondering how many days he would have to wait, but Duvall and Marisol arrived at the camp just before dusk.

"We rode wide around Leasburg and Fort Selden," Duvall said. "They might have trailed behind us, heading north, but they didn't track us or follow us. I'm sure of that. And at Fort Selden, they turned around."

"How do you know that?" Pablo asked.

"The soldiers. I don't know how many men Lozano has with him, but there's got to be a dozen or more of them. A dozen armed Mexicans traveling this deep into the territory? They'd catch the notice of the soldiers."

"You think we're free, then?" Marisol asked.

"I think so," Duvall said. "And if they do go on past Fort Selden, the trail will get them. There's no water for the next ninety or hundred miles. Those men aren't toting casks of water. They don't have the supplies to make it that far. They've been days coming through the desert. They'll turn back, or they'll die on this trail."

"Still, we should keep a watch tonight," Pablo said.

Duvall chuckled.

"Of course we should. We should probably keep two of us on watch. Even if we're free of Lozano, we still have to worry about Apache."

Marisol let out a sigh.

"It never ends. If it's not Néstor Lozano or Armando Basurto, it's Apache. Or dying of thirst."

"Or wolves," Pablo said.

At dawn they broke camp. No one slept well because they kept two people on watch through the night, doing it in staggered shifts. Pablo made coffee while Duvall packed the gear. They made a breakfast out of bacon and biscuits, the biscuits soaked in bacon grease so they wouldn't be quite so dry. Marisol offered to do more than just bacon and biscuits, but Duvall said it was more important that they get moving.

"I want to put as much distance between us and the last place we saw Lozano as we can," Duvall said. "The farther we get, the less the possibility that Lozano keeps coming."

"But you said he wouldn't come this far," Marisol said.

"I said he probably won't come this far. And if he does, the trail will get him. But we've got to be farther up the trail, or it don't matter if the trail gets him or not."

As they packed up the last of the gear, Duvall could tell that Pablo had something on his mind.

"What is it, par'ner?"

Pablo grinned.

"What is what?"

"You got something you want to say."

Pablo nodded his head.

"Si. I just wanted to ask the question, hombre. Like as not, we'll never again be this close to the border – this close to Mexico."

"Not if I can help it," Duvall laughed.

"We shook them men coming after us."

"I hope so," Duvall said.

"Maybe, while we're this close, and we've got this wagon – maybe we should think one more time about crossing the border into Old Mexico. Riding down to that little village, Guadalupe Victoria. Digging up that gold."

Duvall narrowed his eyes at Pablo.

"What's that there above your eyes, Pablo?"

Pablo touched two fingers to his forehead and winced as his fingers fell on a cut.

"That's a cut from where them fellers laid into you, ain't it? You got all them bruises on your face, that cut, that black eye there. They worked you over like a calf on branding day, Pablo. And you're talking about going back down to Mexico? Look here, par'ner. We're lucky to be alive last night. We're on our way out of the hangman's noose. Remember? A man that lucky is a fool to tempt fate. You've got gold in your saddlebags, ain't you?"

"Si. I have gold," Pablo said, feeling like he was being reprimanded.

"Be satisfied with that, amigo. Be satisfied that you got some gold bars and your life. I guarantee you, given a choice, Billy or Bull or any of them others who rode south with us would gladly take a little gold and their lives. You and me? We'd be damned fools to ever go back to Mexico again while Señor Manuel Arellano Hermosillio is still running things down there."

"Si. You're right. I was only thinking," Pablo said weakly.

"Besides," Duvall said. "We don't even know for sure that gold is buried in Guadalupe Victoria," Duvall said. "We had a map and a guess. That's all."

"But Liller said to you that the buried the gold with Billy and Bassett," Pablo said. "Of course they buried the gold in the cemetery. That's where they buried Billy and Bassett."

Duvall shook his head.

"It's just a guess, Pablo. We don't know that for sure."

Pablo shrugged. Duvall could see it already. The little bit of gold they took out of Mexico – a fortune in its own right – it wasn't going to be enough for Pablo. The million dollars of gold they left behind, it would haunt him for the rest of his life. But so long as he resisted that greed, Pablo could still have a long life, unlike their friends who died so young.

Duvall helped Pablo with the mules, and when they had the team hitched, Pablo didn't wait. He started the wagon north on the trail while Duvall saddled Pecas Gris and Marisol's pony.

"Four days," Duvall told her. "We'll get to the north end of the Jornado del Muerto in probably four days. Maybe five. Then we're a day or two out from Las Vegas."

"And then what?" Marisol said. "What will we do in Las Vegas?"

"We can do anything we want," Duvall said. "Buy a little place and some cattle. If you want to run a cantina like you did in Santa Catalina, you can do that."

Marisol sighed softly and smiled at him.

"It sounds nice," she said. "This is what I want."

"It's ours," Duvall said. "At the other end of this trail."

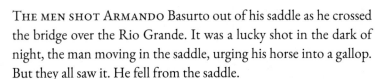

THE MEN SHOT ARMANDO Basurto out of his saddle as he crossed the bridge over the Rio Grande. It was a lucky shot in the dark of night, the man moving in the saddle, urging his horse into a gallop. But they all saw it. He fell from the saddle.

Néstor Lozano himself heard the splash as Armando went into the river.

Lozano and a few others halted on the bridge to try to find the body, but it was dark. They could see nothing, and the noise from the continued shooting hampered their efforts to hear if the man was splashing in the water. A couple of the men fired blind shots into the darkness, but that was a foolish waste of ammunition. They could see nothing and shot at nothing.

But Lozano knew it was Armando who went into the water, because Luis Basurto continued on over the bridge where, within a mile of the bridge, the men caught him. It would have been better if they had taken him alive. The Basurto brothers had answers to questions. But they shot him, and when he fell from his horse, the men trampled him. If they did this on purpose or simply did not see him in the darkness, Lozano never got a satisfactory answer.

When the gringo and Marisol Rosales made their dash into the darkness right in front of him, Lozano was still on the bridge. He shot at them, but they were already disappeared and he was certain his shots were to no effect.

At dawn, Lozano left a group of men to search the bank. His orders were for them to find Armando Basurto – either find him alive or find his body. If he was alive, they were to take him to Juárez and turn him over to Señor Arellano.

"They went north," Guillermo Gomez said.

Through the night, the men were out questioning people who might've seen the gringo. At last, they found a barman at a saloon who said he'd seen a man and woman riding north out of Mesilla.

Lozano left four men to try to find Armando Basurto's body, and with seven others, he rode north to catch the gringo. He'd never been farther than El Paso, and he didn't know what was in front of him. But that didn't matter. His mind was singularly focused on catching the gringo.

"I know there is an old road that runs north to Santa Fe," Lozano said. "I remember hearing old-timers in Juárez talk about how hard a journey it was. No water and Apache. We will see for ourselves if it is so difficult. Eh, Guillermo?"

They were still not far north from Mesilla. They could turn back, and Guillermo thought they should.

"We should consider going back for supplies," Guillermo said.

He didn't know anything about the trail going north to Santa Fe, but he did not like going so deep into los Estados Unidos. They had not yet encountered any gringo lawmen who took an interest in them, nor had the Buffalo soldiers stationed at army forts throughout the territory paid any attention to this gang of Mexicans who looked so much like outlaws. Guillermo knew nothing about the buffalo soldiers, except that even the Apache respected them. Any soldier who could earn the respect of the Apache was a soldier to be feared, Guillermo believed.

"We'll take our supplies on the trail," Lozano said.

"We do not have to keep going," Guillermo said. "We have sent the Mexican back to Juárez. We should let that be enough. If Señor Arellano gets back his gold, he'll be satisfied."

"I won't be satisfied," Lozano said. "And who knows if the Mexican will even talk – or if he knows where the gold is hidden? Maybe the gringo hid it alone."

Guillermo didn't think so. He thought the Mexican probably knew where the gold was just as well as the gringo. But Lozano would not be dissuaded.

Guillermo reined up some, slowing his horse, letting Lozano ride on ahead of him. He fell to the back of the group where Ricardo and Javier rode.

It was a small group now – eight of them in total – and the only men Guillermo knew from the old days in Santa Catalina had been left down on the banks of the Rio Grande searching for Armando Basurto.

"Is this what it's always like in Juárez, working for Señor Arellano?" Guillermo asked.

Javier chuckled.

"Not since Lozano went to Santa Catalina," he said.

"You should not talk like that," Ricardo warned. Then he said to Guillermo, "He's only joking."

Guillermo waved it off.

"Say what you want. You won't offend me, and I'll not say anything to Lozano about what you say to me in jest."

Still Ricardo sent a meaningful glance at Javier, a warning not to say more.

"What are we doing riding so far into America?" Ricardo asked.

"We're going after the gringo so that he can take us to Señor Arellano's gold," Javier said.

Guillermo shook his head.

"I don't think this is about the gold," he said.

"Then what's it about?" Javier asked.

"It is pride with him," Guillermo spoke, but his voice hardly seemed directed to Javier and Ricardo. Instead, he seemed to be making a statement to himself alone – as if he'd reached a conclusion in his mind and by speaking it out loud he was making it final. "He went to Santa Catalina to be the big man there for Señor

Arellano. But he also went there to marry Señor Arellano's niece. But she rejected him. Rejected him for the gringo. That is why we ride north. Don't misunderstand what this is about, amigos. This is about Néstor Lozano's pride."

26

Marisol Rosales rode with a blanket draped over her shoulders. She crossed it under her arms and wrapped it around her so that the blanket offered as much warmth as possible. The wind at night did not blow as hard as the wind during the day. But that daytime wind was hot and stifling and the nighttime wind blew cool.

"I don't know why I'm so cold," Marisol said, shivering under her blanket.

"It's so hot during the day. It's not the temperature as much as it's the change in temperature," Duvall said.

He wore only his coat. His rifle was draped across his lap.

She'd noticed that both Duvall and Pablo had become increasingly vigilant the deeper along the Jornado del Muerto they went.

"Apache," Duvall had said when he told her that he and Pablo had agreed they should travel at night. "That's the biggest reason. We don't want to sit still at night where the Apache can come up on us and we don't see them. It's better on the hosses, too. We don't work 'em too hard in the hottest part of the day. Just like when we were traveling in Mexico."

"I've become like an owl," Marisol said. "Sleeping in the day and staying awake through the night."

They had a sheet of canvas that they could use tie to the side of the wagon and stretch down and stake in the ground to provide shade. But even so, the days were uncomfortably hot to try to sleep.

Two lanterns burned on the wagon, and the moon gave sufficient light for them to see the road.

Their first day on the trail after camping at the Point of Rocks overnight proved all but useless. Pablo's mules didn't want to go in the midday sun, and the horses showed their exhaustion. That's when Duvall and Pablo decided they would travel by night. The spent the rest of the day camped, and at dusk they set out.

"It's hard to remember a time when I was exhausted all of the time," Marisol said.

"When we get back to Las Vegas, we're going to sleep for two days," Duvall promised her.

Marisol laughed.

"I don't know if I'll even remember how to sleep."

There'd been no more talk of going back to Mexico. The gold was gone for good, buried with the men who gave their lives for it. Some of them, anyway. A lot of folks had died over that gold, and their graves were scattered across the desert.

When morning came, Marisol hoped to see grass. But the landscape was still covered in greasewood and sand. Duvall had told her that she would know they were reaching the north end of the trail when te terrain around began to shift from desert scrub brush to high plains grassland. But she saw no grass.

They dropped the blanket down off her shoulders, letting it ride over her saddlebags on Fabiola's back.

The mountains to the left and right seemed very distant, but Duvall had said they weren't far off at all. The valley wasn't but about twenty miles wide, he said.

"I've come through here a couple of times before, driving cattle for Ben Callahan. When we get back to Las Vegas, I'm going to go see old Ben and see if he won't sell us some cattle so we can get a place started. Of course, we'll have to find the place, first. Figure out where we're going to make our home."

"It will have to have many rooms," Marisol said. "We're going to have so many children that we will need lots of rooms for them."

Duvall laughed.

Riding in the morning sun was not much better than riding at night. The sun got hot fast. Not insufferable, but hot enough. And being able to see where they were going quickly gave Marisol a sense of how slowly they traveled. She would pick a spot out on the horizon and watch it. It never seemed to get any closer, and inevitably she would lose the spot she was watching because one spot on the horizon looked like every other spot on the horizon.

It was hard traveling, but they were coming off of days of hard traveling. The creaking and banging of the wagon became the rhythm of their thoughts. The clip-clop of the horses' hooves was like a lullaby as heavy eyes closed and heads nodded. The Mexican desert was no better nor worse than the American desert. All of it was sand and brush hardly taller than their ankles. All of it was harsh.

"Monotony," Duvall said. "That's what the desert is. The same thing over and over again and every time you think it can't go on, you break the horizon and see that it just keeps going."

Marisol found herself daydreaming of a ranch and a cantina and small voices calling "Mami."

Around midday, Pablo said he couldn't sit another minute in the driver's box of his wagon. So they stopped in the middle of the trail.

Marisol drank from her canteen. The water was warm and not refreshing at all. Pablo stretched his legs, walking in a straight line for forty yards or so before turning and coming back.

Duvall dropped down from his saddle and grunted when his feet hit the ground. He leaned against Pecas Gris and stretched his legs.

Marisol nearly fell over when she climbed down from the back of her pony. Her inner thighs felt like fire.

They unsaddled the horses and unhitched the mule team. They poured feed into a small trough and water into another.

"Don't overdo it with that water," Pablo said. "I'd rather put more in there later because they drank it all than have to dump out even a drop of water when we're ready to leave."

They stretched the canvas and Marisol put out a blanket, and she dozed in the hot breeze. Now the flapping of the canvas was the rhythm of her thoughts, and all her thoughts were hot.

They took turns sleeping. Two stayed on watch. It meant none of them got much sleep.

First Marisol slept, and she knew the two men let her sleep longer even though it cut into their sleep. Then Duvall slept. Then Pablo.

When they woke Pablo, Duvall had already collected some sticks to make a fire. Enough to boil some water for coffee. Marisol cooked dinner, but there wasn't anything she could do with beans and bacon other than to make them warm.

It was coming onto dusk now, and Duvall and Pablo were hitching the mules. The animals seemed indifferent to their situation. Stay or go, it didn't seem to matter to them.

Duvall, though, he seemed to be in a rush.

As soon as the mules were hitched and the wagon loaded, Duvall told Pablo to get started.

"Go on and get moving," Duvall said. "We'll catch up to you. And don't light them lanterns."

"What's wrong?" Pablo said.

"I don't know that anything is wrong," Duvall said, seeming agitated. "But I don't know that something's not wrong, neither."

Pablo called to the mules. He snapped his lines. The mules started to pull the wagon.

Duvall turned quickly to the saddles and got Fabiola saddled first, as he always did. While he worked, Marisol scanned the horizon. The change had come over him suddenly, and it worried her.

"What is it Tomás? What is the matter?"

"I don't know," Duvall said, cinching the saddle in place on the piebald pony. "I just have a bad feeling, ever since I woke up. That rig Pablo's driving. That canvas flapping in the breeze. Four mules and two hosses. It all makes for a mighty big sign out in the desert."

Marisol chuckled a little.

"A sign for who to see?"

"We're in Apache country here, Marisol," Duvall said, and his tone shared none of her mirth. "Two men and a woman with a wagon load of goods and hosses to steal? That's a lot for a band of Apache warriors to pass up. Especially if they're hungry. They know we'll have food with us, especially this early on the trail."

Marisol cast her eyes over the horizon, looking in all directions.

"But I don't see anything," she said. "There's nothing out there."

"Well, that's the thing about Apache," Duvall said. "You ain't likely to see them until they want to be seen. And usually, that's when they're right on top of you bashing in your skull."

Marisol's tone also lost its mirth.

"Should we keep moving after dark?" she asked.

"We should. If we keep moving, that might be the only thing that saves us."

"Are you sure they're out there?"

"They're out there," Duvall said. "I ain't sure they've seen us or that they're near us, but they're definitely out there. Now ride on and catch up to Pablo. You stick close to him. Don't leave him. You understand me? Your safety is right there with Pablo."

"What are you doing?"

"I've got to get my hoss saddled. I'll catch you up shortly. There ain't nothing to worry about right now, and I'll be along momentarily."

Duvall held out a hand to help her up into the saddle. Marisol took it and stepped into the stirrup, swung a leg over the back of the pony with a wince from the ache in her thighs. She gave Duvall a last, worried, look.

"Everything's gonna be all right," he said. "Just catch up to Pablo, and I'll be along in a few minutes."

Marisol nodded and dragged a rein to get Fabiola moving.

He lingered some getting Pecas Gris saddled. He watched the horse's expression. Soft ears. Soft nostrils. The hoss didn't sense any danger. Still, Duvall could not shake the feeling that something was wrong, that some threat was just over the horizon in some direction. And then he began to worry that maybe the threat was over the horizon to the north.

It had gotten darker. Still not night, but that gloaming just before the sun fully sets and the darkness from the east begins to take hold. But when he looked north, Duvall could not now see the wagon or Marisol's pony. They'd made good distance, the animals rested. But he wanted to get his eyes back on Pablo and Marisol fast.

He pulled tight the cinch strap and gave the saddle a pull just to be sure it was on well. Then he stepped into the stirrup and swung his leg over. Funny how comfortable he felt getting onto Pecas's back after being so sore getting off earlier.

He urged Pecas forward and then wheeled the horse to face south, just to check their back trail. He reined up, sitting where they were for a moment so he could look over the horizon. And before his eyes adjusted to the dim distance, Duvall noticed Pecas Gris's ears stiffen. The hoss gave a small snort.

And that's when he saw the riders. Too distant to count, but undoubtedly a group of horsemen.

"Dangit," Duvall muttered. "Hope you're ready for a fight, Pecas, because I believe we've got one coming."

27

IT WAS FULL DARK by the time Duvall caught up to Pablo and Marisol, but he didn't need the rattle and clank of the wagon to know he was overtaking them.

"Blow out them danged lights," Duvall called as he neared them. "Didn't I tell you not to light them lanterns?"

He could see Pablo, clear as day, startle and turn in the wagon's seat.

"Ain't no moon yet," Pablo said. "I wanted to make sure I didn't lose the trail."

"Hell, Pablo, I told you not to light them lanterns for a reason," Duvall growled at him. "Get 'em out fast."

They were just going at a quick walk now, and Marisol pushed Fabiola near to Pecas Gris.

"What is it?" she said.

"Riders coming up from the south. They're distant yet, but I saw 'em. No question they're back there."

"Did you say riders, hombre?" Pablo asked.

"Yep. A crowd of 'em, but I didn't hang about to count them."

"Apache?" Pablo asked.

"I don't hardly think so, Pablo."

"Néstor," Marisol breathed.

"Could be him," Duvall said. "He's a danged fool if it is. But it could be him. They were riding with a purpose, I'll say that."

Pablo snapped the lines and called to the mules. Duvall wished that they had a shotgun. If that was Lozano behind them, and if he was going to catch them in the dark, a fight in the dark would be hell. A shotgun would be helpful.

"If this turns into a shooting affair and we start burning powder, you point that pony straight ahead and ride for hell," Duvall told Marisol. "You go and just keep going. When it's done, I'll find you. If they get in front of us and we have to pull up and fight, you get up under Pablo's wagon, and you stay there until daylight. You got that Model 3 in your belt still?"

"I have it," Marisol said. "But I won't leave you."

Duvall shook his head.

"This ain't the time to be stubborn, Marisol. This is the time to stay alive any way you can."

They kept on in the dark. Pablo made those mules move at a steady pace, a quick walk. The moon was slow coming up. It wouldn't be up for another couple of hours, sometime around midnight. The stars gave off light sufficient to follow the trail, but when Duvall twisted around, he could see only a short distance into the black night.

Pablo pushed the mules to keep going. Duvall hoped the animals had the endurance to keep it up.

"They might have stopped and camped," Duvall said, thinking out loud. "Or they could be half a mile behind us."

"If they're half a mile behind us, they don't know we're here," Pablo said.

"I don't know whether to pray for that moon to come on or to pray for cloud cover."

"Cloud cover?" Marisol asked.

"If the moon comes out, we'll have light to know if they're still behind us," Duvall explained.

"But if there's clouds, we won't know one way or the other. But if they are back there, they won't know we're here," Marisol said, catching on.

"That's right," Duvall said.

"I guess I'd rather not know than have them see us and realize we're just in front of them," Marisol said.

"If they decide to break into a gallop, they might ride right into us," Duvall said.

"They could be a hundred yards behind us and we wouldn't know," Pablo agreed.

Another half hour. The mules were tiring. Pecas Gris was tiring, and that hoss had great endurance. The animals were only at a walk now. Out on the eastern horizon, a faint silver glow outlined the peaks of the San Andres Mountains and suggested the moon would be up soon. Another half hour or so, and the moon would be above those peaks, and the night sky was still clear. Another half hour or so, and the landscape would be lit in silvery glow, and if that was Lozano Duvall had seen at dusk and if he was still back there, they might be able to see the wagon and riders in front of them.

"Keep them moving," Duvall said to Pablo. "I'm going to ride back and see if anyone is behind us."

"Oh, Tomás. No. Please don't do that," Marisol said.

"We've got to know. Better to find it out on our own terms. You two keep moving. Don't slow down if you can help it. I'll make sure they don't see me."

"Pablo, talk him out of it," Marisol said.

"No. He's right. If he can sneak around on our backtrail and find them before they happen upon us, it's better."

"I'll be back with you before the moon gets over those mountains to the east," Duvall promised.

DUVALL COULDN'T SAY HOW the Jornado del Muerto was used a hundred years ago. He knew it was a Spanish highway from Mexico City, the route travelers and freight took to reach the northern portions of the Spanish territory. He envisioned long, meandering trains of wagons filled with bolts of cloth and casks of everything from liquor to lamp oil to ink, tools and gunpowder; he believed these wagon trains were accompanied by black-robed Catholic priests with long strides, mounted cavalry, dogs and goats. He didn't know, though. He didn't know who traveled this road a hundred years ago, or how they traveled, or why they traveled.

But in recent years, since this road became part of the United States, Duvall knew that it was mostly cattle that traveled this road. Most freight that reached Mesilla and the frontier forts around the Rio Grande came by way of Texas and into El Paso.

The cattle that used the trail in recent decades, they cut a wide swath, grazing on the greasewood at the edges of the trail, stamping down any vegetation with their heavy hooves. They came from the northeastern reaches of the territory, where they grazed across miles and miles of open land. They went to the forts and the reservations where the federal government paid good prices if a rancher knew which hands to grease with bribes.

That wide swath of trail cut by the cattle and the centuries of black-robed Catholic priests showed up plain at night. The greasewood to the left and right of the trail made the ground appear black, even in the light of a full moon. But the light sand of the road shone white or silver, even with just a sliver of moonlight, and made passage at night easy.

Duvall directed Pecas Gris into the black of the greasewood, but the horse balked at walking where he could not see.

"All right," Duvall whispered. "I'll lead you."

He slipped down from the saddle, took a firm grip on the reins up near the horse's chin, and led Pecas Gris away from the road.

There was no hill to hide behind. No bush tall or wide enough to obscure a man and a horse. The best Duvall could do to avoid being seen by anyone coming up the trail was to walk far enough away to blend into the dark and then hope that moon didn't rise too fast and illuminate the whole landscape.

He kept the freckled-gray horse close. He could feel the horse's warm breath on his neck.

Even at night, the desert was never completely quiet.

A coyote's call. An owl. Some lizard scuttling through the brush. The ever present wind cutting across the landscape.

Pecas Gris pushed his head over Duvall's shoulder. Duvall wrapped his arm under the horse's head and scratch Pecas's cheek and keep a calming hand on the horse.

So he heard it clearly when the horse's breathing made a sudden change. Pecas had gone on alert. Without looking back, Duvall reached a hand up and gave a scratch at the horse's ear. The ear had gone stiff.

"It's okay," Duvall whispered. "Best to stay quiet."

And then Duvall heard the voices. He couldn't see anything, but he was sure it wasn't the wind he heard now.

Then the sound became clearer as it grew nearer. Men talking. A moment later, he was sure they were speaking Spanish.

Now he could hear the footfalls from their horses. Weak. Slow. Horses were suffering from exhaustion. Lack of water, lack of decent grazing.

Lozano had driven his men and his horses up the Jornado del Muerto without supplying first. He'd hardly given them a rest at Mesilla.

The horses wouldn't make it to the malpais – the massive black-rock lava field at the top of the Jornado del Muerto. Duvall could hear it in their steps. The men probably were not in much better shape.

Even as he waited for them to get nearer, Duvall could see a sliver of the moon appear over the mountains to the east. He'd stepped far enough off the trail with Pecas Gris that he didn't worry about Lozano's men seeing him. He also didn't mind them passing by him. At most, Marisol and Pablo were half an hour ahead of these men. When that moon rose fully, Lozano and his men would probably be able to see the wagon on the northern horizon.

Duvall waited, whispering calmly to Pecas Gris to try to keep the horse settled. A snort might not give him away. If Lozano's men were tired enough, they might not even realize that it hadn't come from one of their horses. But Duvall didn't want to chance it.

"We're okay, boy," Duvall whispered. "They got no idea we're here, and we want to keep it that way."

He'd hoped to get a glimpse of them, to be able to count their numbers. But there wasn't enough moonlight yet for that. He did see a shadow or two pass in front of him – a spot of blackness against the blackness of the desert night.

The voices had stopped now. He'd caught the tail end of some conversation.

And then the footfalls of the horses grew quiet and distant.

They'd passed him by, and Lozano and his men were now between Duvall and Marisol. But that was fine. Duvall knew where they were, and that's what he'd come back here for. A bit more of the moon shone above the peaks, now.

He would have to break his promise to Marisol to rejoin them before the moon was fully in the sky.

He waited a minute or two. He took his prayerbook from a pocket and ripped out a sheet. He spread tobacco from his pouch across the crease he'd made. His fingers moved easily in the dark. He probably didn't even spill any of the tobacco. He rolled the cigarette and put it in the corner of his mouth.

He struck a match, keeping it concealed behind his cupped hand, and he lit the smoke.

"We'll go in a minute," Duvall told the horse.

He drew on the cigarette and blew smoke out in front of him. It caught the moonlight, looking like white light for just a second before the wind caught it and scattered it into nothing. Pecas Gris gave him a nudge with his head, nearly knocking Duvall's hat to the ground.

"In a minute."

He drew on the cigarette again and blew deliberately right at the moon. Now the smoke did glow white before the wind whipped it away.

Duvall fixed his hat so that it rode on his head like he liked it.

Something like a plan began to form in his mind. It challenged his first instincts and then waged war. Fight or flight?

They could run. Pecas Gris and Fabiola were rested, at least a little rested. They were fed and watered. Pablo's mules, too.

Duvall could circle around ahead of Lozano, catch up to Fabiola and Marisol. The three of them – even with the wagon – could push their animals hard through the rest of the night and into the morning. They could widen that distance between them and Lozano. Probably by midday, Lozano would find his horses had nothing left to give. A smart man would turn back. If he kept on, the horses would die and the men would soon follow. Either way, without firing a shot, Duvall and Marisol and Pablo would be safe.

Or he could fight it out.

And that was the plan forming.

How close could he stay to Lozano and his men, riding behind them? Fifty yards? Thirty yards?

Exhausted men didn't waste the energy to check their backtrail. Duvall could wait, and either when the moonlight was right or at the first crack of dawn, he could make a charge on his own. He was good with a rifle and pistol. He could get in among them, and in the chaos he could probably bring down two or three of them right away. Enough confusion, and maybe he could take four or five men before they ever recovered from the surprise and started fighting back.

What then?

He'd gotten good at killing. Truth is, he'd always been good at it. It seemed a terrible skill to possess, but it was there all the same.

Anyway, it was something like a plan beginning to form, but it wasn't fully formed yet.

Duvall took another drag from his cigarette and then dropped it at his feet. He stepped on it and then got up into the saddle. He gave Pecas a pat on the neck.

"Be cool and we'll get out of this," he promised the horse. Then he bent down and drew the rifle from its scabbard. He lowered the lever a bit to check the chamber, twisting the rifle into the growing light of the moon. Brass glinted inside.

"Yaw," Duvall called softly to the horse, and he pressed his right knee into Pecas's shoulder.

Pecas gave a little blow and turned left, turned to the north, to follow in the wake of Lozano and his men.

The moon slid up a little higher. It broke beyond the peak of the mountain.

His eyes already adjusted to the night, and now with some added light, Duvall could see a black mass up ahead of him. Riders moving on the road. He couldn't make them out. They were indistinguishable one from the other, but he was within sight of the group of them. He'd ride here until the first gray light of morning, and then he'd charge into them. Maybe. That was the plan beginning to form in his mind. But he knew that plan came from a place of exhaustion – a place of desperately wanting this to be over.

But maybe that's what he'd do.

"WE SHOULD WAIT FOR Tomás," Marisol said to Pablo.

"No. Duvall knows what he's doing. He told us to keep going."

"He also told us that he would be back before the moon was up." Marisol looked over her right shoulder. The half-moon had cleared the peak. The blackness of the sky was clear between moon and mountaintop.

"He was just saying that so you wouldn't worry," Pablo said. "Duvall is fine. If they caught him, we'd have heard shooting."

"That doesn't comfort me," Marisol said.

Pablo chuckled.

"Trust him," Pablo said. "The truth of it is, the only thing between us and getting killed – or worse – is Tommy Duvall. It's best to let him do what he thinks he needs to do."

The mules slowed as they began to climb a small hill. Its slant was all but imperceptible. But Pablo felt them slow. He gave his lines a snap and puckered his lips to make calls at the mules to keep them moving. "Come on, keep it going," Pablo called.

The mules answered the call, getting a little pep in them as they went up the easy slope.

Marisol fell behind a bit, and she clicked her tongue to get Fabiola to catch up. She hardly noticed they were climbing a hill at all. But in the light of the moon, she could see the horizon begin to stretch out some as they reached a point of vantage on the long and level landscape.

GUILLERMO GOMEZ SAID, "THE horses cannot go on like this."

Néstor Lozano gave a start. He'd been dozing in the saddle, and Guillermo's words hit him like a thunder clap, startling him awake.

"Is that right, Guillermo?" Lozano said. "Would you have me turn back, then? Should we tuck our tails like whipped dogs and turn back for Mexico. Should we go to Señor Arellano and tell him that we failed to recover Marisol and we failed to recover his gold and we failed to bring him the gringo's head?"

Guillermo sighed heavily.

"I'm not saying that we should go back to Mexico," he said. "But you have to see the evidence in front of you, Néstor. The horses cannot keep going. Even riding at night and stopping during the day, the horses are too weak to keep on. And we have no idea how far we must go before we get to water. We are poorly supplied for this journey."

"You are weak, Guillermo. You are weak and you lack the instinct to be successful. I could lay my failures at your feet, but I am not that sort of man. I am in command here, and I will accept responsibility for your failures. But I will also lead us to success. A successful man does not give up because he faces obstacles. A successful man presses on."

"Si, Néstor," Guillermo agreed. "But the horses are exhausted."

"Then we will shoot the horses and go on foot!" Lozano snapped at him.

"The men are exhausted," Guillermo said.

"Then we will shoot them men and take with us only those who are strong enough to fight off exhaustion. Shall I shoot you first, Guillermo?"

Guillermo dragged his reins a touch to step his horse away from Lozano's. He did not offer any reply. He also felt it would be worth it – let Lozano shoot him. At least then he would not have to continue to suffer the abuse the man hurled at him.

The moon was finally coming up, finally giving them some light. But what would they do come morning? When the sun directed its scorching heat down on the men and animals. Lozano would insist they keep moving to catch the gringo, but the horses physically couldn't do it. Guillermo knew horses, and he believed they were killing these animals. There wouldn't be a horse left that could be ridden by noon.

Guillermo had half a mind to wheel his horse now, turn back. Get back to water and feed. Get to a place where the horse could rest. And if Lozano shot him in the back, then so bet it. Any fate seemed better than the one Guillermo saw in front of him. In front of him he saw only a terrible death. He lifted his canteen and gave it a small shake. He still had more than half the canteen. He had been careful not to drink too much, though now he could have turned that canteen on its head and drank fully from it.

He was so thirsty.

And tired.

None of the men had slept in days now.

And then one of the men called out.

"Señor!"

Guillermo turned his head and saw that the man was pointing ahead at something on the horizon. Guillermo squinted his eyes into the darkness, and he saw it too.

The ground rose ahead, and at the precipice of a small hill, a wagon and a rider, lit by the silver moonshine.

"It's them!" Lozano called. He gave a shout, a guttural shout, and Lozano used the ends of his reins to whip his horse forward – a final burst of energy.

At first, none of the men moved. Lozano charged forward without giving an order to follow him. Exhausted men on exhausted horses did not react. But then one or two of them gave a shout to their mounts, and then the whole crowd of them dashed forward. And Guillermo, who had no desire for it, followed them because he did not know what else to do.

28

DUVALL HEARD ONE OF the men in that black mass ahead of him give a shout of surprise.

He did not see what they saw, but neither did he wonder what they'd seen.

"Haw!" Duvall called to Pecas, and he leaned forward. The hoss sensed the rider's tension, felt the energy – and responded.

Pecas Gris dashed into a gallop, and in moments, the freckled-gray passed by one of Lozano's men. He came up so fast, that Duvall hadn't even seen him until he was right on top of him. Maybe the man was sitting still, waiting for something, but suddenly he was there, and then he was in Duvall's dust.

Duvall's attention was on the men at the gallop in front of him. Those were the ones who would get to Marisol ahead of him if he couldn't stop them. He'd worry about that one later. Now that mass in front of him began to take shape. He could distinguish an individual rider from the rest of the group. He tried to count them – four or five. No. One just became two. There were six of them. Again, no. There was one out ahead of the others. Seven.

Seven ahead of him and one behind.

Now, Duvall could see what they'd seen. Marisol and Pablo at the top of a small rise up ahead. Glowing like a beacon.

And then Duvall was coming up on those at the back of the group. He'd overtake the first of them in just a moment. He stretched out his arm, rifle in a firm grip. He was just feet behind the man. The man's back so near to the muzzle of the Yellow Boy that Duvall could not miss. He squeezed the trigger.

The crack of the rifle ripped across the desert floor. So loud in that thick silence, that Duvall could almost head the thunderclap of the Winchester echo from mountain range to mountain range and back again.

The man he'd shot fell away from the race. If he was unsaddled or killed or still in the fight, Duvall didn't know. All he knew was that the man's horse pulled up and dashed off to the right like it was going into the desert.

He shoved the reins into his mouth, clutching them between his front teeth. Now he gripped the forestock with his left hand and dropped the lever with his right.

This was the plan forming in his mind now forced into action. He swung to the rifle to his left as Pecas Gris overtook another horse and rider. Duvall aimed down the barrel of the rifle. With each stride, Pecas Gris bounced him up and down so that gaining his target was nearly impossible. The man, too, bounced in his own saddle. Duvall couldn't steady the rifle to get a clear shot. The front rider was less than a hundred yards from the wagon now. There wasn't time for perfect. Duvall would have to settle for close enough and hope for the best.

He squeezed the trigger and knew he'd missed his shot. He dropped the lever and tried again, a fast shot that also missed. Now the man realized the shooting he'd heard was directed at him. He reigned up and Pecas Gris dashed past.

But Duvall didn't have time to worry that he now had at least two men in fighting shape in his wake. He was already coming even with another rider – this one he would pass by with horse and rider on his right side.

Duvall didn't even try to take the shot. Pecas Gris was so close that Duvall could feel the horse's back shoulder brush against his leg. He gripped the rifle tight in both hands and jabbed it like a club, the rifle butt smashing into the side of the man's head. The man fell from his saddle in a heap, but the riderless horse kept running right along with the others, the empty stirrup brushing against Duvall's shin as Pecas Gris passed by the horse.

This was the chaos he'd anticipated.

All around him now, horses and men. Duvall aimed at a rider directly in front of him. Unconsciously, he squeezed the trigger, not even realizing he was doing it. The man reared up and then slumped forward.

Now there were just three – two men very near him, and one out ahead, whipping his horse and seemingly oblivious to the threat coming behind him.

Duvall swung his rifle to get a shot at the man on his left, but he felt a hand grab at his shoulder and clutch a wad of his coat. And then an almighty jerk.

Duvall felt the reins pull away from his teeth.

He felt the sensation of being upside down in the air. A tremendous crash. He was on his back on the ground, all the air rushing out of him so that he was choking on nothing.

A horse running with the pack came past, its hoof nearly colliding with his face. Duvall made a terrible sound as he tried to get a breath and couldn't. Tears like fire welled in the corners of his eyes.

Horses stomping all around and men shouting.

Duvall tried for another breath, but still he could not get any wind.

Néstor Lozano knew something was going on behind him, but his attention would not be diverted.

He heard some shots and shouted over his shoulder to stop shooting.

"We must take the gringo alive!"

But he still his hand swung the reins against the horse's rump.

"¡Ándale! ¡Ándale!" he shouted.

The wagon was picking up speed, the driver rushing to get away, but the rider had wheeled the horse and was turning to face him. Lozano dragged his revolver clear of its holster and fired a shot into the air. But the man in the wagon kept going, the four-mule team at a run now. And as he came even with the rider, Lozano swung out with his revolver and felt his hand strike the face of the rider.

If he'd realized it before he didn't know, but as his hand struck, he realized that was Marisol Rosales.

She let out a cry and fell from the saddle, and Lozano reined up, wheeling his exhausted horse. He thought it must be the gringo in the wagon, and if Marisol was on the ground, then the gringo would stop and come back for her. He had them both, now.

Lozano leapt out of the saddle. His dander up, his anger propelling him.

Marisol was on her back on the ground, grunting and struggling with her leg. At first, Lozano thought maybe she had broken her leg in the fall from the horse, but then he realized she was wrenching a revolver from its holster. And then she had it free and was bringing it toward him. But Lozano was above her now, and he reached down and grabbed her by the wrist and turned her wrist until she squealed and dropped the gun.

He felt the fullness of his strength when he turned it on a person so much weaker.

Lozano jerked Marisol from the ground and then slung her down again. Riders were coming up now, reining in. He looked over his shoulder, and just as he expected, the gringo had stopped the wagon about forty yards beyond them. In the moonlight, Lozano could see the gringo jump from the wagon, a rifle in hand.

"Get him!" Lozano shouted to the two riders who had just come up level with him.

One of them started to urge his horse forward, but the crack of a rifle stopped him. Both men got down from their horses. They took up their own rifles and began firing into the darkness at the man ahead of them.

Lozano, though, turned his attention immediately back to the woman.

He grabbed her by the arms and dragged her to her feet. Holding her with one hand, he slapped her across the face.

"I will teach you to respect me!" he shouted at her.

He gave her another slap that knocked her to the ground again.

Now Lozano looked around. His fury overcame him. He'd stopped thinking about Señor Arellano's gold or taking Marisol back to her father. He just wanted to quench his wrath.

He heard the shots his men were trading with the gringo.

He'd run from the wagon, into the brush. He was harder to see there. The two men were shooting into the darkness, but each time they fired a volley, the gringo got off another shot. And now, with a crack of the rifle, one of Lozano's men went down with a grunt.

"I'm hit!" he said, clutching at his belly. "I'm shot!"

Lozano ignored him. He grabbed the other man by the shoulder and pushed him forward.

"Go!" Lozano said. "Go down there and get him. He is one man! Go and get him and bring him back to me alive."

Lozano gave the man a push, but he only stumbled a few feet forward before the gringo's rifle barked. The man doubled over and fell to the ground. He didn't make a sound, but his heels dug trenches in the sand.

Lozano wheeled himself around.

"Where is everyone else?" he demanded. He had no idea what had happened behind him. His eyes searched the darkness for the other riders. He saw a two horses with no riders. And then he saw Guillermo and another of his men coming up, their horses at a walk.

Lozano pointed back behind him, down toward the wagon.

"Go and kill that man!" he shouted.

The other man drew his rifle from its scabbard and kicked his horse forward. But Guillermo did not move.

And then Lozano's eyes fell on the freckled gray horse with the black mane. The gringo's horse. And then Lozano saw the gringo on the ground, gasping for breath.

He turned and looked into the darkness ahead, in the direction of the man he thought was the gringo. His soldier charging forward on his horse. Lozano watched just long enough to hear the crack of the rifle and see his man rear back before slumping forward.

Nothing made sense to him now. Lozano's head felt like it would explode.

"It does not matter," Lozano said.

He stormed forward, grabbing Marisol by the wrist. She tried to get her feet under her, but Lozano dragged her so that she fell over, and then he dragged her through the dirt. She struggled, trying to jerk her wrist free from him. He turned and wrapped an arm under her belly and lifted her, carrying her now. And though she squirmed and twisted, she could not get free. And then Lozano tossed her on the ground beside the gringo.

The gringo seemed to be in some pain as he gasped for breath. Lozano saw no blood on him that would suggest he was shot, but the man clearly struggled.

He reached down and pulled loose the leather thong holding the gringo's converted Colt in its holster, and then he pulled the Colt free. He cocked back the hammer and pointed it at the gringo's face.

"Now you will learn what happens to a man who steals from Señor Manuel Arellano Hermosillio," Lozano said. "I give you one chance. You tell me now where the gold is buried, or I will shoot –"

Lozano stopped and looked at Marisol.

"Her."

He swung the gun to his right, pointing it down at Marisol. Then he dropped down, driving a knee into her chest and putting the gun directly against her head, pushing her head with the barrel of the Colt so that she was looking right at Duvall.

"One chance before I open her skull and spread her brain all over you," Lozano said. "Where is the gold?"

THE TEARS BURNED RUNNING down over his temples. Duvall wheezed, trying to draw a breath. He had no air with which to force out the words.

"Guadalupe Victoria!" he shouted, but the words only formed in his mind.

He could see in Néstor Lozano's eyes that the man was on the verge of killing – that the man wanted to kill. His eyes shone with his blood lust. But Duvall couldn't force out the words. And the muzzle of the Colt pressed against Marisol's face.

And when he heard the sharp report of the revolver, Duvall flinched and looked away.

He wanted to kill and he wanted to die. For all the pain in his lungs, it was nothing to the way his heart ripped itself in two in his chest.

And Duvall felt the hands cradle his face.

"Tomás," Marisol said. "Look at me, Tomás. Are you hurt?"

Guillermo Gomez stepped over and with his knee nudged Marisol away from Duvall. He grabbed Duvall's belt with his free hand and hefted him up at the waist, holding him there for a moment until Duvall suddenly felt the air in his lungs again.

"He's had the breath knocked out of him," Guillermo said. "When he fell from his horse. That is all. Give him a moment and he will be fine."

Guillermo dropped Duvall's belt, but Duvall was breathing now.

Guillermo stepped over to Lozano and with the toe of his boot rolled the dead man onto his back. Guillermo cocked the revolver in his hand and pointed it at Lozano's head. He squeezed the trigger, sending another bullet into Lozano's skull.

"He's a bastard, and he will rot in hell," Guillermo said.

Marisol looked at Guillermo with her mouth ajar.

"You saved us," she said.

"No," Guillermo said. "I saved myself."

29

By morning, all of Néstor Lozano's men were dead except Guillermo Gomez. Most of them died in turns over night. The three men who Pablo shot lingered on for hours. Nothing could be done for them. Two of the three were gut shot, and they lingered until nearly sunup. But even applying bandages, the blood could not be stopped sufficiently.

"It's probably better for them that way," Guillermo concluded. "Had they not bled out, they would have died over weeks in terrible pain as their insides rotted."

The third man Pablo shot, the one on the horse, he took a bullet to the neck and was dead by the time anyone checked on him.

Guillermo Gomez, of course, had dispatched Néstor Lozano with two bullets to the head, the second one unnecessary.

Duvall had killed two men, shooting them in the back. They were also dead before anyone found them, but they weren't found until morning when the sun was up.

The man Duvall bashed with his rifle, Guillermo decided that man must have broken his neck when he fell from the horse. He was never conscious, but he continued to breathe through most of the night. Sometime just before dawn, Pablo noticed that he was no longer breathing.

They collected most of the horses, but two of them had run off into the desert.

Pablo and Guillermo gave the remaining horses some feed and some water and tethered them to let them rest.

"What made you do it?" Marisol asked Guillermo as the sun's rays first appeared over the eastern mountain range.

"He was a bad man," Guillermo said with a shrug. "He was never the right man to be in charge of Santa Catalina. We are not like Juárez there. When he put that gun to your head – I'd just had enough of him."

"What will you tell my father?" Marisol asked.

"I will tell him the gringo killed Néstor," Guillermo said. "Or I will tell him the wolves got Néstor in the desert. Or I will just say that Néstor is not coming back and leave it at that."

"What will you tell my father about me?" Marisol said.

Guillermo shot a look at Duvall who stood nearby and wondered if the gringo spoke any Spanish.

"You can come back with me," Guillermo tried. "Come back with me and we will tell your father that the gringo took you against your will. We will tell a story that absolves you from all of this. And you can be with me."

"I will not do that, Guillermo," Marisol said. "I'm with him now, and that's where I will stay."

Guillermo's face fell, but he did not appear entirely surprised.

"Si. Then I will tell your father that you are not coming back, either."

Marisol gave a small nod.

"Tell him he should look after these hosses," Duvall said. "As soon as he gets back to Leasburg at Fort Selden, he should put these hosses in a livery for two or three days. Get them fed and rested."

"I speak English, gringo," Guillermo said.

Duvall shrugged.

"Look after these hosses," he said.

They dragged the bodies some distance into the desert. Seven of them. Pablo had a shovel on the wagon, and they used that to throw sand over the bodies. But they all knew that within a day or two the coyotes would dig those bodies up and scatter them in pieces across the Jornado del Muerto, and the buzzards would finish what the coyotes left.

"I feel like I should thank you, par'ner," Duvall said.

"What I did, I did not do for you," Guillermo said. "I thought about shooting you after. Maybe I should have."

"Maybe," Duvall said with a shrug. "And maybe I should thank you for not shooting me."

Guillermo cast a look at Marisol.

"What I did, I did not do for you."

At midmorning, Guillermo Gomez with a string of horses started south for Leasburg, understanding that Pablo never made it to Juárez and that the only people left alive who knew where to find Señor Arellano's gold were bound to the other end of this restless trail, taking that knowledge with them. What did he care about a rich man's gold?

"We'll ride through the afternoon today and camp at night," Duvall announced as Pablo got into the wagon and took hold of his lines.

"You ain't worried about the Apache?" Pablo asked over his shoulder.

"Hell, Pablo, if there's Apache out there – and we know there are – and they saw how you handled these old boys last night, I expect them Apache will leave us alone."

The animals did well, even in the heat of the day. The mules kept a good walk going. Pecas Gris and Fabiola didn't seem to mind the heat too much if all they were asked to do was walk.

Duvall was drenched in sweat by the time dusk rolled around, and Marisol and Pablo were no different.

But when she finally stepped out of the saddle, Marisol was smiling.

"What are you so happy about?" Duvall asked.

"Look around us," she said.

Duvall scanned the horizon quickly and then gave her a shrug.

"Desert," he said.

"Si, Tomás. But it is grass, not the scrub brush. What do you call it?"

"Greasewood," Duvall said.

"Si. That is it. It's grass, and you said when I saw grass I would know that we were getting close. Getting close to home."

30

Hazel Bassett saw the riders coming from down in the pasture and watched them as they neared the cabin. It was not Jorge and Maria, that was easy to see. One of the riders was on a big gray with a black mane and tail. The other rider was on a smaller, piebald pony. Hazel's initial fears diminished some when she saw that it was a woman on the piebald. A woman and a man probably meant no harm.

She put the baby down in the bassinet as they got closer, and she met them outside the cabin as they hitched their animals to the post.

"Ma'am?" the man said, taking off his hat. He had long hair, but his whiskers looked freshly trimmed. "You wouldn't happen to be Mrs. Bassett, would you?"

The woman with him was very pretty. She looked to be Spanish – dark eyes and black hair, but very beautiful. The sort of woman who could make a woman who'd just had a baby feel very jealous.

"Yes. My name is Hazel Bassett," Hazel said.

"Ma'am, my name is Duvall. Tommy Duvall, and this here is Marisol Rosales. I was wondering if I could have a word?"

"Certainly, Mr. Duvall. The baby is inside asleep."

"Yes, ma'am. That's nice to hear. I've come to talk to you about your husband."

Hazel took a breath.

"Well, then, maybe you'd better come inside."

Duvall took the saddlebags off his horse and hung them on his shoulder, and he and Marisol followed Hazel Bassett inside the cabin.

"Is my husband dead, Mr. Duvall?" Hazel asked as the three of them sat down around a kitchen table.

Duvall winced. He'd not been planning to say it outright like that. "Yes, ma'am."

"How did he die?"

Duvall had already made up his mind, and told Marisol, that he wasn't going to tell this woman more than she needed to know. And she didn't need to know that.

"Me and Bassett – your husband – and some other fellers, we went to work down in Mexico. And Bassett died down there doing the job."

"Mexico?" Hazel asked. He might as well have said Timbuktu. She'd not expected that. She was less surprised to learn that he was dead. In fact, it almost came as a relief to her now.

"He never said anything to me about a job in Mexico."

"No, ma'am."

"I just don't understand why he would've gone all the way to Mexico and not tell me before he left."

"Well, it was a hurry-up sort of thing," Duvall said uncomfortably. "Short notice, if you know what I mean. We all left out of Las Vegas pretty quick."

"He didn't even write to me."

Duvall nodded his head, wondering if he'd made a mistake in coming here.

"The job went well," Duvall said. "We was paid admirably for the work we done. And I brought to you Bassett's wages."

The baby made a noise and Hazel went to the bassinet and picked up the baby. Then she came back and sat down again, bouncing the baby in her arms.

"He didn't meant to cause you hardship," Duvall said. "His idea, as I reckon you understand, was to try to make things better. It was a big opportunity we had in Mexico."

"He missed the mark on that. We've been living off of the charity of our neighbors," Hazel said.

"Well, you ought not have to do that anymore," Duvall said. "There's money enough here to put you on feet."

He reached into the saddlebag and took out one of the gold bars and set it down on the table in front of Mrs. Bassett. Then he took out the other one. And then he set down a sack of gold coins.

"Them gold bars are both worth something around six hundred dollars," Duvall said. "And I think it's another two hundred or so in that sack. It ain't the fortune Bassett went after down in Mexico, but I guess that job fell short of all of our expectations."

The woman sat for some time looking at the gold bars. She didn't have to say it was more money than she'd ever seen at one time in her entire life. Duvall already knew that. It was more money than most folks would ever see all in one place in their lives. Enough there that if she was careful, maybe it would last her eight or ten years without ever lifting a finger to add to it. If she took on some light work – seamstress work or housekeeping or something of the sort – she'd probably still have some of that money left when she went off to join her husband in the grave.

At last she looked up at him.

"What kind of work was my husband doing in Mexico?"

Duvall gave his head a small nod and glanced at Marisol.

"We rode down to Mexico to do some railroad work, ma'am."

"Railroad work pays more than twelve-hundred dollars? And it didn't meet your expectations?" Her tone was something beyond dubious. It was disapproving.

"Well, that's why we was all so eager to take the job. The pay was supposed to have been even better than that."

Hazel Bassett stared at the gold bars a few moments longer.

"I don't know what to say, Mr. Duvall. You could have easily kept this money for yourself and never brought it here, and I guess I'm grateful to you. You'll forgive me if I seem cold. I've long since given up on Mr. Bassett ever returning, and a part of me hoped that he was dead. If he wasn't dead somewhere, then that just simply meant he'd run out on me and our baby. And that would have been hard to bear. As terrible as it is to say – your news almost comes with some relief."

"You ain't got to explain nothing to me," Duvall said. "For what it's worth, there for several days down in Mexico, me and Bassett shared a room at a hotel. And we got to know each other a little bit. And I wanted to let you know – for what it's worth – he was awful high on you and that baby. Talked about you a lot. All he wanted to do was finish up that job in Mexico and then get on back here to his family."

Hazel Bassett's eyes became moist, and she blinked several times.

"Thank you for telling me that," she said. "You were with him when he died?"

"No, ma'am. I was with him all through the days leading up to it, but I wasn't there when it happened."

"And will you tell me what happened to him?"

Duvall shifted and looked at Marisol.

"May I hold your baby?" Marisol said.

Hazel smiled through the tears now sliding down her cheeks.

"Certainly."

Hazel held the baby out, and Marisol stood up and took the baby in her arms. She stood with the child, swaying gently and making cooing noises.

"I can't speak to the details," Duvall said. "I wasn't there when it happened. All I can say is that I appreciated knowing him. I thought a lot of him in the short time we was par'nered up."

Hazel nodded her head.

"Well, I thank you for that, Mr. Duvall."

Duvall waited, counting in his head. He wasn't sure how to change the subject.

"Ma'am, I had a tough time finding you. Not a lot of people know who you are."

"Mr. Bassett and I were here only since last summer. Not even a full year yet."

"Yes, ma'am. When I finally did find someone who could point me in your direction, it was Ben Callahan who did it."

"Yes. Mr. Callahan. He was kind enough to buy what cattle we still had."

"Ben tells me you're headed back to Chicago?"

"Yes, that's right. Just last week I received some assistance from my parents who are paying for my trip home."

"And what are you going to do with this place?" Duvall asked.

"The cabin?" Hazel asked, surprised. The cabin wasn't much.

"Yes, ma'am. The cabin. The land you've got here."

"I suppose, Mr. Duvall, I am going to just leave it."

Duvall looked out the open door. He could see the Sapello River running through the pasture down below the house. It smelt of pines up here, and the breeze blew pleasant through the windows and open door. Whatever else he'd done or not done, Bassett had found a good place to build a cabin.

Marisol pressed her lips against the baby's head.

"Her hair is so soft," she said.

Hazel smiled.

"Do you have children, Miss Rosales?"

"Not yet," Marisol said with a grin at Duvall.

"Well, you seem to be a natural with them."

"Would you sell this place to me?" Duvall asked. "I'd pay you a fair price for it."

"Do you plan to raise cattle, Mr. Duvall?"

"I do. And Marisol wants to open a cantina in the village yonder." Hazel nodded her head.

"Yes. I suppose this place would be perfect for the two of you. Do you know about cattle, Mr. Duvall?"

"I do, ma'am. I've worked for some years at Ben Callahan's place."

"My husband didn't know much about cattle." Hazel nodded her head. "Of course, Mr. Duvall. If you would like to buy this place, I'd be happy to sell it, and glad to know it's going to good people."

"I can't speak to how good I am, Miss Bassett, but I'm honestly trying."

Outside, at the post, as they unhitched the horses, Marisol stopped what she was doing and wrapped her arms around Duvall.

"So that's it?" she said.

"That's it," Duvall said. "Next week she goes to Chicago, and you and me can move in."

Marisol smiled brilliantly at him.

"It took a lot for us to get here, Tomás. We lost a lot and went through too much. But I'm going to spend the rest of my life making sure you believe that it was all worthwhile. Every bit of it. Like we promised each other. We'll go through whatever we have to together. And now we're home."

the end

but there's more to come ...

Thank you so much for riding home with Duvall and Marisol and Pablo. I sincerely hope you enjoyed the journey. But the story ain't over yet. Tommy Duvall and Pablo left something behind in Old Mexico. How long can it be before they decide to go back and fetch it?

For your first look at Chapter 1 of the third book in the Restless Trail trilogy, flip the page and read the first chapter of "Back on the Restless Trail."

FIRST LOOK

BACK ON THE RESTLESS TRAIL

Señor Manuel Arellano Hermosillio took a tentative step forward, placing just the tip of his boot on the wooden step.

"Come, Señor Arellano, we have erected this podium just for you."

The man smiled at him, one arm stretched out ushering him up the steps, the other arm pressing into Señor Arellano's back, urging him forward.

"Your audience is gathered for you. Please do not make them wait."

Señor Arellano swallowed hard and looked out across the crowd. Many soldiers. Some politicians. A few civilians, fewer than he might have expected.

"Si," Señor Arellano said, giving his head a small nod.

"Do you have a speech prepared?" the man asked him as he placed his foot down on the next step.

"I have thought about what I would like to say," Arellano said. "But I do not think anyone in this crowd came here today to hear me speak. So I will keep it brief."

"Si. I think that is for the best. A brief statement will be better remembered than something rambling."

Señor Arellano took the steps deliberately, one at a time, placing his feet carefully so that he did not slip. When he reached the top, he walked to the edge of the podium and stood there for a moment, taking in the scene. He stood on a platform erected for this moment at the edge of a plaza in Mexico City. A crowd had gathered, but not as large a crowd as it would have been if they were in Juárez. That was Señor Arellano's home and had been for all of his life. Were they in Juárez, the crowd would have swelled to thousands, most of them admirers and supporters. Many of them would have served on his payroll at one time or another. Some, certainly, would have been enemies or people who hated him for his success. But a man who rises to the upper reaches of politics in a country such as Mexico cannot avoid being hated by some.

Many of those in the audience were soldiers. They seemed so young. Just boys with fresh faces. Most of them lounged, though a few stood erect, almost at attention. Here and there were officers, but their indifference was palpable, even from the podium.

Others in the plaza were politicians or lawyers, men who had an interest in such things. Very few women or children, though here and there he saw a few watching with curiosity.

Under other circumstances, perhaps, Señor Arellano could have put on a show for the people of Ciudad de México. He could have entertained them, enthralled them. He was good at public speaking. But today he did not feel like entertaining.

"What I've done, I've done for Mexico!" he shouted from the podium. He wasn't sure if people very far out in the plaza could hear him. His voice sounded weak, so he tried it again. "I did what I believe in my heart was best for the people of my country. I make no apologies."

He started to say something else, but the crowd seemed as indifferent as he felt. This was not the show they came for.

A man does not lose one million dollars worth of gold quietly.

It had been five years now since Señor Arellano attempted to start a revolution that would have seen him made El Presidente. He would have gone from being the most powerful man in the State of Chihuahua to being the most powerful man in Mexico. The most powerful man in Central America.

He had made the right alliances. He had secured the right promises from the right men. He had bought guns and ammunition. He had orders for more, thousands of guns were to come from factories in America. And he sent a wagon loaded with a million dollars worth of gold to Monterrey as payment to the top generals and officers of the Mexican army. They were going to lead their men in revolt, and when it was all over, Señor Arellano would be made the political leader of Mexico. Overnight.

And then a handful of gringos with the help of traitors — though Señor Arellano was never perfectly clear about who those traitors were — ambushed the wagon of gold and stole not just the money and the first of the guns but they also stole Mexico's future.

"There is so much I could have done for this country," Señor Arellano muttered, but no one in the crowd heard him.

They stole his future.

And the gringo that led this band of outlaws, he stole Señor Arellano's own daughter. Lovely Marisol. Of all of his children — those he claimed and those he did not — Marisol Rosales was his favorite. Not only because she was so beautiful that she reminded him of her mother, but also because of her happy spirit. A happy spirit that made other people happy. A lovely girl, now living in America somewhere with the gringo who destroyed everything.

"Is that all you have to say, Señor Arellano?" the man asked.

Señor Arellano took a heavy breath.

A man does not lose one million dollars in gold without people knowing about it.

Even before that gringo was across the border with his gold, seemingly everyone in Chihuahua knew about it.

And when one million dollars worth of gold gets stolen, people begin asking questions. Why would Señor Arellano have been shipping gold to Monterrey? What did he intend to buy with that gold? To whom was it going?

And enemies who were supposed to be friends show up.

He went for four years, trying to regain his lost wealth. Not the gold — it was gone. Though he'd made inquiries in America, he'd been unable to track down the gold. He did not understand how a gringo outlaw with one million dollars could be so quiet. He thought at first the man would be easy to find — spending money, living a high life. But he never even got a sniff of the gringo who ran off with his daughter and his gold.

But Señor Arellano did make great strides toward rebuilding his wealth. It was easier for him because he was already wealthy and powerful. It took work, but he saw his fortune coming back. No one can lose one million dollars and not be devastated, but Señor Arellano could look ahead and see a day when his fortunes would be restored.

And then José de la Cruz Porfirio Díaz Mori seized power. He did what Señor Arellano had sought to do. The difference, no interfering gringos who stole Diaz's gold.

Diaz set about destroying anyone he perceived as a threat. And the big man in Chihuahua who had a million dollars to spend on revolution was a definite threat.

The federales arrested him.

Diaz somehow found witnesses who testified against him.

But those witnesses did not matter. A dictator gets the outcome he wants in political trials.

And now here he was.

Six years ago, Señor Arellano believed he was on the verge of establishing himself as El Presidente.

And now they had built a podium especially for him.

A podium? No. A scaffolding.

"If you will step back here, Señor Arellano," the man said. "Allow me to just place this over your head."

Everything went black.

"And now this."

Señor Arellano felt the thick rope under his chin. He felt the heavy knot rest on his shoulder.

"Manuel Arellano Hermosillio," the man said, and his voice sounded loud and clear. "For the ultimate crime of revolution against your country, you are sentenced to the ultimate punishment."

Now the priest who had followed him up the steps was at Señor Arellano's side, whispering in his ear.

"Get away from me, Padre. There's nothing now your God can do for me."

Somewhere behind the scaffolding, a drum roll started.

...

To continue following Duvall and Marisol in "Back on the Restless Trail," grab your copy of the third book in the series at Amazon.com.

ALSO BY ROBERT PEECHER

THE HECK & EARLY SERIES

If you enjoyed The Restless Trail series, I'm confident you'll love the Heck & Early series.

They're a couple of hard bit men.

Heck Espinoza's Spanish roots run deep in the New Mexico soil.

Early Bascomb is a Southern drifter fleeing a murder warrant back in Mississippi.

Heck is a cautious man.

Early's a little bit reckless.

Heck lets his actions speak for him.

Early loves to make an oration.

When the pair meet in a Mesilla boarding house in the 1870s, they become unlikely partners, best friends cutting a trail through the territory, sometimes hoping to earn a bounty on fugitives, sometimes looking for an odd job to earn a wage. But the thing both men are good at is earning a living from behind the barrel of a gun.

If you love a gritty Western where you can smell the gunsmoke and feel the horse beneath you, then cinch your saddle and grab a box of cartridges and ride along on a Western adventure with Heck and Early.

Visit Amazon.com and saddle up with Heck & Early in "Bred in the Bone."

ALSO BY ROBERT PEECHER

RIDE THE OREGON TRAIL

In 1846, the Townes Party takes to the emigrant trail, bound for the green valleys near Oregon City.

Fearful of Indians and the weather and sometimes each other, the families in the party must endure the hardships of the trail if they are going to reach their destination. But they are bound together by a common thread, the hope that in the West they will find opportunity and a better life.

Led by Elias Townes, the party will face dangers and obstacles they expect, and some they could never predict.

They're made of tough stuff, but do they have the sand to withstand the difficulties and threats they'll meet on the Oregon Trail?

If you love traditional Westerns steeped in history and full of action, this two-book series is sure to be an instant favorite.

So saddle up your best riding horse and pack your wagon light; this trail goes on forever. Bring plenty of powder and shot, though, because you never know what dangers you'll encounter.

Visit Amazon.com to start your journey with the Townes Party on the Oregon Trail.

ALSO BY ROBERT PEECHER

TAKE ON THE DIXIE MAFIA

The Dixie Mafia is getting old.

They're losing their grasp.

And a new investigator at the District Attorney's office threatens to ruin everything.

Barnett Lowery never wanted to come back home.

He'd escaped Aintry County and the demons here. The shame of his daddy's legacy. The mama who drank herself to death.

And he sure never wanted to take up the torch his daddy dropped twenty years ago.

But when the District Attorney decides to build his political future on going after the corrupt officials who run Aintry County,

Barnett Lowery is the obvious choice to be the hammer he uses to drive in the final nail in the Dixie Mafia's coffin.

If you love stories of down-home murder deep in the hills of Dixie, small-town crime, and rural justice, then slide into the passenger seat of this classic Camaro and buckle up. You'd better bring along your Colt Python and a cowboy hat, because what gets buried Under the Dixie Moon always comes back up.

Visit Amazon.com and get into the Barnett Lowery thrillers!

ABOUT ROBERT PEECHER

With more than 70 novels, Robert Peecher is one of the most prolific authors of classic Westerns writing today. He's an avid outdoorsman and loves paddling rivers and hiking trails. He lives in Georgia with his wife Jean and a small kennel of dogs. You can follow him on Facebook at Robert Peecher Westerns.

Made in United States
North Haven, CT
27 October 2024

59498234R00176